CALCULATED WHISK

TALES FROM THE DRAGON DINER
BOOK 1

LINDSAY BUROKER

1

The Dragon Diner: Bookkeeper Wanted.

"Finally, someone is hiring." Rylana "Falcon" Avandar reached toward the door, a ferocious dragon artistically burned into the wood.

Sylin's firm hand landed on her wrist. The slender elf assassin possessed far more strength than one would guess, and the grip halted Rylana as surely as shackles.

"You are an archer for the Moon Daggers, one of the most well-known mercenary bands in the southern kingdoms," Sylin said. "Enemies run for cover when they see you on the battlefield with your bow, and even *dragons* speak warily of you since they've felt the sting of your arrows. They speak warily of you while they plot your *demise*. What are you thinking?"

"I *was* an archer for the now-disbanded Moon Daggers. You of all people know the Ore War is over, the unit has dispersed, and Captain Maverick is gone." Rylana's throat tightened as she said the last, Mav's irreverent smirk floating through her mind. Nine months of traveling the world and trying to forget the past hadn't been long enough. "Besides, I'm qualified to be a bookkeeper.

When I wasn't busy perforating enemies with arrows, I handled payroll and the ordering of supplies for five hundred people. I'm *sure* I can run the calculations for a diner. This one doesn't even look that busy." Rylana peered through the window beside the door.

"It's not your pen-wielding ability that I question; it's your intent to walk into an establishment owned by a dragon." Sylin released her grip and tucked a lock of her forest-green hair behind her pointed ear, though her frank blue eyes remained on Rylana. "That would be even more foolish than me visiting the elven enclave while we're here."

"I'm sure the diner isn't *owned* by a dragon."

Sylin pointed at the pyrography on the door.

"I'll wager two gold coins that a human owns this and put *dragon* in the diner's name because it might draw more business. Or he or she liked alliteration. The place also might specialize in meat dishes, the kind carnivorous animals, humans, and crazy elves who were raised by wolves like to eat."

"Hilarious. As if *I'm* the crazy one here, the one contemplating applying for a position under one of the great scaled, winged, and *fanged* enemies that we were paid to battle in the war. Also, meat is delicious. Especially slow-roasted northern elk or herb-crusted star-darter tenderloin."

"Not according to your vegetarian elven kin. I assume your culinary preferences are the reason you won't be visiting the enclave and that it has nothing to do with the fact that elves were allies to the dragons in the Ore War—and that you killed even more of them than I did."

Rylana spoke of their triumphs without pride. Had they even *been* triumphs? Years ago, she had been pleased by the development of her skills and rising in the ranks as a mercenary. But as she'd gotten older, losing comrade after comrade, the unit often being forced to obey dubious orders, she'd started questioning if they had been doing the right thing.

"I am certain of that. You know the old saying: in the depths of night, a single blade may cut a thousand throats." Sylin, who always noticed everything, turned as two goblins approached.

Only a block away from the busy Luminous Lake docks, the shop-lined cobblestone street held many passersby, most minding their own business, but the pair of three-and-a-half-foot-tall, green-skinned males were whispering to each other and pointing at them. No, judging by the lewd gesture that one drew in the air, they were pointing at Sylin. She always attracted more male gazes —species regardless—when she and Rylana were together.

With her own feminine curves and reasonable facial appeal, Rylana wasn't usually ignored by men when she traveled with a less striking companion, but as a mere human, she didn't star in their fantasies the way Sylin did. That was fine with Rylana since she was one who chose companions infrequently and with care. Today, with her short black hair in need of a washing and her trousers and tunic travel-stained, she doubted she would interest even a horny goblin.

"Do you think they'd like to *zerg* with us?" one of the males asked, drawing close enough that their conversation was audible.

"When has a beautiful elf *ever zerg*ed with you?" his companion asked.

"In my dreams every single night. Sometimes *many* times a night." The speaker hurried forward, beaming a smile at Sylin, his wispy white hair sticking out in all directions like a dandelion gone to seed. "Beautiful elven maiden, I was wondering if—"

Sylin drew a knife so quickly that Rylana almost missed it. Sylin flipped it casually up and down at the level of the goblin's face. It was her utility knife, not one of the various blades she used in her profession. Those were in a wooden case in her backpack, tied with a magical red "tranquility" ribbon, courtesy of the peacekeepers who'd searched them before allowing them entrance into the city. A similar ribbon was tied on Rylana's sword scabbard and around her bow and the arrows in her quiver. If anyone tried to remove the knots, the peacekeepers would be alerted, and golems would charge into the streets to deal with the infraction.

The goblin halted midstep and midsentence, his yellow eyes transfixed on the flipping blade. "I was wondering if you might have been going in to eat the special soup at this establishment."

"The special soup?" Rylana asked.

If that was what the diner was known for, there definitely wasn't a dragon inside.

"Yes, the magical spices that the chef uses... Well, they're known to put most species in the mood to, ah..." The goblin looked toward his comrade.

His buddy, who didn't appear daunted by the knife flipping, made pumping motions with his hips. "To *zerg*. You know the word?"

"Everyone knows that goblin word," Rylana said dryly.

"Elves are immune to such substances," Sylin said, "but why would a chef use magical spices in the food?"

"Who knows what motivates dragons?" The goblins stepped back from Sylin and looked across the street, one saying, "Let's see if our cake is ready for Vardok's stag party on the docks tonight."

The pair darted between a horse-drawn carriage and a self-ambulating wagon, a glowing yellow controller embedded in the front guiding it to its destination. A grandmotherly dwarf in an apron opened the front door of a bakery with a sign that promised delicious custom goods for all needs, naughty or nice, no questions asked. The goblins trotted inside.

"I'd forgotten what an interesting part of Tranquility this is," Rylana observed.

"I told you there was a dragon." Sylin pointed to a tea and

coffee shop next to the bakery, a steaming cup painted on its wooden sign. "Why don't you inquire about employment there?"

"Retiring to work at a coffee shop is your dream not mine." Of course, Rylana was almost as much of a fan of a heady dose of fresh brew as Sylin, and she smiled at a memory that arose. She'd first become the bookkeeper for the Moon Daggers—and registered to Captain Maverick's awareness as more than a nameless archer in Fleet Foot Squad—when she'd had a fit because the company had been out of coffee. He'd said that if she was that concerned about the status of luxury goods, she could take over the position of supply officer. He'd been surprised when she'd gleefully agreed. Never again had the company been without such an important substance.

"I think it might be a bookstore too." Sylin pointed at tome-filled cases behind a table visible through the window, then rested her knife across her heart and sighed. "I'm going to investigate."

"And apply for a job?"

"I would be bored serving coffee. Even traveling has felt mundane without any challenges to occupy my mind and force me to keep my skills honed."

"As a barista, you might get the opportunity to slap away handsy men."

"*That's* not challenging. And it's the epitome of mundane."

"Well, for my sake, ask if they're hiring."

Rylana had already inquired at more than twenty establishments and found that nobody was. In the aftermath of the Ore War, a lot of former soldiers had come to Tranquility, the city that welcomed all, as long as they obeyed the laws of the new god that required all intelligent species to exist in peace. Since Rylana and Sylin had taken a roundabout route here, those who'd arrived earlier had acquired all the available jobs and also filled the temporary lodgings, something else Rylana's inquiries had revealed. When she and Sylin had decided to come to Tranquility, it hadn't occurred to them that there wouldn't be work or a place to stay.

Sylin turned back to the door, standing shoulder to shoulder with Rylana. "I won't let you face a dragon alone."

"I still don't believe there's a real dragon. They're not allowed to live in their native form in Tranquility because their fangs and claws are too dangerous—not to mention their *magic*. The gnome peacekeepers can't tie a knot on a dragon's ability to breathe fire."

"It would be amusing to see a three-foot-tall gnome attempt to fasten a ribbon around one of those long scaled necks."

Sylin reached for the door again—nobody had gone in or out in the time they'd stood in front of it, so it definitely wasn't busy.

"Be careful in there," came a woman's call from behind. It was the apron-wearing gray-haired dwarf who'd let the goblins in. She now held a tray filled with miniature cupcakes. "With your beauty, if any of the male patrons have been imbibing the soup, they might try to force a mating on you. Cupcake?" She smiled and held up the tray.

"I assume she's talking to you," Rylana murmured.

"You're more trusting than I and likely to take a sweet from a stranger," Sylin said.

"I meant about the *beauty*."

"You'll want to watch out for the dragon too," the dwarf added, her gaze squarely on Rylana now. "He doesn't take kindly to human soldiers, and you've the look of one." Cupcake in hand, she gestured toward the chain mail shirt visible under Rylana's tunic, the bow and quiver, and the combat boots that had seen a lot of use in the dragon-filled mountains that rose out of the mists of the southern jungles.

"See, there *is* a dragon." Sylin nodded, as if she'd known for certain all along. Maybe she had. Elves had more ability than humans did to sense the magical, and dragons, with their ability to fly, breathe fire, and shape-shift into other forms, were definitely that.

"He's the chef," the dwarf added, then popped the cupcake into her mouth. "I really must stop eating so many of the samples," she murmured to herself, then went inside.

Rylana faced the diner's dragon door again, but all the warnings were succeeding in making her believe this establishment would be best avoided. She still had a few coins. She didn't need a job immediately. Just... soon.

"There have to be alternatives. Didn't you say your wealthy family lives across the lake here?" Sylin waved toward the west where, opposite of the city core that sprawled along the eastern side of the lake, ancient castles that had been turned into manors of wealthy families stood along the shoreline, each on sprawling acreages overlooking the water.

"I'm not asking the father I haven't seen or even written to in seventeen years for money."

"Didn't he offer you a job in the family business once?"

"He tried to *force* me into that job after torturing my brother and me with ten stifling years of nonstop tutoring and testing. If my lute teacher hadn't let me sneak out into the woods to practice with the neighbor's bow, I could have gone insane." Rylana didn't mention the worst part, that her father had tried to arrange a marriage for her to a socially acceptable landowner whose family also had an estate on the banks of the lake. That had been what had ultimately prompted her to flee the city and become a mercenary in a far-off land. "You're lucky you were an orphan, Sylin."

"Oh, yes, all orphans are thankful every day that they weren't born into wealthy families where missed meals were nonexistent."

"I bet the wolves didn't make you learn the lute." Brimming with determination, Rylana thrust open the door.

So what if there was a dragon? If he was hiring bookkeepers, she was a bookkeeper.

Rylana stepped inside to the most wondrous of smells. Was that bacon? With a hint of sweetness like maple? The scent wafted through a tidy dining room with not a speck of food or grime on the tile floors. Illuminated by daylight flowing through the windows, the back half was further brightened by lamps and sconces adorned with paper-thin wooden shades that had been burned with the same dragon logo that was on the door.

Despite the sumptuous scents, only two booths were occupied, one by a man eating skewers of meat while reading a newspaper, the other by an amorous university-age couple, the girl sitting in the guy's lap as they giggled over bowls of stew. Or maybe that was the soup the goblins had warned them of. The other booths and a dozen or so stools at an empty bar in the back were unoccupied. A hallway beside it led toward a swinging kitchen door, what might have been an office opposite it, and to what looked like a large supply room taking up the back half of the building.

A pale-skinned gnome with shaggy black hair, bare feet, and wearing an apron sat cross-legged in a corner of the dining room, next to a toolbox and a knee-high mechanical contraption, a panel open in its side. Busy tinkering, the gnome didn't acknowledge Rylana's entrance. Nobody did, certainly not the giggling couple.

Since the gnome looked like he worked in the diner, Rylana started toward him, but the kitchen door swung open first. A handsome man as tidy as the dining room walked out in black trousers, an apron, and a crisp cream-colored shirt with the sleeves evenly rolled up to reveal muscled forearms. He had short silver hair, emerald-green eyes, bronze skin, and radiated power even though he was carrying a tray, not unlike the dwarf baker across the street. Instead of cupcakes, his held a plate of sliced meat under a precise dollop of gravy and surrounded by cubes of beautifully colored vegetables.

It had been a long time since breakfast, and Rylana's mouth

would have watered, but she was promptly struck by there being something familiar about the man. No, that was undoubtedly a *dragon* shape-shifted into human form. There was a scar beside his right eye that stretched back into his hairline, and when his emerald eyes locked onto her, Rylana rocked back. She'd met him before. She was sure of it.

The dragon in human form roared and lifted the tray, as if he might hurl it at her—or against the wall in a fit of rage—but he caught himself and instead set it on the bar before springing toward her.

Rylana slung her pack and her weapons off her shoulder as she rushed back outside where she would have more room to maneuver. But the cursed tranquility ribbon kept her from drawing an arrow. The presumptuous magic even *zapped* her when she tried to pull one from her quiver. Furious, she threw her bow and quiver to the ground and pulled out her utility knife, the only blade the peacekeepers hadn't tied.

"Problem?" Sylin, who'd waited in the street, asked calmly.

"I've met that dragon before." Rylana backed farther, surprised he hadn't yet charged out after her.

A roar sounded again, not the vocalization that might come from a man's throat but the thunderous heart-rattling roar of a real dragon. It came not from the front room of the diner but the alley behind it.

"*You* met him?" Sylin asked. "Or one of your *arrows* met him?"

"I think he got a real personal introduction to the contents of my quiver, yes."

As Rylana crouched with her knife, a shadow fell over them. Scrapes came from the rooftop of the diner—talons gripping the gutters. A huge silver dragon with great muscles bunching under sleek scales glared down at her, and his fang-filled maw opened, saliva glistening on teeth like daggers. No, like *swords*.

Rylana looked down at the ridiculously small weapon she held. Her knife wouldn't even scratch one of the dragon's scales.

"I'm dead."

2

ALARMS GONGED AS THE DRAGON LEAPED FROM THE ROOFTOP AND onto the street, roaring again as his emerald eyes locked onto Rylana. She had no trouble reading the intent to kill in them. He crouched, not able to spread his wings fully because of the storefronts on either side of the street, but nothing impeded his legs, the powerful muscles that would let him spring at her.

Before the man had changed into a dragon, he'd seemed familiar, but now that he stood before Rylana in his natural form, she remembered seeing him before. She remembered *shooting* him before. It had been from a high perch above a mountain valley while human, orc, and dwarven soldiers had battled against elves and dragons on the battlefield below.

Eyes ablaze, the dragon roared again, drowning out the gongs coming from a pillar in a nearby intersection, and she knew he remembered her too. He opened his maw wider, and all the passersby that had been in the street scattered. Drivers of wagons abandoned them, rushing into doorways or alleys.

Rylana backed farther away, glancing around a corner and toward one of those alleys. She turned and sprinted toward it, and none too soon. Flames roiled from the back of the dragon's throat, spraying the cobblestones where she'd stood. The brilliant light and intense heat followed her into the alley.

She would have sprinted for the end, hoping to lose the dragon in the city, but an authoritative call of, "Halt, dragon!" came from the other side of the diner.

More alarms gonged from pillars in other intersections throughout the area. Soon, the entire city would know about this.

The order to stop didn't keep the dragon from stomping to the entrance of the alley. His long silver neck snaked around the corner, his eyes focusing again on Rylana as he once more opened his maw.

She threw her knife at one of those emerald eyes, then sprinted toward the end of the alley. The dragon turned his head to avoid what would have been a precise strike at her target, and the blade glanced off his scaled cheek. As she'd feared, unlike the mithril-headed arrows she'd loosed on the battlefield, the simple steel blade didn't even scratch him. All it did was piss him off. Further.

The dragon roared again. He was too large to rush into the alley, but he crouched, probably to spring *over* it and land on the street one block over.

But a magical net flew at him from the side, the strands sizzling as they touched his flank and stuck to him. Two twelve-foot-tall golems strode into the alley from the opposite end, their brownish-gray bodies appearing to be made from stone, but magic making them far more impervious. Three-foot-tall gnomes in gray peacekeeper uniforms and armed with stun sticks and net hurlers gathered behind the golems, commanding them to stride past Rylana and toward the dragon. He'd paused in his attack to snarl to the side at whoever had hurled the net. More peacekeepers, presumably.

In most of the world, nobody would consider the diminutive

gnomes, no taller than a goblin and less muscular, suitable for law enforcement, but here, in this city that they'd made with the help of the new god, everyone knew they had the magical wherewithal —and the divine blessing—to ensure people obeyed the laws.

"Halt, dragon!" someone called from the street again.

More golems appeared on either side of his netted flanks.

"You are in violation of the laws of Tranquility. If you do not immediately change into a benign form, we will force you out of the city and close your establishment."

The dragon seethed, tail rigid and muscles taut. Would he have the power or be able to use his fire to destroy the net that covered him?

Perhaps, but, at the gnomes' threat, he looked toward the diner, and he didn't try. Smoke wafted from his nostrils when he glowered back into the alley at Rylana, showing his fangs again before closing his maw. But in the end, surrounded by peace-keepers and their golems, the dragon shifted forms, the air rippling around him like a mirage in the desert.

Once more, he stood as a man, his short silver hair now tousled and his clothing rucked and wrinkled. He plucked at the netting, grimacing as it sizzled and probably zapped him the way the ribbon had Rylana, but he focused on removing it instead of looking at the golems and gnomes that had encircled him. The golems were expressionless, as always, mere automatons doing their duties, but the gnomes looked sternly at the dragon, and one stepped forward to address him.

Rylana thought about slipping away, especially since the peacekeepers might take issue with her having thrown a knife, but she risked creeping forward. Maybe she could retrieve the blade from the cobblestones where it had landed before anyone noticed it.

"Jildarin-grozanarav," the head gnome said.

Was that the dragon's name? Even though Rylana had battled

him, she'd never known it. It did sound familiar, like he might have been one of the generals or clan leaders during the war. Such important beings had been mentioned in the orders and reports that had come down from the kingdom militaries. What in either hell was he now doing here in Tranquility running a *diner*?

"I am Patrol Captain Dindarik, and you are in violation of Tranquility law. You've changed into your dangerous native form outside of your lair, something that is expressly forbidden. Have any been injured or slain?" The gnome peered into the alley and also toward the storefronts and wagons, one of which was in flames. "I see that goods have been damaged. At the least, there will be a fine."

The dragon—Jildarin—sighed and looked at Rylana, curling a lip when she picked up her knife. Sylin appeared, stepping past a couple of gnomes to peer into the alley. Her wooden case of daggers was in hand, but she must have seen the peacekeepers and golems approaching, because she hadn't tried to break the tranquility ribbon tying it closed.

Rylana waved that she was all right.

The patrol captain pulled a mechanical device out of a pocket and started tapping on a button. It glowed with his touches and whirred softly. As the dragon finished extricating himself from the netting, a paper spat out from a slot in the top of the device.

"This is an official warning. Should you change into your dragon form again on public streets, you *will* be forced to leave the city. At the bottom, you will see a fine listed for your infraction. You may pay it at Peacekeeper Headquarters. The address is listed at the bottom." Captain Dindarik handed the paper to the dragon, who accepted it with another lip curl, but, after looking at his diner again, he didn't object.

Maybe it was strange, since the dragon had tried to kill her scant moments earlier, but Rylana felt a twinge of sympathy toward him. After all, he was only being fined because he'd reacted strongly to *her* arrival.

"As you were warned when you entered the city," the patrol captain added, "such behavior is *not* tolerated within Tranquility's borders or near Luminous Lake's shorelines. Should you wish to hunt in your native form, you must first leave the city." Dindarik looked at Rylana to address her. "Given the nature of the incident, and your obvious need to defend yourself, you will not be warned or fined at this time for hurling a blade with the intent to harm."

Rylana had already sheathed the knife and lifted her open hands, resisting the urge to say something snarky. Sylin had disappeared from view again. Had the peacekeepers frowned at her for pulling out her knife case?

When the golems and their gnome handlers departed, the gong noises finally fading, Jildarin glared at her. Rylana tensed. She didn't *think* he would attack again, probably more because he didn't want to lose his diner than because he cared about fines—though he *did* glare down at the paper, the tendons of his hands taut, as if he was tempted to ball it up and throw it away. Instead, he smoothed it, folded it once, and tucked it into a pocket. He also smoothed his clothes as he resumed glaring at Rylana.

"What do you want, foul enemy? To attempt to slay me again? The gnomes will not permit that, any more than they will allow me to kill you. Regretfully."

"My name is Rylana, and I came to apply for the position of bookkeeper at the Dragon Diner."

As he stared at her, his jaw slack with disbelief, Sylin appeared again, stepping into the alley to stand at Rylana's shoulder. The support would have meant more if Sylin hadn't been holding a paper cup with coffee inside, as if she'd wandered off in the middle of the chaos to place an order.

"You are *not* hired," Jildarin stated and walked out of view and back toward his diner.

"Are you sure working for your father isn't an option?" Sylin sipped from her cup.

"Yes." Rylana raised her eyebrows as Sylin smacked her lips in some assessment of the brew.

"Now that he's changed back into a man, a lot of people have flowed out into the street to watch," Sylin said. "The coffee shop owners and the bakery dwarf are taking this opportunity to hand out free samples. This is surprisingly good, all things considered."

"All things considered? Did you think the presence of a dragon or me nearly being incinerated would affect the flavor?"

"No, but I didn't expect a quality beverage to be foisted on me by a street peddler."

"Was it foisted on you, or did you rush over to get it as soon as you smelled coffee? I'll bet you were first in line for that sample."

"I was second in line," Sylin said, sipping again, "behind the fast-moving goblins who'd just exited the bakery with a cake box, a hole snipped out on the top so that a rather erect and large… *zerg* stick could protrude. You're fortunate that dragon isn't interested in hiring you. I can't imagine the indignity of working at an establishment where the food has strange aphrodisiacal qualities that prompt the libidinous diners to order pornographic cakes from the bakery across the street."

"I don't think anatomically-shaped baked goods quite qualify as pornography."

"You didn't see the size of the *zerg* stick. It looked like it was inspired by an ogre, not a goblin."

"How do you know it wasn't?"

Sylin took another sip as they returned to the street. "It was green."

"For someone who isn't usually interested in such things, you got a good look."

"Shall I remind you of my profession? It behooves me to constantly remain alert and monitor my surroundings."

"You're retired, aren't you?"

"Hm," Sylin said noncommittally.

Rylana paused in the street. Jildarin was still outside the diner, and his fists were clenched. Fortunately, he wasn't looking at her but instead faced a male human who wore the kind of blue-tweed frock coat that was popular with bankers and business owners in the city. *Most* people, having seen Jildarin in his native form scant minutes earlier, were giving him a wide berth, but this man adjusted his round brimmed hat and stepped closer to him.

"When are you going to be able to pay your rent?" he demanded.

"Soon," Jildarin said.

"You said that last month."

"It's even truer now." Jildarin glared balefully at the man.

Anywhere except in the city of Tranquility, a human would have quailed under a dragon's glare and the irritated power that Jildarin radiated, even while shifted into a more benign form, but the man knew he was safe here. He straightened his coat, lifted his chin, and said, "If you are not able to pay it in full by next month, including interest for all the delays, I will bring the golems and have you evicted."

"The Golden Whisk is in a week."

"The Golden what?"

"It is an annual culinary competition hosted at the old arena on an overlook of Luminous Lake." Jildarin pointed toward the north end of the city. "I will be able to come current with the rent after winning the prize money."

The man—the *landlord*—scoffed. "You're a business owner. You're supposed to be able to pay your rent based on what you earn from your *business*."

Voice cold, Jildarin leaned forward and said, "I will acquire the funds."

Even from a distance, Rylana could sense his power—and she

well remembered the heat of the flames that had almost scorched her. She wouldn't push a dragon, even in Tranquility. There was no magical ribbon that could keep a dragon from changing into his native—and extremely deadly—form, and Jildarin might well decide the diner wasn't worth the trouble and roast the landlord. Maybe he would torch Rylana as well before flying out of the city to return to his homeland.

What was he *doing* here anyway? Dragons weren't chefs. She'd never even heard of one that cooked its meat. They usually killed and devoured their prey raw. They certainly didn't make *soup* that had strange side effects on those who consumed it.

The landlord took a step back, looking like he might have realized he was being overly assertive, given the nature of the being with whom he spoke. That didn't keep him from saying, "If you don't have your rent money, including what's overdue, in *two* weeks, I will start the eviction process."

"That is acceptable and expected, but I *will* have the funds by then." Jildarin opened the door and stalked inside. Before it closed behind him, his voice was audible, roaring, "There will be no *coitus* in my diner. This is a place of eating! *Get out!*"

The couple that Rylana had seen earlier ran through the doorway, the woman's dress half off her shoulder and the man struggling to pull his trousers up while sprinting away at top speed.

Rylana scratched her jaw, bewildered.

"I knew this city was quirky, but I'm finding our visit more fascinating than I expected." Sylin sipped the last of her free sample.

"Was it fascinating when that dragon nearly incinerated me?" Rylana asked.

"No, that was merely entertaining."

"I trust the only reason you didn't try to save me was that the tranquility ribbon tied your knife case shut. It had nothing to do with a barista wandering over to tempt you with samples."

Sylin grinned. "It was one of the owners, and she didn't come out until after the golems showed up. Even the most entrepreneurial of business owners don't peddle their wares while a fearsome dragon is on a rampage."

Telling herself it would be wise to have nothing more to do with Jildarin or his diner, Rylana started past it, but the fleeing patrons had left the door ajar, and the lingering bacon scents made her pause. That smelled so wonderful. Could he *really* work in the kitchen, cooking over a hot stove to feed humans? It was so incongruous with all things dragon. Usually, if they interacted with humans or any of the non-elven species at all, it was to drive them out of their lands. The occasional hedonistic dragon visited villages and towns and expected offerings of meat *from* the orcs, goblins, or humans that lived there, but Rylana had traveled all over the world, and she'd never seen anything like this.

"It does smell good in there, doesn't it?" Sylin said. "What a wonderful combination of aromas. But, why, do you suppose, is he making a soup that turns people libidinous if he doesn't want them to have sex in his diner?"

"I have no idea."

"Perhaps the workers in that fine establishment across the street can illuminate the mystery, should we care enough to inquire." Sylin pointed to the coffee shop, a woman with a tray still out front, handing out the last of her samples to passersby. "No doubt if we buy beverages, they will be more inclined to share details."

"No doubt," Rylana murmured, following her comrade toward the shop, but she couldn't help but look back and wonder about that dragon.

3

"I FEEL BAD," RYLANA SAID AS THE DELECTABLE AROMA OF HER LATTE wafted up, a touch of vanilla bean sweetening the drink. She sat across from Sylin, looking out the window of the coffee shop toward the Dragon Diner while her friend, who had pushed the other chair away from the table, alternately stood or squatted, her back to a ceiling-high piece of roasting machinery that emanated a faint magical glow.

"About what?" Sylin inhaled the scent of her straight black coffee, then took an appreciative sip, letting it linger on her tongue before swallowing. "This is the best roast I've had since we left the southern kingdoms. Most coffee beans are stale and anemic by the time they reach this latitude, but someone must have paid for a dragon to bring this north on its back."

"Yes, I've heard their kind delight in undertaking freight delivery for humans. More likely, some magical gnomish storage containers were used."

"However the beans came to be here in such a fresh state, I approve." Sylin sipped again and smacked her lips a couple of times. "Based on the robust and nuanced taste, I believe they originated in the equatorial Lazombik Rainforest, from farms at just a high enough altitude in the mountains that the cooler temperatures slowed the bean development to increase the flavor, acidity, and exquisite complexity of the coffee."

"Yeah, I like mine too." By now, Rylana knew about her comrade's obsession with the beverage and didn't comment on the rest, though she'd often joked that it must have been the scent of coffee brewing in a hunter's camp that had first drawn Sylin out of the woods and away from the wolves who'd raised her.

"Yours is a latte." Sylin wrinkled her elegant elven nose. "I don't know how you can tell anything about the complexity of the beans when they're diluted with milk."

"There's vanilla and sugar too."

"Loathsome."

"I feel *bad,*" Rylana said to bring the conversation back to the topic, "because the dragon—Jildarin, I believe it was—was fined because of me."

"It was Jildarin-grozanarav. I remember him and his brother Zilek-grozanarav from the war. They were high-ranking dragons in Clan Killcrusher, some of the archnemeses of the joint kingdoms. And it's not your fault that he lost his temper and shifted. All you did was walk in. He brought all that upon himself."

"I did shoot him last year."

"During the war. In wartime, shooting your enemy is *expected.* Your only mistake was in not hitting him in the eye and killing him. Now, he's nursing a grudge, maybe fantasizing presently about chancing upon you outside of the city boundaries so he can finish what the peacekeepers rudely interrupted."

"My incineration?"

"Precisely."

"He's probably already forgotten me. He's got a cooking competition to prepare for."

"And rent to pay. Who ever heard of a broke dragon? Clan Killcrusher has a legendary hoard, reputedly. Though you'd have to ask a goblin for details. Their kind keep track of *all* the sizable hoards, just in case an opportunity arises to visit one while clutching a purse."

"Yes, thieving from dragons often goes well for goblins."

"So often that their charred skeletons frequently litter the mounds of gold." After another sip, Sylin shifted to gaze out the window. "Maybe he's been disowned. I'd say it might have been because of a poor performance during the war, but those two brothers took out the entire Bloodletters mercenary company. Do you remember?"

Rylana set her cup down with a clunk. "That was them?"

She remembered the annihilation of the mercenary clan, but the Moon Daggers had been fighting on another mountain when it had happened.

"That was they, yes. At the time, I was competing for kills against Salvo, the half-elven Bloodletter assassin who always wanted to show me up but also wanted to sleep with me—strange man. He was one of only three people in his unit who survived to tell the tale. That's why I remember the dragons' names."

"Well, that doesn't change anything about today. Even if all is fair in war—" Rylana waved a hand, not sure she believed the aphorism, "—Jildarin's irritation toward me was founded." She didn't think she could pronounce his full clan name so stuck with the shortened version. "If you want to get philosophical, the prevailing dragon irritation toward *all* humans isn't entirely unfounded."

"No, humans are almost as good at vexing other species as goblins are. Elves, I know, find your people terribly tedious and tiresome."

"Yet you honor me by having coffee with me."

"Elves find me even worse." Sylin saluted Rylana with her cup.

Rylana had never asked her comrade how many of her own

people she'd killed under orders from Captain Maverick and his superiors. It didn't seem to bother Sylin. Little did. Perhaps one couldn't be an effective assassin if moral qualms haunted one's sleep on a regular basis.

"Maybe I can help him somehow," Rylana mused.

"The dragon?" Sylin set her cup down. "Are you daft?"

"I still need a job. Don't you? Since the unit disbanded and the war is over, the traditional mercenary retirement plan isn't going to work for either of us."

"You mean the plan where mercenaries die on the battlefield before they *need* funds for retirement?"

"That's the one, yes."

"I was well paid with bonuses for my work, sometimes from multiple employers." Sylin shrugged. "I'll be fine for a while."

Rylana couldn't say the same. They'd lived frugally as they'd traveled, recovering and relaxing and seeing some of the world to help put the horrors of the war behind them, but her funds were nearly depleted. Since the prosperous city of Tranquility, tucked away between two mountain ranges along its northern lake, hadn't been touched during the war, she'd believed opportunities for employment would be many. It hadn't occurred to her that hordes of refugees and veterans would come up here first.

"Even if you were foolish enough to want to work for someone who couldn't pay his rent," Sylin said, "that dragon doesn't desire to hire you."

"Only because he doesn't know about the years I spent being tortured by mathematics and business tutors. I'm an excellent bookkeeper and can do numbers in my head."

"You almost shot him in the eye. He's not going to care if you can do the most elaborate and complicated..." Sylin waved her hand vaguely in the air. "What's something fancy you can do with numbers?"

"Get someone out of debt."

"That's not as fancy as I imagined."

"We could talk about derivatives and differential equations, but I can't imagine that impressing a dragon. But if I could help him to reconcile his books and streamline his business so he could come up with the money to pay his landlord..."

"When you walked in, there were only three customers, and he threw two out. No amount of streamlining will help that diner."

"Are you talking about Jildarin's place?" A woman with curly black hair, creases at the corners of her brown eyes, and a broad face walked up to take their empty cups and place cookies they hadn't ordered on napkins on the table. "Free samples," she said, though Sylin delved into her purse to rest two silver coins next to the sweets.

"Yes," Rylana said. "Do you know anything about the dragon?"

"He keeps to himself. I just know he makes wonderful food and doesn't charge enough for it. He would have armies of people visiting if not for the reputation of the place. Well, actually people are awfully curious *because* of that reputation, but then he drives them away when his dishes work as... one would think as he wishes." The woman slid the coins into a pocket in her apron. "Thank you, lady elf."

"As an aphrodisiac?" Rylana asked.

"It's mostly the soup that has that effect. And sometimes the stew. He puts his special dragon spices in them, and most people find them, er, invigorating."

"It makes them want to have sex," another woman called from across the shop, heads turning to regard her curiously. She was dumping burlap bags of beans into the great roasting apparatus.

Their server waved at her with a shushing motion. Despite having a head of gray hair and a motherly and mature figure, the other woman stuck her tongue out at her. There weren't any other employees in the room, and Rylana wondered if they might be the owners rather than staff.

"The spices tend to make people amorous, yes," the closer woman said. "I've heard they can affect dragons, too, but only in much greater quantities. I believe dragons only use the spices as a seasoning. I'm Tezilly, by the way. That's my loudmouthed partner who tells it like it is, Brella. Do you want another cup? Or something else? We've got more goods from the bakery next door too."

"These came from there?" Sylin, perhaps thinking of the lewd goblin cake she'd seen, eyed the cookies with more wariness, but there wasn't anything phallic or otherwise sexual about them. Inoffensive disks of chocolate were embedded into the tops and framed by sprinkles.

"Yes, Mya is a wonderful baker and makes treats for everything from children's parties to holiday festivities to..."

"Goblin stag gatherings?" Sylin asked.

"Quite. Let me know if you need anything else." Tezilly left the cookies and took the empty cups to the kitchen in the back.

Rylana again considered the Dragon Diner through the window. She hadn't seen any new customers go in. Jildarin *needed* help. She was sure of it.

"Why don't you give up on the job hunt for today?" Sylin suggested, watching Rylana's gaze. "You said you're tired of sleeping on the ground and want to find a place in the city to stay, right?"

"Yes. I checked a number of hostels this morning, but rooms are as infrequent as jobs right now. Maybe *I* could stay at the elven enclave."

"They don't take boarders, and they would be offended that you not only know me but deign to have coffee with me. Assassins are vile, you know."

"Oh, I'm aware. Where are *you* planning to stay?"

Sylin waved airily. "I'll find a place. I suppose there's no room for us at your family's estate? It's a castle, isn't it?"

"Yes. It's almost directly across the lake from us, on an elevated point that overlooks the water from three sides, offering wonderful views of the magically glowing blue, green, and purple fish and plankton that give Luminous Lake its name. And *room* wouldn't be the problem there, even if my father has remarried or has guests." Rylana grimaced at the thought of a strange woman wandering through the stone halls. "There are eighteen bedrooms and twelve bathrooms. It was reputedly one of the first manors to be remodeled with indoor plumbing when that was invented last century."

"It's amazing that you're not dreadfully spoiled. We worked together for years before I had any idea of your family's vast wealth."

"That wealth won't be left to me. It's been years since I even sent a letter home. As for spoiling, my father was stern and strict, not lenient or loving, and he never gave my brother or me anything that we didn't work for."

"So, you only had, what, eight servants?"

"Hardly. *He* had a personal butler, but we kids had to fend for ourselves after Mother died."

"Oh? Who cleaned the toilets?"

"There was a gnomish clockwork scrubber."

"I knew you were spoiled."

"The wolves didn't have any clockwork servants, huh?"

"Not a one." Sylin peered out the window.

Someone even more impeccably dressed than Jildarin was walking toward the front door of the diner. The man appeared to be of a similar age, with the same bronze skin and silver hair, but his was long and drawn back in a ponytail.

"That's another dragon," Sylin said with certainty. "I wonder if it's the brother. Zilek."

"He's a regular in town," Brella said, cruising past with her now-empty burlap bags draped over one arm. "Goes to the symphony, the opera, the museum galas, the tinkerers' clockwork ball. He seems to be enjoying the offerings that abound in Tranquility."

"A dragon who goes to balls and the opera? Is the whole family…?" Rylana extended a hand toward Sylin.

"Quirky," she said firmly, not making it a question.

"The brothers may qualify in that department," Brella said, "though I know less about the one who set up shop across the street. As my partner said, he keeps to himself and is a touch grouchy."

"A *touch*," Tezilly said, dropping off coffees at a nearby table, then lingering to chat with the patrons there. The owners seemed to be capable of tending the shop and also following multiple conversations.

"Two or three touches," Brella said in agreement, then headed to the kitchen.

"I wonder if Jildarin would kick me out if I tried to buy something to eat," Rylana mused.

"The soup that makes people horny?"

"I was thinking of the bacon that smelled so good earlier. Pork doesn't have any aphrodisiacal qualities that I know of."

"It sounds like the spices are the problem. They could be on *anything*."

"Does that mean you're staying here?" Rylana waved toward the wood-beamed ceiling of the coffee shop.

Sylin raised a finger when Tezilly strolled past. "Another cup of the dark roast, please."

"I'll take that as a *yes*," Rylana said.

"While I enjoy my coffee, I'll monitor out the window to see if you're thrown out."

"I won't be gone long."

"Oh, I'm certain of it. Leave your pack and bow if you want me to watch them."

"Somehow, I think *I'll* need more watching than my belongings."

"Yes, but they'll be easier to protect while I enjoy my next cup. Ah." Sylin almost purred when Tezilly delivered another coffee with two more cookies balanced on the saucer.

Rylana left her bow, quiver, and pack beside the table and stood. "Those dragons aren't the only quirky ones around here, you know."

"I'm quick to recognize like kind, yes." Sylin sipped from her cup. "Excellent. Why don't you ask the ladies that own this place if they need a bookkeeper?"

"Maybe *you* should see if they're hiring and if free coffee is a perk."

"I might consider that, yes. But working across the street from a dragon sounds almost as unwise as working *for* one."

"Mercenaries aren't known for their abundance of wisdom." Which was undoubtedly why Rylana felt compelled to check on the dragons. Hopefully, she hadn't managed to shoot and wound the brother during the war, as well.

"Some aren't, no." Sylin pointedly arched an eyebrow as Rylana walked out.

4

WHEN RYLANA CROSSED THE STREET AND OPENED THE FRONT DOOR of the diner, the only people inside were the gnome waiter and the solo customer who hadn't left his booth, even after the excitement outside and seeing the other patrons being kicked out. He was working on a dessert now, some kind of flatbread that smelled of cinnamon. The scent of bacon that she'd lovingly inhaled earlier lingered in the air, but it didn't smell like someone was cooking it fresh now. She almost slid into a booth and asked the gnome if there was any left, but it had been the dragons that she'd wanted to observe, and they weren't in the front room, nor did she hear voices in the kitchen. Was there a back entrance that they might have gone out?

Rylana ventured into the alley she'd visited—fled into—earlier, then circled around to the block behind the diner. Lined with warehouses and stables, the street wasn't as busy as the shopping and dining thoroughfare out front. She spotted a wide drive that led to large carriage doors and the storage room in the back half of the diner. She almost called it a warehouse. If Jildarin had to pay rent for all that space, no wonder he was behind on his payments.

One of the carriage doors stood ajar, a sign on the wall next to it a copy of the one posted out front. *The Dragon Diner: Bookkeeper Wanted.*

Though certain Jildarin had no more interest in hiring her now than he had an hour earlier, Rylana walked closer to the doors. The only windows were high on the walls, so she doubted anyone would see her coming, but she stepped carefully. Dragons had a lot of innate magic, and she'd learned from personal experience that they had sublime senses when they were in their native forms. It was possible their senses remained nearly as strong when they shifted into other forms.

As she drew closer to the door, the hair on the back of her neck rose. Even though she couldn't see or hear the dragons, her instincts told her they were inside the storeroom. She stepped off the drive and crept closer, then pressed her back to the wall beside the open door.

"Do you actually *sleep* in here?" a man with a rich baritone asked. That had to be the brother. Zilek. "In your true form? Isn't it claustrophobic?"

"During the war, I slept in caves that were smaller than this." That was Jildarin's voice. Also rich in tenor, it was almost pleasant when it wasn't raised to swear at Rylana. "Caves filled with stalactites that jabbed me in the back every time I twitched my tail."

"That doesn't happen *here*? There are crates and barrels everywhere. Where do you lie down? And what in the two hells are all those metal boxes with legs lined up along that wall? Do I sense magic emanating from them?"

"They're gnomish commercial ovens. I'm attempting to make an arrangement with the dwarf baker across the street to make bread, since so many of the patrons seem to think meat should be accompanied by that. I'm still wrapping my head around *vegetables* as a desirable thing to eat. But she's thus far been unwilling to give me a reasonable discount for ordering in bulk. And for being a dragon."

Rylana raised her eyebrows at the comment—at the entire conversation. Spying on dragons wasn't a good idea, even when fully armed. Why was she doing this?

"Because of her recalcitrance, I had to learn to bake bread," Jildarin finished. "And purchase my own oven."

"Yes, but why are there so *many* of them?"

"There was a small mistake during the ordering process. *Processes*. I didn't realize the ovens were custom made and took weeks to craft, so, when the first didn't arrive in a timely manner, I sent my goblin server, Rolf, to order another. I didn't realize he had execrable handwriting that would be misinterpreted. Or that a crafts-gnome wouldn't *check* before filling what should have seemed like a ridiculous order."

"I'm shocked you expected a goblin to be able to write at all. Their specialty is stealing books, not reading them."

"He grew up in the city and said he went to a human school."

"More likely a *thieving* school. I'll wager at least two of those ovens ended up stashed behind a log in a park."

"Yes, yes, my ability to hire minions is questionable, but I have a deadline coming up—the competition is only a week away—and I'm busy perfecting my recipes. I don't have time to deal with goblins, peacekeepers, landlords, or suspicious mercenaries interrupting my day."

Rylana shifted her weight, tempted to leave before the dragons realized that one of the *suspicious mercenaries* was spying on them.

"This is an odd life that you've chosen for yourself, Jildarin-grozanarav."

"Said by the dragon going regularly to operas and theaters."

"I enjoy being entertained by the lesser species. Listen, my brother, the war is over, and it was draining. We all need to recover and decompress, so I can understand taking the time to explore a new hobby or passion—even a strange obsession with cooking, as if meat devoured raw after being torn from the bones of one's prey isn't perfectly delicious. What I can't believe is that you want to *serve* the lesser species. I am here so that they might serve *me*. That is the correct order of the world, and they are most honored to attend to my every desire."

"It helps that you brought gold from Mother's hoard and pay them handsomely to do so."

"That does add to their feeling of honor," Zilek said.

"You spend lavishly on frills like wine and entertainment and that *castle* you've leased, but you won't give any coin to me for my endeavor."

"The wine I purchase is serious and sophisticated. I will admit the box tickets to the dwarven opera might have been a touch frilly, but those bearded ladies can sing. It's brilliant and so relaxing. As to the rest, you know Mother forbade me from giving you gold."

"Even though *I*, during the proving quests of my youth, acquired a large sum of what's now in the clan hoard."

"As I've told you before, she'll gladly share coins with you if you'll fulfill the one request she's made of you since the war ended. I'm here today on her behalf to remind you of your familial duty. I'd even go so far as to consider it a favor if you flew off to obey Mother's wishes so that *I* don't have to hear about how magnificent your strength and athleticism and stamina are and what an utter waste it is that you haven't used your male essence to impregnate a suitable female."

"I suspected it wasn't a craving for my wit that brought you."

Zilek laughed. "Your wit. That's rich. You're too busy being surly to amuse anyone. For the sake of your patrons, I hope your kitchen knives are sharper than your wit."

"With such flattery, you're certain to receive favors regularly."

"I don't regularly *need* favors. I only wish you'd obey Mother's one request. And that I wouldn't have to hear about the desirable physical qualities you apparently demonstrated in such abundance during the war that the Clan Sunclaw females want you above all others to sire their offspring. Never mind that you and I are from the same clutch and practically the same. Further, *I* didn't let a scruffy human archer almost shoot my eye out in the heat of battle."

"Do you *want* to mate with the Sunclaw females?" Jildarin asked. "I'll happily send you in my stead."

"Not particularly. They're as crabby and temperamental as you and have a tendency to pedantically *instruct* all the males around them. I can imagine how mating with one would go. Ahead of the event, she would probably send a list of requirements for her satisfaction and bite my head off if I mixed up the ordering."

"That sounds accurate. And I was only shot because I flew across the valley and over the enemy frontlines to risk their wizards and archers so that I could destroy that dreadful gnomish contraption that was shooting our kind out of the air."

"Yes, you're very brave. I do adore hearing about your exploits. Does the scar itch in bad weather? It was quite a deep gouge and with a mithril arrow. Those are painful."

"I'm aware," Jildarin said. "The female who was responsible came today to the diner."

"What? The human archer?"

"Yes."

Out in the street, a horse pulling a wagon clopped past.

A moment of silence followed, and Rylana wondered if the brothers were looking toward the open door. Had they realized someone lurked outside?

Since humans had no inherent magic, not the way so many of the other intelligent species did, they generally made good spies and assassins because magical beings couldn't detect them, but a dragon might see, hear, or *smell* a human.

"Did you slay her?" Zilek asked. "You must not have, or you'd be in a better mood. To slay an old nemesis is most satisfying."

"You know the laws of Tranquility forbid *slaying*. Or changing into a dragon outside of one's lair."

"Yes, it's tedious to obey the mandates of such lesser species as gnomes, whether they and their city are backed by the new god or not, but it is also appealing not to be hunted down by overly ambitious soldiers out to prove themselves. Was the human archer here to slay *you*? That should also not have been permitted by the peacekeepers."

"Her weapons were tied, and I did not detect mithril in her quiver." Jildarin's voice held a growl when he added, "She *did* throw a knife at my eye."

Rylana bristled, forgetting her wariness and half-tempted to stalk in to defend herself. She'd only thrown the knife because he'd turned into a dragon and tried to incinerate her.

"She must be drawn to those atypical emerald orbs of yours. I believe that's one of the attributes the Sunclaw females find appealing. It can't be *only* your strength and stamina that draw them."

"I doubt it's *appeal* that sends the human female's projectiles in my direction. You can tell Mother that I'm busy and will not mate with anyone right now."

"Are you certain you can't fly away for a couple of days? As I already said, it's tedious for me to have to be the intermediary. Besides, you know that we dragons lost a significant number of our kind during the war. As mighty as we are, the enemy had so very many troops to hurl against us. Orcs, dwarves, humans, and even ogres and trolls who are usually too busy beating upon their chests to band together with the other species. We need to do our part to replenish the numbers of dragons soaring up and down the Icefang and Skyfang Mountains."

"I understand, but I have no desire to spend time with the Sunclaw females. They're Mother's contemporaries, almost past egg-bearing age, and, as you yourself pointed out, they're more aggressive and overbearing than our sisters."

"Aggressive and overbearing?" Zilek asked. "You are describing all dragon females."

"So, naturally I should want to fly home and spend time with them."

Rylana shifted as another wagon passed, the driver peering curiously in her direction as a breeze stirred her hair. This wasn't the conversation she'd expected to listen in on, and she felt guilty for eavesdropping. All she'd wanted to learn was if there was a way she could help the dragon she'd wronged, but she couldn't do anything to assist him with his home life.

"You need only lend your essence to the procreation process," Zilek said, "not bond with one forever. I'm certain, if you did so, Mother would reward you with gold from the clan hoard."

"That's not how you got *your* coins, is it?"

"The species must be perpetuated, my brother."

"My essence isn't for sale."

They fell silent again as another breeze riffled through Rylana's hair. With a start, she realized that breeze might carry her scent to the dragons. She stepped away from the entrance, intending to hurry back to the coffee shop, but one of the doors flew open and banged on the side of the building. She snatched the sign off the wall as the two brothers stepped into the doorway, both scowling at her.

"Were you spying upon dragons, human?" Zilek asked, his amber eyes flaring with indignation.

"No." Rylana waved the sign in front of her, as if it were a shield that might protect her. "I'm here about the job."

"This is my enemy, the female archer who shot me." Jildarin looked at his brother as he thrust an accusing finger at Rylana.

"Oh, really?" Zilek's indignation faded as he looked her up and down, and was that a hint of a smirk on his lips? "She's scarcely five-and-a-half feet tall, and rather normal-ish in appearance. Her bow can't be *that* huge."

"I never said it was," Jildarin said.

"The story you told after you were wounded suggested an ogre-sized female with arms like tree trunks launched arrows with such power that they might have been blown from a cannon."

"My aim is excellent," Rylana said, worried that Jildarin's darkening scowl would lead to her being attacked again, perhaps in a more calculated manner that wouldn't bring the peacekeepers. Even in human form, dragons had great strength. Maybe Jildarin would throw one of the oversupplied ovens and crush her. "But I'm an equally good bookkeeper. That's why I'm an ideal candidate for you to hire. My handwriting is also excellent. *I* wouldn't fail to order an accurate number of kitchen supplies and equipment for you."

"You *were* spying." Jildarin lifted an arm, starting to surge forward.

Rylana leaped back, but his brother also caught him from behind, keeping him from reaching her.

"Don't slay her," Zilek said. "You may need her."

"*Need* an archer who enjoys *shooting* dragons? Who would need *that*?"

"Someone with ten gnomish commercial ovens crowding his cave," Zilek said blandly.

Jildarin turned his scathing scowl on his brother. Unintimidated and still smirking, *he* didn't leap back.

"Earlier, you didn't let me explain my qualifications," Rylana said. "I grew up here in Tranquility—across the lake actually—and, despite eventually becoming a mercenary, I had a formal education. I can perform basic and advanced mathematics and have real-world experience from keeping the books for the Moon Daggers for almost ten years. I never accidentally ordered extra ovens or anything else, and I am sure I can help you with inventory as well as running your business. By my calculations, you *need* help."

"Look, she wants to serve you." Zilek thumped Jildarin on the chest with the back of his hand. "That's how it's *supposed* to work. Humans serve dragons instead of the other way around."

"I'm seeking employment, not to be a servant," Rylana said calmly, though she was developing a distaste for the brother. Too bad she hadn't had an opportunity to shoot *him*.

"Of course, dear human." Zilek smiled condescendingly at her.

"It's Rylana. Rylana Avandar."

"It was Sergeant *Falcon* during the war, wasn't it?" Jildarin asked, eyes slitted as he regarded her.

"It was. I'm impressed that you learned my name. I was third in command of the Moon Daggers, and our unit merely worked for the joint kingdoms, so I wasn't an important player in the grand scheme of things."

Jildarin's eyes slitted further. "When we captured and interrogated one of your spies, I *asked* who the archer was who shot me."

Unease crept into Rylana at the reminder of the many dark atrocities that had taken place during the war and that yet haunted her nightmares. She had little doubt that the spy he spoke of hadn't survived that interrogation.

Refusing to appear weak or cowed before the dragons, Rylana lifted her chin. "That was wise. One should know the names of one's enemies."

"Thus to more easily identify them when they show up in your place of business as part of a plot to finish what they started a year earlier," Jildarin said. "Do you think it's not blatantly obvious why you're here?"

"We've established that it's not your wit that drew her." Zilek appeared far less offended by Rylana's appearance—and spying—than his brother. Probably because she hadn't shot *him*.

"Believe it or not," Rylana said, keeping her focus on Jildarin, "I didn't know that you were in the city or had anything to do with this diner until I saw you inside. I haven't been looking for you. The war is over, and dragons haven't been in my thoughts at all." Aside from the nightmares she'd just been thinking about. They'd grown less frequent these last couple of months, but they still reared up, causing her to wake with her heart pounding and sweat plastering her nightshirt to her body. If she actually succeeded in getting this job, would working alongside a dragon cause the bad dreams to grow more frequent again?

Maybe Sylin had been right. Maybe this was a bad idea.

"If you hired her to serve you," Zilek said, "you could more easily keep an eye on her than if she's out here in the streets, skulking about the city."

"My usual hobby," Rylana muttered.

"I'm not hiring her," Jildarin said. "I don't need help."

"You don't need help?" Zilek pushed the carriage doors fully open.

Light flooded into the storeroom, revealing an even more crowded space than Rylana had imagined while listening to their conversation. Crates, kegs, and sacks of oats, flour, and other bulk ingredients were stacked along the walls from cement floor to beamed ceiling. Piles also bulged outward, encroaching upon an empty area in the center and an aisle stretching from the carriage doors to the hallway leading to the dining room.

Zilek pointed at ovens lined up along one wall. "You need a *lot* of help. Let her count your money and order your supplies. That is the work of a servant, regardless, not a dragon."

"It's the work of a bookkeeper," Rylana said, "and it's clear from the numerous signs you've put out that you're in dire need of one."

"There are *two* signs." Jildarin snatched the one in her hand, then pushed the doors closed and glared at his brother again.

"By serving you and assisting you with this enterprise, perhaps she can make amends, and you will forgive her for shooting you," Zilek said.

"She is my *enemy*. She'll try to shoot me again!"

"That's not allowed in Tranquility. She would have to stab you with a kitchen knife, and surely you're capable enough, even in this diminished form—" Zilek plucked at his brother's shirt fabric, "—to keep her from succeeding at that."

"I am capable. You wouldn't be here with Mother's request otherwise." Jildarin opened his mouth, as if to say more, but then he squinted suspiciously at Rylana again.

Was he wondering if she'd heard the portion of the conversation about his mother wanting him to share his *essence* with a female dragon?

Having no interest in bringing that topic up, Rylana pointed at the sign. "This doesn't mention what the starting wage is."

"And yet you wish to work for me, regardless. That is a sure indication that you plan duplicity."

"No, I smelled the bacon cooking and was hoping meals would be included."

"Bacon?" Zilek's nostrils twitched. "I thought I caught the lingering scent of that even in the back. Are you making more of the seasoned bacon? Or the kind rubbed in alcohol? Bourbon, was it? I wouldn't mind some. It was delicious."

Jildarin was still squinting suspiciously at Rylana, but did his scowl lighten ever so slightly when his brother showed interest in his food?

"It *is* delicious," Jildarin stated. "And I do feed my staff meals that occur during their work hours. But how would you trust that I wouldn't poison yours?"

"Because you need me. I can find buyers for your surplus—*very* surplus—ovens to bring in some coins so you can pay your rent."

"That sounds like a more reliable way to obtain gold than from Mother," Zilek pointed out.

"Having an assassin pretend to work for me while scheming my death sounds reliable?" Jildarin asked.

"I'm an archer, not an assassin." Rylana kept herself from mentioning that she was traveling with a comrade who held that occupation. That wouldn't be a point in her favor. "An *educated* archer," she said.

The way Zilek nodded with certainty at his brother, as if he actually knew Rylana, made her wonder why he cared about this. He was even pushing for Jildarin to hire her. He couldn't *want* his brother assassinated, surely.

"Maybe," Zilek said, "she'll have such skill with the piddling affairs of running a business that you can leave for a few days to fly south and..." He glanced at Rylana, then finished by whispering, "put your wings to resolving affairs."

Ah, was that the reason for the brother's interest? Setting Jildarin up to end their mother's nagging?

"I'm not putting my wings on the Sunclaw females," Jildarin said.

"Mother will reward you." Zilek winked, fished in a pocket, and withdrew and rubbed together two gold coins.

Jildarin shook his head and turned his sour expression on Rylana again. "Come in and assess the numbers, if you wish. Should you try to slay me, I'll end you, the peacekeepers be damned."

Without waiting for her response, he stalked inside.

Zilek grinned and wandered down the street, whistling cheerfully.

Why didn't Rylana feel like she'd won a victory?

5

JILDARIN HAD LEFT ONE OF THE CARRIAGE DOORS OPEN, AND RYLANA was about to venture into the storeroom when Sylin walked out of the alley with their belongings and joined her. She looked down the street to an intersection where Zilek was disappearing around the corner.

"Other than arranging meals, you didn't discuss salary or benefits," Sylin said.

"How long were you spying on us?" Rylana asked, though it wasn't as if she could be affronted when she'd spied on the dragon brothers for twenty minutes herself.

"I was observing potential targets to determine if my blade services might be needed to protect a colleague."

"So... five minutes? Ten?"

"You should be grateful that I care enough to bother. Except when orders from a superior officer were involved, I've bestirred myself for few others."

"Was your bestirring prompted because you got kicked out of the coffee shop?"

"Certainly not. I'm a polite, quiet, and well-paying customer."

Rylana squinted at her.

"An elf walked in," Sylin said. "Though he didn't speak to me, he gave me a long, thoughtful look, so I decided to leave. After seeing an enemy recognize you, I judged it possible that even in this northern locale, many hundreds of miles from the war, I might also be recognized."

"And you don't need the entire elven enclave after you." Rylana took her bow, quiver, sword scabbard, and pack from her friend. "I'm going to look at Jildarin's books. I trust that won't interest you."

"Unless you refer to mystery, history, or adventure books, not in the least."

"Financial books." Rylana mimicked a pencil solving equations in the air.

"I will leave those to you. But did you get a sense that you'll be safe in there with him? Alone?" Sylin arched her eyebrows. "Tranquility law allows dragons to change into their native form within their lairs, doesn't it? And it sounds like he's sleeping in there."

Rylana hesitated. Was it possible Jildarin had invited her in simply so he could change without alarms going off? And then blast her with fire and chomp down on her with that great fang-filled maw?

"He seemed more concerned about *me* attempting to kill *him*," she said.

"We accuse others most often of what we've contemplated doing ourselves, that which is top of mind."

"I'll risk it."

Sylin cocked her head. "Why?"

"I told you why."

"Guilt?"

"Yeah. It's a powerful human emotion. So is a desire for bacon." Rylana had been intrigued when the brother had mentioned seasonings. And a bourbon rub?

"If you say so. I'll leave you and check a few more hostels to see if there are any rooms available. If not, I suppose we can sleep in a park or in the woods or farmlands outside the city. It isn't as if we've gone without shelter before."

"True, but it rains and snows a lot up here. A roof would be nice."

"There's always your family's castle."

"I told you I'm not going over there, not even to sleep on the lawn outside."

"Maybe the dragon will let you stay in his lair. Ask him that when you're inquiring about benefits."

"Oh, I'll be sure to. Salary, sick days, vacation pay, and whether it's acceptable to sleep sprawled across the gnomish ovens are all things that should be covered during a job interview, right?"

"I believe so, yes." Sylin saluted her, then headed off down the street.

Rylana stepped into the storeroom, hoping she hadn't irritated Jildarin further by keeping him waiting. But he hadn't remained in the crate-, keg-, sack-, and oven-filled space.

In the hallway at the other end, she spotted a goblin peering through a side door—that was the kitchen, wasn't it?—and speaking with someone. Jildarin?

Rylana left her belongings beside the carriage doors, trusting thieves didn't venture into a dragon's lair often, and walked slowly past the crates and sacks, reading labels and starting a mental inventory of items. The goblin watched her curiously before scurrying toward the dining room where a couple of new customers had arrived. Before reaching the kitchen, Rylana passed a tiny office with a desk and filing cabinets, but there weren't any papers or logbooks in sight. Unlike the packed storeroom, it was tidy with the trash bin empty.

The kitchen door opened easily on hinges that let it swing in both directions. Though the spacious room undoubtedly saw a lot more use than the office—with pots, knife blocks, utensils, and stacks of plates out on and above counters—it was also tidy. Surprisingly so, given the number of jars and pouches of spices and other ingredients scattered about with meal preparations in various stages of progress.

Jildarin stood at a butcher block, slicing potatoes. Scintillating scents wafted from a stockpot with the flames burning low. Alas, Rylana didn't see any bacon being fried or left over from the morning meal. She might have to wait until breakfast rolled around for a sample.

Without pausing cutting, Jildarin looked over at her. His expression wasn't any more inviting than before, and Sylin's question came to mind. Why *was* Rylana doing this?

Yes, she needed a job, but she didn't know if this one would pay. And Rylana had never been the type to do foolish things for the sake of a man, even an appealingly handsome one. Given what Jildarin was, his handsomeness was irrelevant. Humans and dragons didn't have relationships, even when they *weren't* former enemies. Besides, she was still getting over Mav. She wasn't looking for a relationship with anyone.

"What are you doing, my enemy?" Jildarin asked.

Why had she thought *former* enemy? He clearly believed she was still one.

"You said I could come in and look over your numbers, but I didn't see any ledgers in your office. Where are you keeping track of inventory and profit and losses?"

Jildarin stopped chopping for long enough to touch his index finger to his temple.

"I'm beginning to see why there's a problem," Rylana said.

"There's *not* a problem."

"You're behind on your rent."

"Are there any conversations I've had today that you *haven't* spied upon?"

"You had the rent one in the open with your landlord. And the other… Well, you had it by an open door."

"I am a fool for allowing you into my diner." Jildarin growled and returned to slicing his potatoes. Vigorously. The knife went *thunk, thunk, thunk* on the cutting board.

"It's a good idea to keep written records of everything for your business," Rylana said. "I trust someone is tallying sales at the end of the day, right? Do you have any papers at all? Or at least an empty ledger I can get started with? It would be a good idea to record all your existing inventory and figure out what orders you need to make on a regular basis and how much your typical ingredients and expenses are. That'll help you figure out how much to charge for meals."

Jildarin eyed her. "What is a *ledger*?"

"An empty book for recording debits and credits."

He looked blankly at her.

"I could start with some paper, I suppose," she said. "You do have that, don't you? And pencils?"

Jildarin looked around the kitchen thoughtfully, then walked to a locker door in the back, a magical button beside it glowing a soft orange. He tapped it, and the door swung open, a cool draft wafting out. He grabbed a frozen slab of meat that had been wrapped by a butcher and clunked it down on a metal counter. Rylana watched with bemusement as he unwrapped the meat and handed her the slightly bloodstained brown paper. Then he fished in a drawer of thermometers, shears, and other kitchen utensils and plucked out a half-used charcoal stick.

"You can write with this," he said.

"I may need something a little more sophisticated. Even as a mercenary living in a tent, I had ledgers and pencils. One Winterfest, Mav got me an abacus, though the kinds of calculations we did for ordering weren't that sophisticated, and I could do them in my head."

Jildarin, having provided what he apparently deemed suitable materials, returned to cutting potatoes.

"I know where a stationery store is," Rylana said. "Why don't I buy what I need and put it down as an expense for the business? Maybe you can pay me back once we sell your extra ovens."

Jildarin grunted without looking at her.

As Rylana headed for the dining room, she decided she wouldn't ask about a salary until she'd proven herself. For now, if Jildarin believed she was scheming his demise, he wouldn't give her money or anything else. Once she helped him turn a profit on his business and catch up on his rent, he might be more cooperative.

"Do you work here?" a middle-aged man asked when Rylana stepped into the dining room. He was seated at the bar with a woman about the same age, both wearing brown dockworker uniforms and matching marriage bracelets.

Rylana started to shake her head, but hadn't she just talked herself into a job? Sort of?

"Yes, but I'm new. *Very* new. And I'm the accountant. You probably need..." Rylana looked around for the gnome she'd seen earlier. His toolbox and pile of parts were in the corner, but she didn't see him.

"We don't need anyone in particular." The man glanced at the woman—his wife?—and lowered his voice. "We're looking for two orders of the special soup. Well, really only one is necessary, but we'd both like to try it. We're hoping to rekindle sparks. With, uhm, kindling."

The wife rolled her eyes. "He has trouble getting his *zerg* stick up these days and is hoping magic will help."

"It couldn't hurt, and don't tell *strangers* that, Mulivy. By the old and new gods." He rubbed his face, including reddening cheeks.

"I'm not sure..." Rylana looked down the hall, thinking of how Jildarin had thrown out the earlier amorous couple.

He made the soup and presumably knew how the dragon spices affected his clientele, but were there rules about who could get it? And how large a dose? And was one supposed to then promptly leave the premises before engaging in amorous activities? Maybe Rylana should have asked about that instead of ledgers and pencils. But she was applying to be the bookkeeper, not a server. Hypothetically, the only information she needed was the price Jildarin sold the soup for and how much the ingredients that went into it cost him.

"Please," the man said. "I've tried everything."

"He has," his wife said. "That includes all foods that are reputed to be aphrodisiacs, the special vigor and dilation herbs from the apothecary, and even a potion from the wizened half-elven alchemist in the Forbidden Market, but he's not had a twitch lately."

"There's been *some* twitching." He elbowed her, his cheeks redder than before. "Just not enough for, uhm, you know. And Mulivy is pining, you see. I don't want her to turn to another."

"I'm not pining that much," the woman told Rylana. "I've actually been enjoying evenings with my tea and books and not having to worry about being poked in the back."

"I…" This time, Rylana rubbed *her* face. As a mercenary, she'd heard everything—and far cruder talk than of twitching *zerg* sticks—but that didn't mean she *wanted* to hear the sex details of strangers. Never had she thought a desire to return to bookkeeping would lead to this.

"I'll handle it, new lady." The goblin that Rylana had seen in the hallway bounced up to her arm. "The special soup is eight copper," he informed the couple. "*Each*."

"It's six copper for a bowl," came a call from under a table.

Oh, *there* was the gnome that Rylana had seen earlier. He waved a wrench when their eyes met. Whether he was repairing a wobbly leg or had simply wanted a quiet nook to work, she had no idea.

"There's a mandatory tip for delivery," the goblin said, smiling at the couple while gesturing at the gnome. It was the two-fingered get-out-of-here-before-I-poke-these-into-your-eyes gesture popular with his kind.

"For delivery from... the kitchen to the table?" the man asked, though he was delving into the purse fastened to his belt.

"Yes," the goblin said. "Hazard pay. Did you know there's a *dragon* in the kitchen?"

"Isn't he the owner?" the woman asked.

"Yes, but he's *very* grumpy. He talks about how he wants to introduce dragon spices to the world while inventing new and innovative dishes, but I don't think he really likes people. Especially *green* people."

"*Six* copper each." The gnome came over, unfazed by a second finger gesture from the goblin, though he was six inches shorter and less muscular than his green-skinned colleague. "And Chef Jildarin isn't grumpy as long as you don't interrupt him when he's working."

The man counted out the coins, and the goblin reached for them, but the gnome's hand darted in first, sweeping them off the table, then depositing them in a metal cashbox bolted to a shelf under the bar. It took a finger press to a slightly glowing oval-shaped button to open the lid. For the sake of her future accounting work, Rylana hoped the goblin didn't have access to the cashbox.

"Who are you, and what do you do here?" she asked the goblin as the gnome went to retrieve the order.

"I'm Rolf, and I make deliveries and work for tips. *Gniknik* rudely proclaims that I have to wait for those receiving the food to think of their own accord to give me a tip. As if anyone voluntarily *tips* goblins. It's much more logical and lucrative to add my fee to the total preemptively."

"Or liberate it from their purses if they're not generous enough?" the gnome asked, returning with two steaming bowls that smelled wonderful.

Chunks of meat and vegetables floated in a rich broth with herbs sprinkled on top. Slices of bread with small ramekins of whipped butter accompanied the soup. It all looked wonderful, and Rylana couldn't see or smell anything suspicious about the meal. Her mouth watered, and she wanted to taste it herself. It had such an allure that she had to stick her hand in her pocket to keep from grabbing one of the spoons and helping herself.

"Do not share," Gniknik warned the couple as they accepted the offerings eagerly, inhaling the scents with as much interest as Rylana had. "There should be one bowl only for each person. I've already filled them fuller than is advised by the chef since I heard that you *seek* to feel amorous afterward, but he doesn't desire that outcome and is still experimenting with portions. He wants to make food that all species love but not that makes them *fall* in love." The gnome winked and headed back to his table.

Rylana scratched her cheek. Was that what all this with the dragon spices was about? Jildarin wasn't trying to turn his customers, er, *amorous,* as the gnome had said? Only make the best recipe he could? Perhaps to win that competition and be able to pay his rent?

Hinging financial security on something called the Golden Whisk was a gamble at best, so Rylana would help Jildarin get his affairs in order the old-fashioned way. With numbers.

Nodding to herself, she started for the door, intending to go buy a ledger, but someone walking past the window paused to look in. With sunlight limning the well-dressed gentleman from behind, and a beaver-fur hat low on his forehead, Rylana couldn't see him clearly, but her gut recognized him faster than her mind, and dread slammed into the pit of her stomach. Was that...

Before she could tell for certain, he backed away from the window and walked off. Maybe she could have opened the door and peered out for a better look, but her instincts were to skulk out the back door instead. Unless her gut had been wrong, that had been Vernest Vormalt, the man her father had long ago tried to arrange for her to marry.

6

With Jildarin turning a baleful eye on her each time she walked past his kitchen, Rylana spent the rest of the day taking inventory of the supplies and equipment in the storeroom. She'd started, with Gniknik's help, by opening the cashbox and counting what was in there and searching for records, but that hadn't taken long. There hadn't been any tallies—even on scraps of butcher paper—of the earnings from the previous months, weeks, or even days. Apparently, Jildarin took money from the cashbox when he needed to order food. Given how modest the amount inside had been, Rylana had a feeling he was in debt with a lot of his vendors. She would have to quiz him on that when he looked less... cranky. For now, she would do what she could and hope that he would come to trust her, though that might be asking a lot. After all, she *had* shot him.

Every time she passed through the dining room, Rylana glanced out the windows, worried Vormalt would be out there, peering in again. It had been a coincidence, she kept telling herself. He couldn't yet have learned that she was back in the city, and he certainly wouldn't be looking for her. Not after seventeen years. He must have married someone else by now. Even when he'd been attempting to court her, she hadn't gotten the impression that he was infatuated with her or even cared that much for her. It had been more that, because he'd been an up-and-coming employee in her father's business, and from a family of appropriate social standing, Vormalt and her father had thought it a logical idea. The man had come around the castle for months, bringing Rylana gifts and trying to get her to set a date for their wedding, even though she'd rejected his proposal. Three times. Until Father had tried to force the matter by accepting on her behalf.

"A coincidence," she told herself firmly and went back to her inventory project. In a city the size of Tranquility, Rylana would probably never see Vormalt again, especially if she avoided the west side of the lake, where his family lived a mile down the road from her father's estate.

"Hello?" A half-elven waitress who'd shown up to work the dinner service leaned into the storeroom. A pretty woman in her twenties, she had red-blonde hair, pale skin, slightly pointed ears, and a voluptuous figure that doubtless came from her human side. "Your name is Rylana, right?"

"Yes."

"I'm Zalani." The woman glanced back up the hallway before heading toward her.

Rylana lowered the inventory book, one of a handful of purchases she'd made at the stationery store. She could ill-afford extra expenditures right now, but a bookkeeper *needed* pencils. While working, she'd been flirting with the idea of asking Jildarin if she could sleep here until the diner became profitable enough for him to afford to pay her a salary. But maybe she was delusional to believe he would let her stick around long enough for that to happen. Sylin hadn't returned, however, with word of having obtained affordable lodgings, so Rylana would have to find a place to spend the night soon. The dinner service was almost over, and darkness and rain had arrived outside, so the thought of sleeping in a park lacked appeal.

"Someone came in looking for you a little while ago." Zalani stopped in front of Rylana and peered at the inventory book. "Are you actually here for... accounting purposes?"

"Yes."

"Rolf and Gniknik were here earlier, and they, uhm." Zalani waved toward the front of the diner. "They saw and heard your discussion with— Well, they said you were the person who gave Jildarin his scar." She touched the side of her eye.

"Yes." Rylana was more interested in hearing about the *someone* who'd come looking for her than discussing the past.

"Your arrow must have almost taken his eye out."

"That was the goal."

Zalani blinked.

"We were on opposing sides during the Ore War."

"Oh, yes. Of course. We got some of the details of the fighting up here, but..." Zalani shrugged and waved, as if to suggest it had all been so far away that the citizens of Tranquility hadn't worried about it. Maybe that was true. With the cold drizzle falling outside, it was easy to think of the steamy southern jungles and mountains as belonging to a far-off world.

"They've got a bet going about how long it will be before you try to kill Jildarin again, and if it'll work or if Jildarin will kill *you*. The odds are in favor of that. He *is* a dragon after all, even if he gets distracted by his cooking projects."

"I see."

"Goblins and gnomes aren't that great at reading humans. To me, you don't seem very..." Zalani looked at a pencil that Rylana had tucked behind her ear. "You don't strike me as an assassin."

"No, I was a soldier doing my job—defending my unit from dragons. You said someone was looking for me?"

"A man with a well-groomed beard and mustache who was wearing a beaver-fur cap and a fur-trimmed cloak. Dark hair with a few flecks of gray in it. Gray eyes. Pompous. I figure he was in his early forties and he was obviously of the monied sort, but he wouldn't give me his name. Even when I flirted with him."

The dread stirred anew in Rylana. Her gut had been right. That *had* been Vernest Vormalt she'd seen through the window.

"I don't *usually* flirt with the pompous ones, but sometimes it's worth enduring their arrogance for a good tip." Zalani made a motion of rubbing fingers together in the air, then cocked her head. "Even though he wouldn't tell me his name, he was looking for Rylana Avandar. As in the Avandar family with the big castle estate across the lake and the huge shipping business that runs freight all over the world." Zalani arched her eyebrows.

"It's not that uncommon of a surname. There are Avandars all over the north." The words came out automatically. Though Rylana had spoken of her family to Sylin and some of the other mercenaries she'd come to know well over the years, she hadn't proclaimed her heritage to all, never caring to be associated with her father or the estate. In the south, few would have recognized the name, being familiar only with the shipping business and not who owned it, but, every now and then, she'd come across someone else who'd spent time in Tranquility and knew of her family.

"Oh, sure," Zalani said. "Anyway, I didn't tell him you were back here. He had a dubious... *qora*."

Yes, Rylana well remembered the dubious *qora*. The elves liked that term for one's spiritual and magical force, and she wondered if Zalani had spent time among them. Most half-elves ended up being raised by their human parent since elves were snooty about their blood. They only considered purebred elves worthy of immersion in their culture, a place in their enclaves, and protection under their gods.

"His name is Vernest Vormalt, and it's been a long time since I've seen him," Rylana said. "I can't imagine what he would want with me. I don't suppose he said?"

"Just that he heard you were back in the city and looked forward to reacquainting himself with you." Zalani grimaced. "You're lucky he didn't stay for a bowl of soup. Even though I don't usually mind the companionship of men—all right, I seek it out regularly—I prefer to choose who and when. When they get randy after slurping the soup and try to forcibly choose me, I'm less delighted."

"I'll bet," Rylana murmured.

She eyed the hallway, half-expecting Vormalt to stalk into the storeroom at any moment. She had no idea what he wanted but reluctantly accepted that she would have to deal with him. An unpleasant thought, but she told herself that she was a much different person now, not a young and inexperienced girl of scarcely eighteen being pressured by her father. Now, she was a veteran and a seasoned fighter. Though she preferred the bow, she'd sparred with Sylin and the others often, not to mention engaging with actual enemies who'd made it to the shooting lines on the battlefield. She could handle Vormalt.

Not that he'd ever been overly physical with her. He'd tried to charm her with his wit—his wit and his gifts. The last gift he'd brought had been a collection of sugar cookies from a renowned confectionary in town, little purple and red sprinkles adorning the tops. They'd been speaking in the library, perusing some of the old tomes there, and one of Father's dogs had gotten into the cookies before she'd tried one. The hound had eaten a couple before they'd caught it. Shortly after, it had run outside and thrown up all around the grounds before slinking off into the woods. She'd shooed Vormalt out of the library and chucked the cookies into the trash. A week later, she'd departed for the south and hadn't returned. Until now. Maybe coming back had been a mistake.

"No coitus!" came Jildarin's booming voice from the dining room.

"I'd better get up there and help him usher out the guests." Zalani hurried for the hallway as a great thump came from the front room.

"That sounds like very physical ushering," Rylana said.

"That's how dragons do it." Zalani shrugged and smiled before disappearing into the hallway.

"You will eat in this establishment and nothing more!" Jildarin bellowed, another thump sounding, followed by the door slamming.

Rylana returned to her inventory, trusting her assistance wasn't needed up front, though she yawned and rubbed her lower back. She'd been on her feet all day and wouldn't mind sitting down, but she wanted to get through everything, and there was a lot of *everything* in the large storeroom.

So far, she hadn't discovered anything unexpected except that the quantities were sometimes odd. Did even a professional chef need two *dozen* spatulas? And an entire *box* of meat thermometers? Yet there'd been scarcely a pound or two left in the bag of oats, a measuring cup left inside suggesting it was drawn from often. She hadn't yet seen sign of dragon spices, though she'd found racks of rosemary, dwarfbeard, thyme, and elfmoss, staples in most northern kitchens.

"My enemy is still here." Jildarin stood in the hallway, eyeing her.

"There's a lot to inventory." Rylana held up the logbook, then turned the pages to show him how much she'd filled. "I thought I'd wait until tomorrow to look for buyers for your gnomish ovens. Do you want to give me a list of your suppliers—butcher, fishmonger, grocery, that kind of thing? Or, I suppose it's in your head, so maybe *recite* me a list. Then I can work with them to get totals for what you owe and what you typically order in a week."

Jildarin gazed at her, his face difficult to read. She had to *guess* what he might be thinking. Probably that she was going to great lengths if this was all a ruse to allow her to get close and try to kill him.

Behind him, the dining room had fallen silent, and the hallway was dark, lamps extinguished. Rylana wondered if he'd sent the rest of the staff home after kicking out the randy customers. If she was going to ask him if she could sleep here tonight, this would be the time, though maybe she was foolish to contemplate spending the night in the same building as a former enemy. A former enemy bearing a permanent scar from one of her arrows. Just because *she* felt guilty and wanted to make amends didn't mean that *he* wouldn't enjoy seeing her dead.

"Come with me," Jildarin finally said and headed for the double doors in the back.

"Are you... going to recite your list for me?"

"I will show you where I get those items." Jildarin glanced at her bow where she'd deposited it and the rest of her belongings earlier, then opened one of the carriage doors.

"So I can visit in the morning and learn about your accounts myself? I suppose I can do that."

"Yes." His gaze was cool as she picked up her cloak and joined him. Chilly air whispered through the doorway, and puddles dotted the drive and street outside.

"You're not thinking of instead showing me the dark alley where you plan for my body to eventually be found, are you?" Rylana asked.

His eyebrows twitched, and he walked outside. "The alarms would go off again if I attacked you in an alley."

"Probably only if you turned into a dragon first. There *are* occasionally murders in the city that are carried out with items the peacekeepers don't classify as weapons and tie up with their ribbons. Even by bare hands from time to time. Determined killers can find a way."

Jildarin looked at her again as they stepped into the street, lanterns on posts brightening the way.

"You knew that, right?" Rylana asked. "Maybe I shouldn't have given you that information."

"I've heard that the peacekeepers employ necromancers who can communicate with the souls of those who were killed in their city and find out who was responsible. The killers are then driven from Tranquility and memories of them magically stored in the guard pillars to ensure they may never return."

"I've heard that too. I'm not sure how much consolation it is to the dead to know their killers are on the pillars' naughty list."

"Will you come with me, or not?" Jildarin didn't sound like he cared one way or another.

Rylana sighed. "I'll come."

7

DESPITE HER RESERVATIONS ABOUT ACCOMPANYING A DRAGON INTO the night, Rylana pulled her hood up against the drizzle and walked beside Jildarin. If she showed him some trust, he might be more inclined to trust her. And when he pointed out a butcher shop two blocks from the diner, she believed he might genuinely have decided to show her where he got his supplies. After guiding her past a grocery and through the open-air market where he picked out mundane herbs and spices, he led her along the waterfront. To visit a fishmonger?

Many docks stretched out from the shoreline into the miles-long Luminous Lake, hosting everything from private sailboats to public ferries to cargo vessels. Some of the latter wore the sun-and-harpoon logo of her father's shipping company. Those vessels were being loaded and unloaded, laborers undeterred by the late hour. The crew came and went, often with a drunken lurch to their steps as they departed noisy taverns facing the lake.

Even in the misty night with poor visibility, some of the glowing blue, green, and purple fish were visible flitting in the water. A few pools of similarly luminescent plankton gathered between and beyond the docks, their colors never mingling, as if they represented different species that held grudges and didn't visit each other.

"Is your fishmonger in this direction?" Rylana asked as Jildarin led her farther than she would have expected down the waterfront street, dark warehouses looming on the side opposite the lake. The docks grew less frequent, the pedestrians fewer.

"Yes."

"You wouldn't lie to me, would you?"

"In the human world, is honesty customary among enemies?"

"For many people, yes. They try to treat even their adversaries with honor. But are we still enemies, Jildarin? The war is over."

"You tried to kill me," he said softly. "And you succeeded at killing other dragons with your bow."

"Just as you killed humans. I'm sure you would have delighted in chomping me in half if you'd had the opportunity. Many of my colleagues *did* die in exactly that manner. With elves peppering us with arrows, our soldiers fell to dragons who flew down from above and bit us in half or burned us to death with their fire."

Rylana had only meant to point out that they'd both participated in the war, not bring painful memories to mind, but they came nonetheless. For a moment, she saw the faces of the dead, many of the bodies so badly burned that they'd been unrecognizable in the aftermath. More keenly than the deaths of the others, she felt the loss of Captain Maverick. He'd fallen to an elven warrior with a sword, one who'd been targeting the leaders of the various military outfits. It had been in the last weeks of the war, before the kingdoms had retreated from the mountains and diplomats had eked out an unsavory truce with few of the concessions that the human, dwarf, and orc rulers had wanted.

"Your kind invaded *our* mountains," Jildarin said.

They'd passed the last of the buildings, and dark gardens and parks with trails stretched to the left, an area that nearly marked

Tranquility's southern border. A pillar along the walkway ahead reminded Rylana that they were still within the peacekeepers' protection, but the patrols were infrequent beyond the borders, and it would take longer for help to arrive if the alarms sounded.

"Several of the joint kingdoms also claimed those mountains," Rylana said, debating what she would do if Jildarin tried to lead her past the last pillar. "For generations, the dragons and elves didn't object to their presence or dispute the borders."

"Our kind *ignored* the human, dwarf, and orc infestations. Until you brought magic- and steam-powered machines to excavate great mines and forever scar the wilderness and drive game away."

Since Rylana had later in the war come to question whether humans had been right in fighting for those mountains, she didn't argue further.

Jildarin stopped before two lampposts framing the entrance of a wide boardwalk that stretched for almost a half mile into the lake toward Lucky Island, a popular destination for weddings and other ceremonies. There was also a scientific outpost for studying the unusual fish and plankton of the lake, as well as an observatory with a huge gnomish telescope that had been there in Rylana's youth. Unable to imagine Jildarin's fishmonger having a shop out there, she raised her eyebrows.

He was looking at her. Waiting for a response to his last statement?

"I was just a soldier, a mercenary at that, and not from the kingdoms you were fighting, so I don't honestly know what started everything and who was right or wrong."

"Yet you fought to slay my kind."

"It was my job. Like bookkeeping but with more clarity about what's expected and when I'll get paid."

Jildarin squinted at her. Why did she feel like she was at an inquisition?

"Look, there are reasons why I left home when I did and got into that line of work. I loved being out in nature and loosing arrows at targets, and, back then, I *hated* math and accounting and everything related to what I'd been taught to do. Archery was my only other skill, and I wanted adventure and to see the world. And to escape..." Rylana caught herself. The *last* thing she wanted was to go into details with a surly dragon about her upbringing and being pressured into marriage. "The job with the mercenaries suited my needs at the time. But years of war sanded away my desire to be a soldier. That's why I ultimately came back here."

Jildarin looked out along the dock. "Walk this way with me."

"You're taking me to Lucky Island? For what? Romance? It's not a warm moonlit night, and you're not..." Rylana trailed off when he looked at her again. "My type," she finished, though he *was* handsome. If he hadn't been a dragon who was possibly contemplating her death, and she hadn't been mourning Mav's loss, she might have been attracted to him.

Jildarin pointed at the silhouette of a rowboat out in the water, the illumination from pools of plankton making it visible on the otherwise dark night. When he strode onto the boardwalk, curiosity rather than wisdom prompted Rylana to follow him.

A few boats and ships dotted the lake to the north, some cargo vessels on their way in from the Troll Gulf River, and others belonging to fishermen who ventured out at night since it was easier to tell where the luminescent fish and eels were lurking after dark. Many varieties of those were considered delicacies by the Tranquility residents. To the south of the boardwalk was the marshy end of Lumi Lake where the waters were shallow, and it was easy for ships to become mired. Once, a ferry had carried people out to Lucky Island, but the city had built the boardwalk to make access easier and also as a barrier to keep ships from venturing into the shallows.

"You are familiar with the name of that outcrop?" Jildarin

asked over his shoulder halfway out to the island while pointing at a lump of rocks that rose from the lake between the boardwalk and the last of the docks in the city. A magically glowing lamp stuck up from the center, making it visible from the distance.

"We call it the Dragonspit," Rylana said.

"So I recently learned."

"A lot of ships have wrecked on it over the centuries. That's why the gnomes put that lamp out there."

"Humans like to name things they do not like after dragons."

"They name things that are *deadly* after dragons."

They hadn't reached Lucky Island, but Jildarin stopped and looked into the lake, his hands gripping the railing. Was that rowboat heading in their direction?

"Your kind," Jildarin said, "see my kind as savage beasts, but we have a culture, a history, a heritage, and we are as educated as your people—often *more* educated since we live longer lives and have seen much."

"Are you looking for sympathy? Dragons are incredibly powerful, deadly, and dangerous. You're nothing like gnomes or goblins that have historically been targeted for slavery because they're small and can't as easily put up a fight."

"I do not seek *sympathy*," Jildarin said, a growl in his voice, and turned toward her, "but I do seek to change the opinions of humans, dwarves, and orcs toward dragons. Only the elves, perhaps because we've shared the same mountains and forests for eons, understand our kind. But through my excellent cooking, I will show humans that dragons are a sophisticated species who can perform and appreciate the arts, including culinary arts."

Rylana had stopped a few steps back but had to fight the urge to back farther under his dark gaze. Out here on the dock, they were far from any peacekeepers, and she was well aware of how strong dragons were, even in their shape-shifted forms. While she believed she could win a fight with Vormalt, Jildarin was another matter.

"That sounds like a worthwhile goal," Rylana said.

Jildarin tilted his head. They'd moved far from the lampposts at the entrance to the boardwalk, and the glowing fish that flitted past below didn't illuminate the air above the water, so she couldn't see his face well. She did, however, sense that his expression was less hostile.

"Not many humans have said that. When I came to open the diner as a way to show off my art, a newspaper proclaimed that the food was doubtless poisoned, being distributed by a dragon bitter due to losses during the war."

"You'd think Tranquility would be open to a dragon chef. The whole background of the city is that it's the only place in the world where all the intelligent species can live and intermingle and have peaceful relationships with each other. Those who don't want that... aren't supposed to live here."

"Few want to *intermingle* with dragons, regardless of the location." Jildarin lifted a hand, directing the rowboat toward them. It had drawn close enough that a single fisherman—or was that a fisher goblin?—was visible rowing and attending nets that trailed behind him and into the water.

"Greetings, dragon patron," came the raspy voice of the goblin as the rowboat bumped gently into one of the dock pilings. "You've brought a female tonight? Will you attempt to get lucky on Lucky Island?" He cackled.

"I will not. You've acquired rare and delicious fare?"

"I've caught eight eels this evening. Do you want them all?"

"Yes." Coins clinked as Jildarin delved into a pocket. He waved for their visitor to show his catch before handing them over. "Elder Wognov doesn't deal in credit," he told Rylana. "One must pay in coin."

"What's the going rate for rare and delicious fare?" Rylana asked.

"Five copper for eels, three for thunder fish, and two for simple purple trout." The goblin opened one of several insulated boxes in the rowboat, revealing a stack of eels. Their glows had faded with their deaths but were still prominent enough to easily count them in the dark.

"Last week, it was *four* copper for eels," Jildarin said.

"Because I didn't have any eels." The goblin cackled. "But I'll give you a discount of two coppers if you take the lot. Three silver, eight coppers for all eight."

"You are aware of where we are?" Jildarin asked, his tone cool.

"Oh, I'm always aware of where the pillars are in relation to the dragons that I deal with. But you are a noble fanged one, and I believe you will not slay the brave goblin who dares sell to such a fearsome individual."

"I will not slay you if you honor your previous price and do not add on a goblin *tip*."

"Very well. Four coppers per eel, but *no* discount."

"I will give you three silvers for the lot."

"That is a discount of another two coppers! When I've already lowered the price."

"Your math skills are excellent."

"Unfortunately, yours are as well. You not only refuse to give me a tip but you barely acknowledge the many hours of work that went into the catch."

"I trust your tip is already calculated into the prices and that little has changed in the last week in the effort that is required to obtain eels."

Rylana, watching the exchange with some bemusement, decided the diner's messy financial situation probably had more to do with Jildarin's inexperience in running a business, and possibly a disinterest in anything that didn't deal with the cooking itself, than a lack of intelligence.

The goblin sighed dramatically as he placed the eels in a portion of netting, rolled them up, and lifted them like a bundle of kindling. Jildarin dropped three silver coins into his hand and accepted the offering.

"Enjoy your female," the goblin said as he used an oar to push the rowboat away from the boardwalk. "Or," he added with another cackle, "is she an enemy you brought out to this particular location intentionally?"

"She *is* an enemy," Jildarin stated. "One who attempted to price gouge me."

Jildarin touched his temple. He and Rylana both knew a different type of *gouging* had been involved. She shifted her weight, uneasy that he was still classifying her as an enemy. Even if he was joking with the goblin—or were the words intended more as a warning?—there was likely some truth to how he felt about her.

"Then I will depart before I accidentally witness something the peacekeepers will ask me about later." With the rowboat turned, the goblin put his oars into the water and stroked away.

The rain was picking up again, and Rylana wanted to return to the city and somewhere dry, but she couldn't help asking, "What's significant about this location?"

Since she'd grown up in the area, she would have assumed she knew more about Tranquility and the lake than a newcomer dragon, but she couldn't guess.

"It is between the last of the pillars at the edge of the city and the sole pillar on that island." Jildarin pointed. "Both are sufficiently distant from each other that approximately one-hundred feet of the boardwalk is not monitored for the use of weapons, magic, or dragons changing form."

"Interesting." Rylana still couldn't see much of his face and tried to determine if he was contemplating *acting* on that information. Would he be telling her about it if he intended to kill her? "Did you bring me out here to slay me and toss my body in so that the eels would eat it before the peacekeepers found it?"

"Freshwater eels, even interestingly glowing ones, consume insect larvae, snails, worms, and small fish."

"So, you don't think my body would appeal?" As rain pattered on the surface of the lake, Rylana pulled her cloak more tightly about her, feeling a chill for more than one reason.

"The carrion birds in the area might enjoy it."

"I don't know if we're engaging in delightful if grim banter or if you're going to attack me any moment."

"When I invited you to join me, I contemplated bringing you to this spot so that I could physically overpower you and question you under duress about your motives in coming to my diner. Were my hands about your throat, I judged that you would answer honestly."

"Have you changed your mind about interrogating me, or should I be figuring out how best to wrap an eel around the neck of an opponent who's stronger than I am?"

"You've been a less belligerent companion than I expected on the walk out here."

"I'm starting to like you too."

Jildarin cocked his head as he regarded her. "That was sarcasm, I believe."

"Yeah, but not belligerence."

He snorted and walked toward her. She eased to the side, lifting a hand in case he decided to attack. But he strode past without touching her, save for the eels that brushed her sleeve. The boardwalk wasn't that wide.

Rylana watched him, not sure if it would be safe to follow him or not. After walking about ten steps, he paused and stabbed a finger toward the dock at his feet.

"Beyond this point, the pillars can sense magic being used or weapons drawn."

"Or a dragon shifting into his native form?"

"Indeed." Jildarin took two steps forward. "Since I desire to keep my diner and must already pay *one* fine, you are safe from me at this point."

"I guess that's something," she murmured and followed him back into the city.

8

Even late at night, the streets of Tranquility were safe, but as Rylana walked back along the waterfront with Jildarin, she kept her ears perked and her eyes open, peeking into alleys and behind wagons and carriages parked in front of warehouses and taverns. She'd spent most of her adult life in much more dangerous parts of the world, so it was habit to be wary, and Jildarin pointing out that he had chosen *not* to interrogate her on the boardwalk didn't leave her certain that he would help out if someone attacked her.

That *should* have been unlikely here, if only because of the late hour and the drizzle that had driven pedestrians inside, but her instincts itched. A few times, she thought she saw movement in the shadows of an alley or deep doorway. Vernest Vormalt's face floated through her mind, but, unless he'd changed a lot over the years, she doubted he had the inclination—or skill—to tail a target through a dark city without being noticed.

"You will handle the ordering of my supplies going forward?" Jildarin asked, his mind clearly elsewhere.

"Yes. Just tell me how much of what you use for the diner in a week, and I'll take care of the ordering and recording costs. Since you're a regular customer, maybe I can also barter for discounts."

"Sometimes, I require special ingredients for a single-use purpose."

"Like dragon spices?" Even after he'd pointed out his various ingredient supplies, Rylana remained vague on what those were and where they came from. He hadn't once mentioned them that evening. Did they come from a furtive merchant in the Forbidden Market?

"Only a *dragon* may acquire dragon spices."

"They're not sold in the city, I'm guessing."

"One must fly deep into the southern climes and up to high mountain caves in the sides of steep, rocky cliffs that are guarded by magic—and the scaled inhabitants within." Jildarin touched his chest. "The various luminescent mosses, lichens, and fungi that, when dried and pulverized, we call spices grow on rock formations that hum with dangerous power. They are attuned to the magic of the dragons that live nearby and exist only where we live."

"So, you can't get the spices delivered, then?" Rylana envisioned a goblin on a winged bicycle attempting to reach one of the caves to collect the ingredients.

"You cannot."

"Resupplying seems like it would be a pain in an ogre's *bukok* even for you."

"Collection does demand a journey since there are not dragon caves in this area. My kind prefer the warmer southern reaches."

"I remember. Can you grow them in your storeroom with your own bodily emanations?"

"I..." Jildarin paused to look thoughtfully toward the lake.

They were only a few blocks from the turn up to Acorn Street and the diner, and nobody had attacked Rylana yet, so she tried to loosen her tense shoulders. Even if someone *was* following her for some reason, walking beside a dragon, even one distracted by a discussion of spices and emanations, ought to be a suitable deterrent.

"I hadn't considered whether that would be possible," Jildarin said. "This climate is temperate, not warm, but the heat from the kitchen *does* drift back to the storeroom in cool weather. The growth of the mosses and fungi has not spontaneously happened, but perhaps I will ask one of our scientists if it might be possible if one inoculated the area."

"Dragons have scientists?"

Jildarin looked balefully at her. "As I informed you, our kind are more educated and sophisticated than *your* kind believe."

"Sorry. It's hard to look at someone with fangs longer than swords and think of sophistication. Or science."

"You judge us by our appearance."

"No, I judge you by the fact that dragons ate my comrades during the war."

"Human meat is unpalatable. I assure you they weren't *eaten*."

"Fine, but they were eviscerated or burned beyond all recognition and left for dead."

"Dragons are fearsome predators when their ire is raised, which your kind are sufficiently talented at doing." Jildarin touched the scar near his eye.

"I received a lot of injuries too, you know. The war was rough on both sides." Rylana almost untucked her tunic to show him a scar along her side that had almost eviscerated *her*, though it had been delivered by an elven sword rather than dragon fangs, but the streetlamps didn't provide that much illumination. Besides, if someone *was* following them, she didn't want to provide material for a peep show.

"Yes. Cooking is more relaxing than battle. The special ingredients of which I spoke can be acquired in the city. They are not components in my regular recipes, but I am practicing with them for the Golden Whisk. You know the details of it?"

"I don't know anything about it. My brother, cousins, and I didn't jump to attend cooking contests when I was growing up."

"It is strange that you think *dragons* lack sophistication."

Rylana wanted to reply with a witty retort, but a yawn derailed her. All she managed was, "Oh, I'm sure," and to think longingly of a comfortable bed.

Jildarin, perhaps contemplating growing fungi, turned to walk toward Acorn Street. Rylana rubbed her gritty eyes and debated asking what she'd considered and dismissed earlier. The worst he could say was *no*, right?

"I've already passed the first step of having my meals chosen during a blind taste test," Jildarin said, "so I am officially one of only a dozen contestants in the Golden Whisk, but I must now practice developing recipes and executing dishes made from myriad different ingredients, some unusual. At the least, the combinations of ingredients required to be used in the dishes are atypical. For the contest, we may bring our own knives and our own spices, but everything else will be supplied at the venue, and we will not know in advance which ingredients we will have to showcase in meals for the judges. From what I've researched about past years' competitions, it is usually a mixture of mundane and exotic ingredients." Jildarin held up his bundle of eels.

"Just make a list—or recite a list for me—and I'll check the prices at various merchants to get what you need."

"Check the prices?"

"Yes, to ensure you get the best deal."

"Quality and trustworthiness are more important than price when selecting a supplier."

Rylana was about to say that he was in debt to his landlord and not turning a profit, so he couldn't be picky about *quality,* especially for practice dishes, but he spoke again.

"One disreputable half-orc with a grudge toward dragons *poisoned* the ingredients I ordered from him. He mixed in wolfsbane, a substance as deadly to my kind as yours. The peacekeepers have no way to detect a weapon such as that. If not for my superior olfactory senses, I might have consumed it and also served it to others."

"Er, did you report it to the peacekeepers?"

"I did, even taking the ingredient with his label on it, to them. They accepted it and claimed they would investigate, but the half-orc has not been arrested and continues to run his store. The gnomish authorities here are quick to suspect dragons of improper behavior but do little to defend them against the same."

Rylana doubted the gnomes wanted dragons in their peaceful city and wasn't that surprised. When the founders of Tranquility had built it, writing on the main entrance pillars that all species were welcome within its borders, they probably hadn't expected their kind to be drawn to visit. If the poison incident had been recent, it was no wonder Jildarin was on edge and suspicious of her.

"Tell me the name of that store so I don't order from it," Rylana said. "Though I doubt the owner would poison me."

If the half-orc proprietor was still in business, he presumably didn't poison *most* of his clients.

"I'm friendly and charming and hardly ever roar at people," she added.

"Instead, you shoot them with your bow."

"Yeah, but I can't do that here."

"You will avoid the establishment, regardless. The word will soon get out that you are shopping for a heinous dragon."

"So far, I haven't heard anyone call you that." Rylana didn't mention that no fewer than three people had referred to him as *grumpy*.

"Once I have won the Golden Whisk and satisfied the tastebuds of many in this city, they will be eager to visit my diner and won't call me *anything*. Except perhaps talented."

"And sophisticated?"

Jildarin squinted at her, perhaps trying to decide if she was teasing him—maybe a little—but said only, "Yes."

"Since you've decided you're not going to kill me tonight," Rylana said as they reached the intersection near the diner, a fountain in the center gurgling next to a pillar, "I'm going to ask if I can spend the night."

"Spend the night?" Jildarin stopped and stared at her.

"In your diner. It's raining, cold, and I don't have lodgings. Also, I'm short on funds. You haven't suggested that you'll pay me anytime soon, and there aren't many vacancies in the city anyway. My friend and I checked several hostels earlier." Rylana wondered where Sylin had found shelter for the night and also hoped she hadn't run into any trouble. What if the elf who'd seen her in the coffee shop earlier had reported her presence to the other elves in the city, and they'd objected to her visiting? Like Jildarin, they might also know of gaps where the peacekeepers' magical coverage was incomplete.

"Why would you want to sleep in the lair of a dragon?" Jildarin's tone had shifted from thoughtful to suspicious.

"Like I said. Rain, cold, and nowhere else to go. It also seems fair that you would give me *something* for the time I've put in working for you, at least until you've got enough funds to start paying me a salary."

"You've put in *one day*."

"It was a *long* day."

Jildarin looked past her shoulder and toward the diner and didn't answer. Someone tall and wearing dark clothing with a hood pulled up against the rain—or against being *seen*?—was peering in the window by the door. Whoever it was turned enough to see them, then scurried off down the street in the opposite direction.

Again thinking of Vormalt, Rylana grimaced. "Should we chase that person down?"

"To what end?" Jildarin walked toward the diner but didn't look like he had chasing in mind. The person disappeared into the same alley that Rylana had fled into that morning.

"To learn why they were peering through your windows?"

"People sometimes show up in the depths of the night, hoping to acquire leftover soup. Your kind are overly preoccupied with sexual acts." Jildarin looked at her with condemnation.

"Some people enjoy them. Do dragons not..." Rylana didn't know how to finish the question. She knew dragons *mated*, especially after the discussion she'd overheard between Jildarin and his brother, but, in all her years as a mercenary, she couldn't remember anyone talking with authority on the subject or whether, when they shifted into human form, they experienced human... *urges.* She didn't think dragons discussed such things with outsiders, and the soldiers had always been a lot more concerned about dragons using their human forms to spy rather than for liaisons.

"Engage in sexual acts? For mating purposes when a female is in heat, yes, but not *all the time* like humans and orcs, and do not even bring up goblins. They are like rabbits. I cannot imagine being so preoccupied by coitus."

"I'll keep that in mind if I have the unwise urge to ask you on a date."

"Do so." Jildarin stopped at the door to the diner and looked at her. "You are still here. The employment will not start again until the morning."

"Does that mean you're denying my request to sleep here?"

"*Yes.*"

"The storeroom would be fine. I left my things there anyway."

"The storeroom is my *lair*."

"What if I slept in the diner? Or the kitchen?"

"You are an *assassin*."

"No, I'm an archer, and I can't use my bow while there's a tranquility ribbon on it. I don't have any mithril arrowheads anyway. My normal ones wouldn't pierce a dragon's scales." Rylana could hardly believe he viewed her as a real threat. Even if the half-orc *had* tried to poison him recently, what could she do to such a powerful being without an army beside her? "You sleep in your dragon form, don't you?"

"I am usually compelled to spend hours regenerating in my natural state, yes."

"Then you'll be impervious to my weapons, right? I'd have to stab you in a vulnerable spot like your eye, and I assume that's closed when you sleep." The rain had picked up, droplets falling from the edge of Rylana's hood, and her cloak was already soaked through. She longed for dryness. "What's the problem?"

"I do not share my lair with others, even those incapable of menacing me."

"I'll sleep under a table. Or in a little corner behind an oven. Anywhere dry would be fine." She shook the water droplets from her hood.

"My enemy," Jildarin said slowly, as if she were dim, "I do not trust you."

"I'm the one who's going to be vulnerable sleeping next to a dragon in his native form. You could chomp me in half at any point during the night."

"When I am in my native form, I can't fit through the hallway to the tables."

"Then we'll both be safe from each other."

Jildarin made an exasperated noise and opened the door, chopping an ambiguous wave that could have been an invitation to follow or a promise that he would hit her in the head with a mallet. "You will sleep in the storeroom in a corner where I can keep an eye on you, and you will not leave at any time during the night, lest I suspect you of inimical intent."

Rylana stepped inside, willing to agree to anything to get out of the rain. As if the matter were settled, he was already heading for the hallway.

She didn't want to argue but couldn't help but ask, "What if I have to pee?"

"You will not leave your corner."

"That sounds messy."

"It had better not be," he said darkly over his shoulder.

9

THE FLOOR IN THE CORNER OF THE DINER'S STOREROOM WAS DRY AND the air warmer than Rylana had expected, given that the kitchen ovens had been allowed to burn down for the night. Since dragons preferred southern climates, maybe Jildarin had a magical implement that provided warmth. Or maybe his giant dragon body put out heat.

During the night, Rylana had been very aware of the powerful, winged, and fanged predator sleeping scant yards away in the center of the storeroom. Only after she'd seen his silver-scaled body on the cement floor, tail curled around it, snout resting on the end, had she realized that what she'd initially considered haphazard and overflowing stacks and mounds of crates, kegs, and sacks were arranged to form a cozy space around him as he slept.

Or *did* he sleep? Whenever Rylana had stirred and looked over, she'd caught one of his silver lids open, an assessing emerald eye gazing in her direction.

How strange that he worried about *her* when she kept thinking how vulnerable she was. Her sword, bow, and quiver were inaccessible to her, thanks to the ribbons, and neither her knife nor unarmed combat skills would save her if such a strong, powerful, and fast foe attacked her. How ludicrous that she'd thought sleeping in a dragon's lair would be better than enduring a night on a park bench in the rain.

When Rylana had been a mercenary, she'd traveled with a small tent as well as her food, water, and medical supplies, but, when she'd left, she'd turned in her gear to the remnants of the unit, never planning to return to a soldier's life. Even though she and Sylin had traveled for several months first, Rylana had planned from the beginning to end up back in Tranquility. During those last years of the war, when the battles had dragged on and on, fewer and fewer comrades surviving after each engagement, she'd longed for a less bloody existence, one filled with more peace. She'd daydreamed of starting fresh here and reestablishing relationships with old friends. And, after Mav had died, there'd been no reason to linger in the south.

Half-asleep, dreams lingering, Rylana didn't hear Jildarin rise or change back into his human form. It wasn't until the scent of frying bacon wafted back into the storeroom that she came fully awake. That smelled *amazing.*

She swigged from her canteen, pulled on her boots, and touched the previous day's clothing to see if it had dried. Despite being draped on a crate, everything was still damp, so she fished her spare clothes out of her pack. After dressing, she started for the hallway. Her nostrils twitched like those of a hound, and her mouth watered in anticipation, but a knock at the carriage doors made her pause.

Unpleasant thoughts of Vormalt, stalkers, and bacon getting cold filled her mind, and she wanted to ignore it and hurry up the hallway. But what if Jildarin was expecting a delivery? Since she *was* working for him, however vaguely and noncontractually, and would be ordering supplies soon, accepting deliveries would probably be her responsibility. That didn't keep her from drawing her utility knife as she walked to the doors. It was, after all, early for deliveries.

The knock came again. Windows were high and sparse in the storeroom, so Rylana couldn't see out. She opened one of the doors warily.

Sylin stood in the same clothing as the night before, but she wasn't damp, and she looked as beautiful and unrumpled as ever. As Rylana had observed before during the years they'd worked together, elves seemed incapable of rumpling.

"You slept with the dragon?" Sylin asked with amusement.

"I slept... *adjacent* to the dragon. With crates between us." Rylana waved toward her corner, her belongings visible. Oops, maybe she should have tucked her corset and drawers away, but they needed to finish drying.

"I'm surprised you trusted each other enough for such intimacy."

"It was raining. And there were a *lot* of crates between us."

"Which wouldn't be an obstacle in the least to a dragon who decided to slay you in the middle of the night. The pillar alarms wouldn't have gone off since he was being dragonly in his own lair."

"I'm aware."

Sylin tilted her head. "There are rumors that if a woman screams, the golems will hear and come of their own accord."

"If *anyone* screams and they are within auditory range, yes."

"There are two golems standing at that fountain, but I don't know how long they've been there." Sylin pointed down the street toward the intersection.

Rylana frowned in that direction and walked up the drive far enough to see the spot. In addition to the two magical, stone-skinned creatures, a pair of uniformed gnomes were pointing about, one holding a small notepad. The rain had stopped, but large puddles remained on the cobblestones.

"The golems weren't there last night," Rylana said, "but the peacekeepers run patrols around the clock throughout the city, so spotting them isn't unusual. Where did *you* sleep? I'd wondered if you'd found a place. This was a last resort."

Sylin's eyes crinkled at the corners. "I assumed."

"It was fine. He didn't bother me other than by looking mistrustfully in my direction every time I moved."

"You should be used to that. Mercenaries get mistrustful looks all the time, even from allies. The kingdom soldiers never trust those who hold no oaths and work only for coin."

"Yeah, but the soldiers don't have the giant eyes of a predator that pierce unnervingly into your soul."

"It's the *fangs* I'd be more worried about piercings from. I slept in a room above a tavern only a few blocks away. I was doing my evening jog to stay fit when two drunkards were thrown out into the street not ten feet in front of me. Apparently, they'd been brawling, and the owner said their rooms were forfeit. I swooped in like a hawk on a field mouse and took one of the new vacancies. You would have found it delightful. There was a mattress, a pillow, and blankets."

"I assume you slept on the floor."

"Well, of course. Assassins can't let themselves go soft. Last night, I came back to see if you wanted to share the room, but the front door was locked, the lanterns were out, and nobody was there." Sylin spread her arms.

"I accompanied Jildarin on an excursion along the waterfront."

"A romantic excursion?"

"He showed me a place on the boardwalk between the city and Lucky Island where he could kill me without the peacekeepers knowing."

"As an assassin, I wouldn't say that would necessarily destroy my mood for intimacy." Sylin's nostrils twitched. "Is that bacon? And... some kind of egg dish?"

"I think so." Rylana peered at a metal and ceramic smoker burning outside near the door, with the smell of fish wafting from it. Or was that where the eels had gone? Rylana was surprised she'd slept heavily enough as morning approached that she hadn't heard Jildarin rummaging around, setting up the smoker.

"There are eels in there," Sylin said. "I already checked. They smell good. I'm surprised passersby haven't taken samples."

Given how few humans Rylana had encountered who craved eels, *she* wasn't surprised. Though the scents wafting out were more appealing than she would have expected.

"Why don't you come in, and we'll see if my new dragon employer will feed us?" Rylana waved for Sylin to follow her toward the hallway.

"As a chef, that's his duty, isn't it?"

"I get the feeling that, while he *does* want the common man—and dwarf and orc and gnome—to experience and appreciate his food, his primary concern is winning the upcoming Golden Whisk."

"The what?"

"It's a cooking contest."

"Huh." Before entering the hallway, Sylin gazed around the storeroom. "Why are there so many of the same kind of appliances?"

"Ordering mishap, I understand. I'm going to help him refine his purchasing system—or lack of a system—and get rid of excess inventory. You aren't in the market for a gnomish commercial oven, are you?"

"Not at this time. Your new employer sounds quirky for a dragon."

"Yes." Rylana peered into the kitchen as they drew even with it, though she could see Gniknik and Zalani seating people in the dining room and was tempted to head straight there. But the staff, as she'd learned the day before, ate in a back corner of the kitchen.

Not certain how Jildarin would feel about Sylin joining her, especially when he had suggested several times that he didn't find *assassins* appealing, Rylana knocked on the swinging door before entering. "Mind if my friend joins us for breakfast? And by the old and new gods, your food smells amazing."

Opening the door allowed them to enter a heavenly mixture of sumptuous aromas. There was the bacon, of course, but Rylana picked up the scents of herbs and spices, baked eggs, melty cheese, and other foods she couldn't identify but longed to try.

"Yes," Jildarin stated, barely glancing at them as he took pans out of the oven. For some reason, he was shirtless, revealing a lean but muscular physique, and Rylana blinked at the choice for kitchen work. Didn't he worry about hot spatters? "For your friend, it is four coppers for breakfast. Only employees eat for free."

"That's fair," Sylin said, waving that she had the coin.

Rylana was tempted to object, but, as Jildarin had pointed out last night, she *had* only worked one day for him. And a partial day at that. Once she'd fixed all the inefficiencies and his business was turning a profit, she would ask for more benefits. Like wages.

Inhaling deeply and with a pleased smile, Sylin hurried to stools at the staff table in the corner of the kitchen.

"Is there a reason you're not wearing a shirt, Jildarin?" Spotting a row of hooks with chef's coats and aprons dangling from them, Rylana pointed, offering to grab clothes for him. "After our conversation last night, I assume you're not hoping to attract women."

With a whisk dripping an egg mixture in hand, Jildarin looked blankly over at her.

"I thought not." Rylana held up an apron in offering.

"When the bacon spatters in its pan, it flings droplets of grease that leave unappealing stains on my garments," he said.

"Yeah, but that's better than hot grease spattering your chest. That has to hurt."

"Heat rarely fazes a dragon."

"Let the chef cook topless if he wants," Sylin murmured, waving to an empty stool, "and simply appreciate the show."

Jildarin *was* nice to look at without his shirt on—in all states, really—but Rylana was surprised Sylin would remark on it. She'd been devotedly single all the years that Rylana had known her, only indulging occasionally in one-night flings—or *esylanta*, as the elves called them—with partners that had been enemies as often as allies. Rylana had never pried. Even though Sylin had opened up more to her than most of the mercenaries, she had always been close-lipped on personal topics and spent more time alone than with others.

"I didn't know you enjoyed looking at men with grease-spattered chests," was all Rylana said.

"The grease is irrelevant. The chest is nicely symmetrical, muscular, and not overly hairy."

"So, you're in love."

"*I'm* not the one who spent the night in a storeroom with him."

"Separated by crates. *Many* crates."

Jildarin had returned to whisking eggs and appeared oblivious to the conversation. He grabbed a pinch of a ground green herb to add to his concoction, then picked up a dish of chopped meat—or maybe some of the eels. As he focused on his work, Rylana decided he didn't just *seem* oblivious to everything else but likely was, so she allowed herself, per Sylin's suggestion, to admire the fine view.

But not for long. Gniknik entered carrying a tray, the swinging door almost bumping Rylana in the rump, and she skittered to the corner table with Sylin.

"Chef Jildarin, we've got *six* customers this morning," the gnome said with excitement. "That's a record for the opening hour. For *all* hours. And only two requested the special soup."

"The soup is not served for breakfast," Jildarin growled.

"Oh, I told them. And they decided not to leave. They said the aromas wafting out of the kitchen smelled too good not to try. They'd like some of your eggs and the bacon flight."

"The bacon flies?" Sylin murmured.

"I think that means there's a variety of types," Rylana said, having vague memories of her father hosting wine tastings at the castle and the visiting vintners using that term for a selection of their offerings.

"Crusting or rubbing bacon with different enhancements is one of my specialties." Jildarin sounded a touch smug. "Today, there is maple-bourbon bacon, spicy chili bacon, blueberry-glazed bacon, and one of my newest creations, bacon encrusted with spruce tips."

Rylana blinked. "Spruce? As in... the tree?"

"The needles," Jildarin said, "have an excellent flavor with hints of bright citrus and pine."

Rylana made a face. As a mercenary, she'd eaten a lot of dubious fare, but the cook had never fed the troops tree branches.

"They're a common foraging staple in temperate forests," Sylin said.

Of course, leave it to an *elf* not to bat an eye at the thought of eating pine needles. *Spruce* needles.

"They're good for you too," Sylin said. "They boost the immune system."

"Improving health is always my goal when eating bacon."

When Zalani came in, also carrying an empty tray, Jildarin removed pans of bacon from a warming oven so his servers could make up plates.

"I've also created four varieties of soufflé to test my baking skills, which are much improved since I've focused on them." Jildarin withdrew circular pans of baked egg dishes, the tops puffed over the sides and a beautiful golden brown.

Despite the conversation about spruce tips, Rylana's mouth

hadn't stopped watering, and she couldn't wait to try the food, but she made herself let the servers go first. They were, after all, attending actual *paying* customers, and, as the bookkeeper, she approved of that.

"That is a blended herb soufflé," Jildarin said, pointing, "that one is cauliflower and goat cheese, that one features spinach, and *that* one," he said, beaming with pride, "is a new recipe made with eels."

"Eels?" Zalani had been in the process of loading plates onto her tray but paused.

"Fresh eels," Rylana murmured. "Fresh *glowing* eels."

Jildarin nodded at her but lamented, "The baking process destroyed the glow, unfortunately. I suspected that would be the case since I've also had that experience grilling and roasting fish from that lake."

"It's all right," Rylana said. "Humans don't want their food to glow blue. Trust me."

"You are certain?" Jildarin asked. "I've heard the gnomish chefs here often employ what they call magical and molecular gastronomy to create dishes with unique textures, flavors, and colors."

"That is true," Gniknik said, hopping onto a stool so he could reach the plates that Zalani had prepared, then sweeping them onto his tray and heading back toward the dining room, "but they rarely glow in the dark."

"Hm." Jildarin's contemplative expression suggested he thought that making food glow sounded like a challenge rather than something to be avoided.

After the servers departed, Sylin laid five copper coins on the counter, grabbed a plate and filled it with bacon and soufflé, not hesitating to try the more interesting dishes. In fact, she took extra pieces of the spruce-tip-encrusted bacon.

"Maybe you should target elven customers, Jildarin," Rylana

suggested as she filled a plate for herself. "They're adventurous eaters."

"The spruce-tipped bacon is excellent." Sylin saluted her with a piece. "It's clear the needles were recently harvested, young and fresh with the spring. You don't want old spruce needles. They get tough and resinous."

"I do loathe resinous food." Rylana popped a piece of the maple-bourbon bacon in her mouth. It was excellent—and didn't taste at all of a forest.

The door opened, and Gniknik hopped in, waving his empty tray. "Chef, a *food critic* is here."

Jildarin lowered his whisk and faced the gnome.

"From the *Lumi Lake Chronicles*," Gniknik said. "I've heard of him. Each week, he does an article featuring a different diner or tavern in town. He said he wants a tasting menu and that he'll write up what he thinks about the food. If he likes it, the diner could get a lot of new people coming to try it. Even if he writes scathing things, it could bring in extra business."

"Never has such a person come to this diner. What is the protocol? Do I go out and speak with him?" Jildarin curled a lip, as if interacting with a food critic would be beneath him.

Rylana hadn't seen him go out and schmooze the guests and ask how they were enjoying the meal either. Maybe he wanted people to experience his artistry, not him.

"Put on a shirt or at least an apron if you go out to speak with him," Rylana said, believing a degree of professionalism would be in order.

"As his bookkeeper, are you allowed to make sartorial suggestions?" Sylin murmured.

"*Someone* has to."

"I can ask if he wants to meet you, Chef," Gniknik said, "but I don't think you need to go out there. That might be considered an attempt to influence what he writes, and food critics notoriously resist bribes, coercion, and hands around their throats."

"I will remain here then. You may prepare tasting dishes for him."

"Yes, Chef."

The gnome hurried to the counter, hopping onto the stool again, and grabbed fresh plates as a yawning Rolf walked in, his white hair sticking out in all directions. He grabbed bacon from pans, then headed to where dishes had piled up in the sink.

"Er, Chef?" Gniknik asked. "Shall I stick with the more *normal* recipes or also give him the eel soufflé and the spruce-tree bacon?"

"They are spruce *tips*," Jildarin said, "and you will share *all* of my excellent creations with this critic. Let him judge the full panoply of my offerings and write of them in this newspaper."

"Yes, Chef."

"It's all good." Sylin had moved on from the bacon to sampling the egg dishes. She placed her fork in her mouth, only slowly withdrawing it, then chewing thoroughly to savor the bite.

"I think so, too," Rylana said, "though my palate isn't the most refined after years of eating Cook's food."

"My palate is excellent. I keep it honed by tasting and assessing coffees from around the world."

"Hence your ability to tell a good spruce tip from a resinous one."

"Precisely."

Rylana started to say more but was diverted when Jildarin walked to the kitchen's exit, donned a white coat, and peered over the top of the swinging door. He shifted and craned his neck.

"Are you trying to see the critic to tell whether he's enjoying the food?" Rylana asked.

"His enjoyment is of no more consequence than that of any other patron."

"Of course. You can't see him from there, can you?"

"He must have seated himself in one of the booths to the side."

"Want me to go out and spy on him?"

"Certainly not."

Rylana popped a piece of maple-bourbon bacon into her mouth, then stood. "I'll go out and help clear dishes then. Next to his table."

Jildarin pursed his lips in apparent disapproval, but he also stepped aside to let her exit. "See if he wants a beverage. There is cow and goat milk, apple juice, and water."

"You need to make coffee."

"I do not care for flavored water, and there is a shop that specializes in it across the street. My serving it would be redundant."

Sylin lowered her fork and mouthed, "*Flavored water*," with a horrified expression.

"People like coffee," Rylana said, "and you don't want customers to leave to get a drink elsewhere, right? If you serve it here, you can charge a profitable amount, and folks will linger and chat amiably."

"I don't want people to *linger*." Jildarin made a shooing motion. "Go clear the plates next to the critic's table."

"But you don't want me to spy?"

"Certainly not."

"Right. I'll let you know if I hear good things." Rylana smiled as he shooed her out the door again.

But her smile dropped as soon as she reached the dining room, looked around, and found the booth where a bespectacled man sat across from another man, a notebook and pencil on the table beside numerous plates with different menu items between them. The critic was somewhat familiar—someone from the west side of the lake who'd been a kid about the time Rylana had, she thought. But the man across from him was *very* familiar, and she groaned as his gaze swung toward her. Vernest Vormalt.

10

RYLANA RESISTED THE URGE TO FLING HERSELF BEHIND THE BAR TO hide from Vormalt—after all, he'd already seen her. She needed to deal with him. Reminding herself that she was a combat veteran who'd faced *dragons*, she walked to the table.

The food critic looked up, blinking curiously at her a few times. "Rylana Avandar?"

"Yes," she said. His name clicked for her between one breath and the next, and she added, "Yerin Molingvar, right? You've changed."

He hadn't worn spectacles as a kid, and his freckles had been more pronounced, but she remembered him riding past the castle on his bicycle and asking if she or her brother wanted to come out and play. He'd been fond of making elaborate sandcastle villages on the beach while lecturing the other kids on proper structural support and engineering challenges. The rest of the children in the neighborhood, Rylana and her brother included, had been more interested in throwing balls or tossing sticks into the water for the dogs to fetch.

"You've changed too." Yerin adjusted his spectacles and considered her face—or maybe her hair.

"Yes, quite. What did you do to yourself, Rylana?" Vormalt waved at her hair. "That used to be lush and long, and now it's... Did you cut it yourself?"

"Actually, a comrade did. She's skilled with knives."

"Not that skilled." Vormalt smirked.

"I'll admit her blade moves are more for assailing enemies than cutting hair, but the only scissors in our unit were in the doc's medical kit, and I was loath to be trimmed by something used for snipping off sutures and removing bloody bandages. Besides, I've found it practical to have my hair shorter. And you're not as charming as you used to be, Vernest."

The smirk turned into a dazzling smile in a face that remained handsome, the flecks of gray in his hair doing little to detract. "You remember me too. I'm touched."

"Why are you lurking at the Dragon Diner?" Rylana looked at his wrist, relieved to spot a golden marriage bracelet there. Whatever had brought him by, it wasn't a quest for a wife.

She'd asked the question to Vormalt, but Yerin lifted his notepad and answered. "The newspaper sent me to try the food and learn if there's a story here. This diner is developing quite a reputation." He raised his eyebrows, as if to ask if she knew more and would gossip. "Do you... work here?"

"Yes, but only since yesterday." Rylana eyed the notepad, glimpsing lists of ingredients, several with question marks after them.

Was Yerin trying to deconstruct Jildarin's recipes? She had no idea if that was typical for a food critic but supposed it might be. He would want to mention specifics in whatever write-up he did. Hopefully, he wouldn't pick out the spruce tips and make scathing comments about being fed tree branches.

"Are you a waitress now? At a diner a block from the docks?"

Vormalt's smile shifted back into a smirk—a condescending one. "Does your father know? He would be terribly disappointed in you working such a menial job, I'm certain."

"I'm the bookkeeper. But I used to kill people for a living."

Vormalt blinked. Maybe that wasn't the wisest thing to announce, especially in Tranquility, but Rylana felt the need to let him know that she'd changed and that she wouldn't be pressured by whatever he wanted.

"Gavlin Avandar might also be chagrined by that career choice," Yerin murmured.

"I didn't tell him about it," Rylana said. "Vormalt, you must need something since you keep coming by this lowly diner a block from the docks. Do you want to step outside and discuss whatever it is in private?"

"I would like to speak with you, yes."

"I gathered when we saw you peering through the window last night." Rylana arched her eyebrows as she waited to see if he would deny he'd been the window-peeper. He did not. "I assume it wasn't a desire to monitor the bacon preparation that brought you by."

"The bacon *is* excellent. Write that down." As Vormalt slid out of the booth, he waved at Yerin, almost knocking over a water glass near the edge of the table. It wobbled but remained upright.

"The *Chronicles'* hobbyist archaeology journalist isn't going to advise me on my restaurant column," Yerin said.

Since when did Vormalt write for the newspaper? Or have an *archaeology* hobby? Rylana vaguely remembered him enjoying reading history books, but hadn't he been assiduously climbing the ranks in her father's business when she'd last seen him?

"*Excellent* is a pedestrian word with no inherent descriptive meaning," Yerin added.

"I'm always fortunate that you're willing to tutor me in the ways of scribes." When Vormalt stood straight, he towered over

Rylana, as he always had. He'd been gangly at twenty-five but had filled out since then.

"I remember why we didn't play with Yerin when we were kids," Rylana murmured as she walked toward the front door with Vormalt. She glanced down the hallway, wondering if Jildarin was still peering out of the kitchen, but he must have returned to his work.

"He's all right." Vormalt held the door open for her. "Just ambitious with a need to prove himself."

"Are you doing anything to prove yourself these days? Writing for the newspaper instead of working for my father?"

"He let me go years ago. Shortly after *you* left, as I recall."

"He didn't blame you for that, did he?"

"I think he was more upset after someone told him a story that I'd poisoned one of his dogs." Vormalt gave her a sidelong look.

"You *did* bring the cookies that made Darter sick."

"Your father should have held the baker accountable. As to my ambitions with the newspaper, my contributions are infrequent, usually made after I go on digs. I have become an archaeologist and take expeditions into the mountains every year." Vormalt looked up and down the street, his gaze lingering on two dwarven females who walked out of the bakery with a box similar to the one Sylin had described the day before—maybe that particular cake was a popular menu item. Vormalt pointed to the coffee shop. "A drink?"

"All right, but I can't stay for long. I'm on the clock."

Vormalt regarded her as they navigated around a wagon and across the street. "I *do* remember that you had a knack for numbers. Your father badly wanted you to go into the family business, not be an empty-headed trophy on some man's arm." He smirked as he looked at her hair again.

"*That* wasn't ever going to be my fate."

"Are you going to let that grow out again? Now that you're

not... what did you say you did before? I assume you were jesting to intimidate Yerin."

Yerin wasn't who she'd been delivering that message to, and Rylana bristled at the insults to her hair. "Until recently, I was a mercenary and fought in the Ore War."

Vormalt stopped in front of the coffee shop and stared at her. "You're not joking?"

Rylana showed him her right hand. In addition to scars on the back, her palm was calloused from training with swords, and the tips of her draw fingers were in a similar state. "I don't know what I'll do with my hair now, but it's hardly any of your concern. I see that you're married and presumably not looking."

His eyebrows lifted. "After you fled from our engagement—"

"We were never *engaged. Father* was the only one to agree to your proposal."

"I thought our marriage was a certainty. Regardless, I did indeed, after nearly perishing from a broken heart, have to seek the embrace of another. Pennigrew Timberport, in fact."

"An older lady, goodness. But quite well-endowed, so an obvious choice, I suppose."

"Well-endowed in family assets, certainly. Less well-endowed in *personal* assets, alas. We've had an open marriage, and, as far as looking goes, I do occasionally seek the company of others."

"Is it as open for her as it is for you?"

"Certainly."

Rylana grimaced as she perched on the edge of a chair at a table for two, less interested than ever in speaking with Vormalt.

"She's an agreeable enough wife, especially given the great wealth that she was raised amid, but I travel quite a bit, and pining with loneliness prompts me to seek out others from time to time."

"I don't need the details of your affairs," Rylana said. "What do you want with me?"

"I simply heard you'd arrived back in town and was quite

curious what became of you and what you've been doing all these years."

"It had to be more than curiosity that prompted you to come by three times in the last two days."

"It was only twice."

Vormalt waved for a blue-haired gnome—or maybe she was a half-gnome, because she was on the tall side for one of their diminutive species—to bring them coffee. One of the owners—Brella—was roasting beans again, and the air smelled wonderful.

"A latte for me," Rylana told the girl. Then, feeling obligated to at least *attempt* to turn this into a work-related business excursion, she added, "Will you ask the owners—I met them yesterday—if they have any interest in purchasing a better-than-new gnomish commercial oven?"

The girl blinked.

"They mentioned that they get their cookies from the bakery next door, but it would be less expensive if they made their own here in the shop. Further, you could incorporate your coffee into the batter. I enjoy dipping a wafer biscuit into my lattes, don't you? I'm certain all manner of treats could be enhanced with espresso powder if not whole delicious beans from your fine local roastery." Rylana waved toward the equipment.

"I… will see if they are interested."

"Your father must lament daily that you chose not to go into the family business," Vormalt said dryly. "You almost make *me* want to buy an oven from you. At the least, the cookies one could make sound appealing."

Turning back to Vormalt, Rylana asked, "You weren't the one stalking me in the streets last night?"

"Certainly not."

"Just peering in the windows?"

"I was hoping to speak with you and thought you might remain at the diner after closing."

Rylana debated if she believed him. She hadn't *seen* anyone following them the night before, with only her instincts alerting her to the possibility. Still, with his height and a tendency toward clumsiness that appeared to have lingered, he was, as she'd considered then, an unlikely stalker.

"What do you want to talk about?" she asked.

"You said you haven't been to the castle to visit your family?"

"I haven't, no."

"Hm. I used to enjoy sitting with you in the grand library by your room. Remember the sofas with the view of the lake?"

"I remember them." Rylana watched him as their drinks arrived, little cookies again on the saucers.

She would have to join Sylin for evening jogs if she were going to be a regular at such a calorically abundant establishment. Not to mention the danger of working in a diner overflowing with wondrous food. Her life as a mercenary had kept her in good shape, with Cook's meals *never* tempting her to overindulge, but Tranquility offered many more culinary delights.

"How *much* is the oven?" the girl asked before leaving. "Tezilly wants to know. Also, how is it *better* than new?"

"Ninety gold coins, down from the original price of one hundred." Rylana was glad she'd researched that the day before. "And it's been meticulously kept in Jildarin's storeroom where he sleeps in his dragon form at night, the magic his body emanates flowing into the items nearby, including the oven." Rylana had no idea if Jildarin's *emanations* could convey any power to nearby objects, but, after hearing his story of how dragon spices came to be, it seemed *possible*. "I'm not sure what exact power might now lurk in the oven," Rylana said, catching Brella glancing their way as she took empty bean sacks toward the back, "but maybe cookies made within it would be less likely to burn or be dry."

"That's a lot of coin," the girl said, "more than I've ever seen, but I will pass your words along."

"Thank you."

Rylana faced Vormalt again, expecting more dry comments and amusement in his eyes, but he was gazing thoughtfully out the window.

"I suppose the castle is about the same," Vormalt said, as if he hadn't heard the oven conversation, "since your mother passed long ago, and your father wasn't the sort to bring in decorators. Your brother, Frodin, and his wife lived there for a few years, but they eventually got their own place in town. Have you kept in touch with your family? Do you know what they've been up to this last… what's it been? A decade and a half?"

"Seventeen years." Rylana sipped from her latte.

"Goodness. Other than the hair, you look really good after all this time. At least from what I can tell under those mannish clothes you're wearing. I suppose dresses aren't practical for mercenaries."

"They aren't. It's a wonder that I once found you somewhat witty and charming."

"I was angling for something then." Vormalt winked at her.

"Thus greasing your words with flattery?"

"Yes, that's typical for all men courting women." He winked again.

She didn't think *all* men had that tendency, but she didn't want to prolong the conversation and said only, "Since you're apparently more prone to honesty now, tell me what you want."

"I would appreciate it if you could take me to your family's castle for a visit. As I was saying, I always loved the library, and there were a few old tomes that would be of particular interest to me now that I not only read about history but have a career researching it."

"Uh-huh. Why won't my father let you in?"

"His grudge."

"Over the dog?"

"He adores his hounds."

"That, I know, but he liked you almost as much. He wanted you to *marry* me, after all."

"I think that was less about adoration and more about me being apt enough with numbers and his business that he believed you and I would produce suitably scholarly offspring. He had fewer hopes pinned on your brother, you know. I'm surprised *he* wasn't the one who ran away."

Rylana waved that away, hardly believing her father had held a grudge against Vormalt for all this time. "I'm sure he would let you in if you asked."

"I did ask. Several times. Did you know there are magical security wards to keep trespassers off the grounds and out of the castle?"

"I did know that, yes. Father had them installed when I was a kid. His hunting hounds love people too much and weren't good deterrents."

"Well, after all these years, your father hasn't let me step foot inside, not that I've made a habit of pestering him. Pennigrew has a castle, too, you know." Vormalt sipped from his cup, smirking around the edge. "A *bigger* one."

"Yet, it doesn't satisfy you fully."

"It's not as ancient and steeped in history, and it's a bit gaudy and grandiose if we're being honest."

"Why would we be anything but? *Honesty* was always a hallmark of our chats." When Rylana had been eighteen, after briefly being flattered by an older man's interest, she'd assumed it was more her family's status and money that had prompted Vormalt to pursue her. And maybe it had been partly that, but now… she was curious what about the *castle* drew him. And had that been his reason all along for wanting to marry her? No, that would be silly. Still, he wanted *something* there.

"Do you think you'll be visiting your father soon?" Vormalt asked.

"No. I'm staying here in town and not going to see the family, so I can't get you into the castle. And I need to return to work." Rylana finished her latte and dug into her purse, having to part with a few precious coins to pay for the drink, and stood. "Don't lurk around here, all right? I can't help you with your problem, and there aren't any libraries in the diner."

She kept herself from saying there wasn't even paper that wasn't wrapped around meat from a butcher shop. She found herself wanting to protect Jildarin's reputation rather than complaining about his quirks. At least *he* hadn't sneered at her haircut.

"Of that I'm certain. Dragons *burn* libraries instead of reading books."

Rylana almost objected but remembered how, a few years earlier in the Danbar Kingdom, a squadron of dragons and elves *had* torched a university in a stealth attack behind the frontlines. They hadn't targeted the library, but so much of that portion of the city had been built from wood that the flames had spread to disastrous effect.

"Keep those." Vormalt pointed at her change and laid a gold coin on the table. "You've scintillated me with your conversational skills, so I can't let you pay."

"That's enough for twenty cups. Don't you carry smaller coins?"

"I've no need." Vormalt waved airily. "And I might stay and have another drink. The coffee is quite good, isn't it?" He gazed toward the book-filled shelves in the back.

"It is. And maybe *they* have books that would interest a historian. Some could be filled with ancient treasure maps."

Vormalt snorted. "Yes, I believe most archaeologists start their research at the local coffee shop."

Rylana's fingers twitched toward the table—since he'd offered to pay, she was tempted to take back her coins—but she stuck her empty hand in her pocket. Even if Vormalt was leaving a ridiculous amount, she didn't want to feel she owed him anything.

His eyebrows arched, but he didn't comment on her choice. Irritatingly, despite his suggestion that he might stay for another round, Vormalt rose to follow her out of the coffee shop.

Rylana was tempted to veer off in another direction, even if she would ultimately circle the block to go in through the storeroom, but the gnomes and golems that Sylin had pointed out earlier had moved to Acorn Street. Even if she wasn't doing anything wrong, she was reluctant to walk past them, lest they question her about who knew what. Why were patrollers lingering in the area anyway?

Yerin was waiting outside the diner, his notepad tucked away. Hopefully, he and Vormalt would walk off together.

"Did you find the dragon fare satisfactory?" Vormalt asked him in an amused tone.

"Surprisingly so."

"Did you get a chance to try the fabled soup?"

"I would prefer to do that in the comfort of my own home with a lady friend on the premises," Yerin said. "Otherwise, if its reputation is to be believed, I might leap into your arms after a few spoonfuls."

"Neither of us wants that."

"Certainly not."

"I'd have to repel such an advance and toss you to the nearest available *lady friend*." Vormalt turned his amusement toward Rylana, though his gaze drifted upward to her hair again.

She bared her teeth, not wanting to participate in the insipid conversation. They were blocking the door, so she made a shooing motion, hoping to stem off any further comments they might make about their sexual preferences, though she knew Vormalt's perfectly well. Assuming they hadn't changed in the intervening years.

The men didn't move, and the reason why opened the door and stepped out. The goblin, Rolf, strode out, smiling and clutching a bag in his arms. His step faltered when he saw Rylana. He recovered quickly and held the bag toward Yerin.

"Your leftovers, sir," Rolf said.

Yerin accepted it and handed the goblin a silver coin.

"Is it Jildarin's policy to charge people for leftovers?" Rylana asked.

"Oh, that's a tip, my lady." Rolf kissed the coin, bowed to the men, then hurried back inside.

Yerin smiled, not disagreeing, and headed off down the street with his bag.

"Do see to your hair, Rylana," Vormalt said before following his comrade. "It's *much* more flattering when it flows lushly about your shoulders."

Rylana borrowed from the extensive variety of goblin hand gestures to make an appropriately scathing one as he walked off. He was lucky because, if not for Tranquility's peace laws and the lurking gnomes, she would have found something to hurl at the back of his head. Her aim was, after all, impeccable. Instead, she was left staring after him and wondering if he would be more trouble.

"Probably," she muttered and stepped inside.

She almost walked into Jildarin. He was peering out the window, watching his food critic depart, but his gaze shifted to her. She braced herself, expecting him to comment on her departure in the middle of the day for coffee with a man.

"That food critic is Yerin Molingvar," Jildarin stated, barely acknowledging her as he continued to look out the window, though the two men had disappeared from view.

"Yes. Did he introduce himself?"

"He did not."

"But you know him?" Rylana asked in surprise, though she supposed it would make sense that he would read restaurant reviews in the newspaper and have heard of a food critic.

"He is also *Chef* Yerin Molingvar who works up the hill at Celestial Ceremony."

Rylana had never been to the fancy restaurant but recognized the name. It was the kind of upscale place people of her father's ilk visited when they deigned to cross the lake to take in the food and culture of Tranquility. It was considered an honor to work there and even the servers and kitchen help came from well-off families.

"One would think having a restaurant review column would be considered a conflict of interest for him."

Jildarin waved away the suggestion and said what must have been more important to him. "He is one of the chefs who passed the preliminary rounds and was accepted into the Golden Whisk competition."

Ah, *that* was why Jildarin knew him.

"So, he's one of your archnemeses."

"I would not suggest that precisely. After all, *he* has never shot me." Jildarin looked pointedly at her.

Rylana sighed, suspecting it would be a long road to win Jildarin's trust—and forgiveness.

While he was looking at her, his gaze drifted upward. "Why did the assistant of Chef Molingvar comment on your hair?"

Rylana almost laughed at the idea of Vormalt being someone's assistant, but she didn't correct Jildarin. "Because he's a pompous ass."

"Would not long hair be impractical when battling enemies? It could easily be grabbed in a fight, yes?"

"*Yes*. That's why I cut it when I became a mercenary. That's exactly what happened."

"Practical." Jildarin nodded. "You will not depart the premises during work hours. My understanding of human, dwarf, and gnome culture suggests that is not desirable behavior from an employee."

"It's not," Rylana admitted, though her first instinct was to bristle with indignation. He wasn't wrong. Even Captain Maverick would have made her do push-ups, if not help Cook scour pans, for leaving the unit without permission.

The door opened behind her, and Rylana stepped out of the way. The coffee-shop owners, Brella and Tezilly, stepped into the diner together, carrying a bag of coins.

They looked heavy. Were they *gold* coins?

"We're here to purchase the gnomish commercial oven," Brella said.

Jildarin's mouth drooped open in surprise.

"There's more than one, and they're in the storeroom back there." Rylana pointed. "You can take your pick."

"Which is closest to where the dragon sleeps?" Tezilly asked.

"I'm sure his body hasn't *really* exuded magic that will improve the oven," Brella said with an eye roll.

"Hush. We've already discussed this." Tezilly lifted a hand to her partner's lips and pinched them shut. "I've researched that such things *are* possible."

After sharing another eye roll, Brella stepped back to free her lips. "You read two chapters in the book on dragons that we usually use to level the wobbly table near the lavatory."

"*Research.*"

"Foolproof, I'm sure."

With a hair flip, Tezilly turned back to Rylana. "The oven?"

"I'll show you." Hoping Jildarin wouldn't object to Rylana leading strangers to what was his *lair* as well as the storeroom, she hurried back without checking with him first. Even if he wouldn't make a profit, he would be able to pay the back rent in full with the coins from the sale of the oven.

The ladies followed her and *ooh*ed and *aah*ed at the ovens. They were gleaming without a speck of dust on them, and Rylana pointed out a couple next to the spot where Jildarin slept.

"This one, please." Tezilly patted it lovingly. "I absolutely believe there's dragon magic in it."

"That's silly," her partner said, "but it *is* gnomish, so we know it'll be of high quality." She handed the bag of coins to Jildarin, who'd followed them back but hadn't said anything to imply he was offended by their presence. He probably wanted to sell the ovens, even if it meant an intrusion upon his lair.

"We'll have it delivered," Rylana said.

"Yes." Jildarin nodded.

"Perfect," Brella said.

Rylana had imagined the entire staff banding together, perhaps with the use of a wagon, to carry the oven across the street, but Jildarin pushed open the carriage doors, squatted, and hefted the large heavy appliance by himself. Rylana gaped. Two hells, dragons truly *did* retain a lot of their strength when they shifted into human form.

Was he going to carry it all the way around the block like that? He headed for the doors, so apparently so. Before walking out, he looked back at Rylana.

"You may depart during work hours any time you wish," he stated.

"I... thank you."

"He's warming up to you," Sylin said, appearing in the hallway with a piece of spruce-tip-encrusted bacon in hand.

"I'm a quality employee."

11

Rylana sold another oven the next day and deposited another bag of gold on Jildarin's desk, which prompted him to suggest she spend even *more* time away from the diner during work hours. She wouldn't take him up on that. There was too much to do to stabilize his business and set it on a sustainable path forward. Her latest project was calculating the costs of all the meals that Jildarin made and coming up with prices for a menu that they could post outside the door. That would ensure the diner didn't lose money on any of the dishes and that the amounts didn't fluctuate depending on who served the patrons. Rolf, in particular, always added a *goblin tip*.

By the end of the day, Rylana had posted the menu and felt accomplished. Needing a touch of exercise, she took off before the dinner hour to accompany Sylin on a jog. She vowed not to be gone for long in case the servers needed help. As the bookkeeper, carrying trays and washing dishes probably wasn't one of her duties, but, since she wanted the place to succeed, she felt obligated to assist whenever it was useful.

"There's plenty of space in the room I've leased if you want to sleep there," Sylin offered as they trotted through the streets of Tranquility. With spring creeping into the northern city, the days were growing longer, and twilight hadn't yet descended, but the gnomish fire-fliers were out, the buzzing contraptions applying flame to the streetlamps that brightened the intersections after dark. "I've paid for it through the next two weeks, and, as we discussed, I'm not using the bed."

"That does sound more comfortable than sleeping on the hard floor of Jildarin's storeroom." Rylana wiped sweat from her brow.

The air was cool, but Sylin's pace always pressed her. Since Rylana didn't plan to return to the mercenary life, she supposed she didn't *need* to keep training, but she'd continued sparring and doing jogs with her elven comrade since they'd left the south. It seemed wise to remain fit, for more reasons than her increased consumption of delicious food. She *hoped* she wouldn't see Vormalt again but couldn't help but believe she would—and that trouble might come with his appearances. There was also something unsettling about the peacekeepers being around the diner so often. Maybe it was simply because Jildarin had changed into his native form the other day, but she had a feeling that walking at a dragon's side—and working in his diner—might also deliver trouble.

"There were only two drunken knocks on the door during the middle of the night," Sylin said, "by men who'd seen me go upstairs and hoped I was lonely and pining for their company."

"Only two men bothered you? That's a quality establishment."

They turned onto the waterfront street, jogging north, away from the cargo docks and deeper into the heart of the city. With the weather decent, numerous humans, dwarves, gnomes, orcs, and people with mixed blood were out. In a bump-ball court on a sandy beach, a goblin team battled a dwarf team, none of the contestants daunted by the net being strung for taller competitors.

"You'd think my aloof and chilly demeanor would deter men," Sylin said.

"No, they like a challenge, and they're always certain they're the ones with the ability to melt the ice statue." Rylana didn't find her elven comrade *icy* but had heard many others describe her that way.

"I've noticed alcohol further bolsters their self-confidence."

"It's a powerful elixir, yes."

As they neared the ferry that could carry passengers, horses, and wagons across the lake to the estates on the monied west side, Rylana had a view of her family's castle perched on its rocky point to the south of the landing on that shoreline. Though plumbed and otherwise modernized, it still looked like a vestige from the time when Tranquility had been little more than a troll-fishing village with a few family farms stretching between the water and the forests. Back then, the gnomes, who'd eventually traded for much of the land, had lived in the mountains, much like the dwarves, many of whom remained there, preferring subterranean homes.

"Of course, you might get an even more appealing room if you visited your family there," Sylin said, following her gaze across the lake. "One less frequented by drunk males."

"True. The men in my family haven't been that prone to drink, unless my uncle Chanlin was visiting."

"Even if he were, I would assume he wouldn't knock on the door to your room seeking a mating experience."

"Probably not," Rylana said. "High society frowns upon incest, though there have been some plays involving the topic published and performed and lauded by critics. But my beauty isn't as great as yours and as likely to tempt men to foolishness."

"Your beauty is fine. It's not your fault you don't have any elven blood." Sylin veered to run up a street perpendicular to the waterfront.

As Rylana followed, she saw the reason why her comrade had rerouted. Two elven males in green cloaks with blond-green hair to their shoulders and bows on their backs had been heading toward them. Their weapons were knotted with tranquility ribbons, so their arrows weren't a threat, but Sylin picked up the pace, regardless.

"Are you going to avoid the elves who live in the city for as long as you're here?" Rylana asked.

"As assiduously as the drunks in the tavern, yes. And as assiduously as you're avoiding your relatives." Sylin slanted her a don't-judge-me-lest-I-judge-you look, and Rylana waved her fingers in acknowledgment.

But as they jogged up the slope away from the waterfront, she looked thoughtfully back across the lake. As part of her return to Tranquility, she'd hoped to reconnect with some of the friends she'd grown up with, but they likely still lived over there on their family estates. If Rylana crossed the lake to visit others, she would feel compelled to see her father. Maybe she should have felt compelled to do that regardless, out of a sense of familial duty, but the thought made her grimace.

Ahead, on one corner of an intersection, Rylana spotted a gnomish newspaper dispenser.

"Hold up," she said, remembering Yerin's visit. It was probably too soon to expect a review of the diner, but more people than usual had visited during the breakfast and lunch hours, so she wondered if a piece about it might have already been published. As Gniknik had said, even a poor review could increase business.

"Are you tired already?" Sylin asked. "We've only run four miles."

"Yeah, but the last mile was uphill at a flee-from-wyverns pace." Rylana wiped her brow again, then fished in her pocket to find a copper for the dispenser.

"A flee-from-elves pace only."

"For you, that's as brisk. Do you think your people will attack you if they see you? Here in Tranquility?"

"They attack with words as readily as with weapons. I do not seek to engage with them." Sylin looked back down the slope as Rylana exchanged her coin for a newspaper. "Since you also battled elves for years, I would think you would likewise desire to avoid them."

"I doubt any of them would recognize me." Rylana opened the paper and found the culture section where events such as the dwarven opera, ogre wrestling matches, and the latest plays were reviewed. "If I see one with an arrow scar beside his eye, I'll run the other way."

"They are all arrogant, supercilious, and best avoided. Unless, of course, one has an assignment to eliminate one." Sylin said the latter words as if she were remembering a pleasant experience, one she hoped to relive one day.

"You're going to have a hard time transitioning to a new line of work, aren't you?" Rylana ran her finger down the columns, looking for something about diners.

"I also enjoyed the challenge, and I was among the few to lament the end of the war. I even debated remaining with the mercenaries in the hope of more unrest arising. Tranquility is..."

"A brilliant and blazing start under the leadership of an atypical bellwether."

"I assume you refer to the diner and not the city," Sylin said.

"*Yerin* refers to the diner that way."

"Though the gnomes are atypical, and some people with peace-loving demeanors do think the city brilliant."

Busy reading the column, Rylana didn't answer. "Huh. It's approving."

"That is a review by the food critic?"

"Yeah, he even liked the spruce-tip bacon."

"*All* of the bacon was good."

Rylana lowered the newspaper. "When Jildarin said Yerin was a fellow chef and a rival in the cooking competition, I assumed he would write a scathing review."

"Maybe he's honorable."

"He stole my bicycle chain and hid it in the flower garden when my brother and I wouldn't come play with him."

"Mischief undertaken at a young age, presumably. People can mature."

"Like the people who knocked on your door in the middle of the night?"

"*Some* people can mature."

Rylana supposed that was true. Unlike Vormalt, she didn't have any reason to be suspicious of Yerin. He'd been a quirky kid but not a mean one, crimes against bicycles notwithstanding.

Trusting the elves had passed on the waterfront street, Rylana gestured that she wanted to head back. She'd had enough exercise and wanted to show the newspaper to Jildarin.

Sylin allowed Rylana to change their route, but she eyed the waterfront warily and turned a block before it to walk back on a parallel street.

"Is it more than wanting to avoid some unpleasantness that has you dodging elves?" Rylana looked across the lake to a stone manor perched three estates down from her family's castle. Assuming the property hadn't changed hands in the years she'd been gone, it belonged to the Molingvars—Yerin's family.

"There are many reasons why doing so is prudent."

Rylana gave Sylin a sidelong look but didn't pry further. Her elven comrade opened up to her more than she did most people, but she knew Sylin didn't share everything. The captain had known some of Sylin's secrets that Rylana had never learned, and he'd never spoken of them, even after he and Rylana had become intimate. It wasn't healthy to dig deeply into the pasts of assassins.

"All right," Rylana said as Sylin started jogging again. Rylana would have been content to walk back, but she coerced her cooling muscles into a trot with thoughts of visiting the coffee shop or the bakery for some cookies later. "Let me know if you need me to cover for you if any elves come to the diner to seek you out."

"I assume you will cover for me whether I suggest it or not."

"I suppose that's true. You've saved my life multiple times over the years, and I would be bereft of companionship if something happened to you."

Two blocks from the diner, Sylin slowed, then stopped altogether, easing behind a fountain featuring two goblins wrestling while spitting water from their mouths. She swept the hood of her cloak over her green hair, putting her face in shadow.

With eyes practiced at picking out targets at great range, Rylana had keen vision, almost as good as that of an elf, and she spotted what had made Sylin pause. A figure with blond-green hair, who wore a green cloak and a bow on his back, was peering through one of the front windows of the diner.

"I believe that fellow's ears are pointed." Rylana joined Sylin behind the fountain, though she continued to watch the elf through a gap between the goblins.

"It's one of the males we saw on the waterfront."

"You're certain?" Rylana asked, though she agreed. "Elves all dress so similarly, and most have some green in their hair."

"I'm certain, and so are you. But where's the second one?" Sylin looked around, her gaze lingering on the nearby rooftops. Probably more because she was thinking of vaulting up to one and disappearing into the city than because she believed an elf was perched up there.

The door of the diner opened, and the other green-cloaked figure walked out holding a bag that reminded Rylana of the one Rolf had packed for Yerin.

"Acquiring a dragon-spice aphrodisiac apparently," she said.

"I do not believe it's a coincidence that they are visiting an establishment where I've been lately," Sylin said.

"Probably no more of a coincidence than Vormalt knowing to seek me out there. Do you think there's a spy at the dragon diner that tells the world when interesting new customers—or employees—arrive?" Rylana asked the question jokingly, but she did wonder how Vormalt had so quickly learned she was in the city and at the diner. She supposed he might have found out via Yerin, who might be keeping an eye on the establishments of his competitors. And the elves… Well, they were an observant people, and Sylin had mentioned spotting one at the coffee shop the day before. As an assassin, she was good at seeing others without being seen herself, but if she'd been sipping coffee at a table, and distracted by assessing the elevation at which the beans had been grown, she might not have been applying all her talents at remaining unnoticed.

"While I've been about in the city," Sylin said, "I've heard several different people mention that diner. Dragons visiting Tranquility are rare, and one opening a business is unheard of. I do not know who would pay to have it spied upon, but I don't doubt that many are keeping an eye on it."

Two gnomes in peacekeeper uniforms walked past the fountain with a short-furred, copper-colored dog on a leash, the animal wearing a green vest that said *LOG INSPECTOR*. They were doubtless on the way to one of the parks or beaches to look for stolen goods stashed by goblins or—even more likely—pixies, stumps and logs being a favorite spot for them to tuck items. Rylana doubted the search team had anything to do with the diner but thought of all the times she'd seen peacekeepers and golems loitering nearby the last couple of days and decided that Sylin was right. A lot of people *were* keeping an eye on the diner and its dragon owner.

"I will depart." Sylin pointed up a side street. "Should you desire to sleep separate from the dragon, my room at the Dockside Lodge will be available."

"Will *you* be in it?" Rylana wouldn't be surprised if her comrade left the city to avoid the elves.

Sylin waved noncommittally and trotted into an alley.

By the time Rylana reached the diner, the elves were walking away with their bag. Their faces were beautiful but haughty and aloof, and they gave her long, cool looks as their paths crossed. They didn't, however, stop her. For Sylin's sake, Rylana hoped the elves weren't holding a grudge after the war and looking for assassins.

12

Scintillating scents filled the dining room when Rylana walked in. Rolf, Gniknik, and Zalani were all there, tending the needs of customers seated in the booths as well as on the barstools. In addition, a wheeled gnomish contraption circled the dining room, a tub fastened to its back so that people could set their dishes in it. Small nozzles sprayed soapy water onto glasses and bowls as they were deposited.

So far, none of the couples seated in booths were engaged in amorous acts. Maybe Jildarin wasn't serving soup tonight—or maybe he was refining the amounts of the spices he used so that their effects weren't as strong.

"Let us know what he did with the freshwater conch," Zalani said as Rylana headed toward the kitchen. "They're so hard to get tender."

"Er, all right," Rylana said.

"It's a favorite goblin food that few outside of our species can properly cook," Rolf said. "It's right up there with fermented freshwater shark, scorpions, and mealworms. He did a good job with those ingredients in his taste test last week. For a non-goblin."

"Other species cook with those too," Zalani said as she carried a water jug to one table.

"Not with the *zest* that goblins cook with them."

"Goblins do *most* things with zest."

"We're a joyful species." Rolf patted a pocket that jangled. With tips? Or had he absconded with a few purses today?

"I won't argue that," Zalani said.

She jangled a little bit too as she sashayed around the dining room, filling water cups and smiling at unattached men. They both appeared to be in good spirits, maybe due to the increased patronage. If the busyness was a result of the review in the newspaper, Yerin had done Jildarin a favor. At the least, he'd done his job fairly when, as a competitor, he might have been tempted to sabotage others in the contest. Maybe he thought, after tasting the food, that his own was better and Jildarin wouldn't be a threat. Or maybe Sylin had been right, and Yerin had grown up and become honorable.

"My bicycle would be surprised by that," Rylana murmured.

As she stepped into the hallway, the dwarf baker from across the street walked into the diner with a tray full of tiny loaves of bread, cookies, and biscuits. She looked around—in surprise?—at the full room, then walked from table to table, offering samples.

Rylana paused, wondering if she should object, but she'd spoken earlier in the day with the baker, trying to convince her that she needed to buy a gnomish oven, so maintaining a good relationship would be ideal. Besides, it was possible this happened regularly, and the dwarf had a deal with Jildarin to do this.

Smiling, the baker reached the hallway and held her tray out toward Rylana. "Cookie? Honeyed biscuit?"

"Not right now, thanks. I haven't eaten dinner yet."

"Nor have I. I was told to come hungry." She winked and lowered her tray for Rolf when he came over. "I'm Mya Stonehammer, by the way. Did I mention that this morning when we spoke?

This is not my first time coming over here, but it is my first time being invited in to eat."

"I'm Rylana. I've, uh, seen some of your cakes go out."

"Naughty or nice?" Mya winked and pushed one of her red-gray braids over her shoulder. "I admit, after I lost my husband in the mines and needed a new career to have something to do with myself now that my young ones are grown, I thought I would use my baking talents to make tasty treats for children's birthday parties, weddings, and summer- and winter-fest galas. But when the dragon opened his diner and started drawing people with that *soup*... Well, they needed desserts."

"Naughty desserts?"

"Apparently! I do charge more for those. I'm not a prude, mind you, but it's more of a challenge to bake and affix various somatic appendages than to simply make and frost a round or square cake."

"I imagine the *zerg* sticks fall over if you're not careful."

"Yes, and nobody wants a limp *zerg* stick." Mya pointed toward the kitchen. "Is the chef ready for us?"

"I don't know. I wasn't invited to anything."

"No?" Mya tilted her head. "When Jildarin-grozanarav mentioned wanting new people to try tonight's creations, I assumed he would include you."

"You can pronounce his full name? That's impressive."

"I can't *easily* pronounce it, but you know how dragons feel about their clans and their heritage. I wouldn't want to insult him. Does he allow you to simply call him Jildarin?"

"So far, he has, but he probably doesn't expect much from someone who shot him in the war."

Mya blinked and mouthed, "*Shot*?"

Maybe Rylana shouldn't have mentioned that, but she shrugged and tapped her temple.

"Enter, diners," Jildarin's voice boomed down the hallway.

"You will sample my dishes now and not gossip outside of my kitchen."

"I'll take that," Rolf said cheerfully, pulling Mya's tray out of her hands, some cookies and miniature loaves remaining, "and finish handing out your samples."

"Hm," Mya said, though she let the goblin depart with her goods so she could walk obediently into the kitchen.

Rolf had already shoved two loaves into his mouth by the time Rylana followed the dwarf through the swinging door. She doubted many more samples would be handed out. It was impressive that goblins could have such lean musculature despite a propensity to eat as much as dragons. And far more sweets than dragons.

Jildarin scrutinized Rylana and Mya before nodding to himself and pointing toward the table in the back. "I have placed sample plates under cloches, much as they will be delivered to the judges at the Golden Whisk. Of course, you know that *I* made the dishes —as long as everything is done according to the rules of the contest, the judges won't know which chefs prepared which items —but I will not tell you what the dishes are or about the ingredients, thus to not predispose you to certain opinions."

"I've already heard about some of the ingredients," Rylana murmured, eyeing the small silver cloches clustered in front of the stools, numbers written with a charcoal stick atop each. Three seats were set at the table, each with a torn-off piece of butcher paper next to the cloches. Rylana wondered who else Jildarin expected to join them.

"You will sample each dish and rate them on a scale of one to ten, with ten being the most excellent." Jildarin guided Rylana and Mya to the table.

"The lengths I go to for free food," Mya murmured, taking the seat by the wall.

"You have a thriving business," Rylana said. "You can't *need* free food."

"No, but I've been curious about the fare here for a while. And the owner." Mya looked over her shoulder, lips twisted thoughtfully. "He is a quirky dragon, is he not?"

"Those of us who survived the war all are, I think. If we weren't before, all the years of fighting and death made us so." Rylana had meant it as a joke, but it wasn't really, even if *quirky* wasn't quite the appropriate word to describe the survivors. Damaged, maybe.

"In order to be of most assistance," Jildarin said, "you should keep your conversation centered on the food."

"I'm not sure *war* can explain him," Mya said.

"You may discuss the dishes," Jildarin said, as if he couldn't hear the comments about him, "but I suggest you first independently rate them on your own. Someone else's strong opinion might sway your own."

"Thanks for the life advice," Rylana said dryly.

"Certainly. Begin when you wish, but where is your elf comrade? I've been told there will be two elves among the judges, so I desire to test my fare on her palate as well."

"She had to leave, and her name is Sylin."

"You did not introduce me to her, so it is not a cultural error that I do not know how to address her." Jildarin pointed his spoon at Rylana.

"That's fair. I didn't think you'd want an introduction or to formally meet someone who was a mercenary with me and… may have targeted your kind during the war."

"I did not even wish to formally meet you."

"But now you're delighted to have made my acquaintance, right?" Rylana smiled at him.

"How many gnomish commercial ovens did you sell today?"

"I haven't closed a deal yet today, but I did propose to Mya here that she could use a new one. She already has one, though, so she needs to think about it and consider her books first."

Mya, who had lifted a couple of her cloches and was sniffing the food with appreciation, didn't answer.

Jildarin squinted at Rylana. "I will determine whether or not I have delight over your acquaintance after you judge the food. Sit, Miss Rylana." He patted the empty stool beside Mya, then walked toward the doorway and peered left and right down the hall.

"That's the first time he's used my name," Rylana mused.

"What does he usually call you?" Mya removed the rest of her cloches and set them aside, revealing more of a tasting arrangement of small dishes than a traditional meal, but there was plenty of food to fill a belly.

"Sometimes *bookkeeper.* More often *my enemy*."

"I suppose if you'd shot me, I might have a similar appellation for you. One surrounded by more adjectives."

"It was during the war."

"Miss Zalani," Jildarin called toward the dining room. "I require you for a tasting."

"He doesn't usually call her *miss* anything, that I've heard." Rylana removed her own cloches and stacked them nearby. "Maybe he's learned the human custom of flattering the judges."

"That's a custom among *most* of the intelligent species, I believe." Mya picked up a spoon and pointed it toward a tiny bowl. "Do you think that's one of his legendary soups? I'm not sure if I dare try it. With my husband passed, I don't have anyone available to, ah, satisfy my urges. What if I'm moved to spring upon the goblin male who stole my sample tray?"

"I haven't tried any of the dragon spices myself yet, but I'm not sure any herb, magical or otherwise, would be capable of making a sane woman spring upon a goblin."

"There *are* such beings as half-goblins in the world."

"Yeah, but that usually goes the other way, with human men

deciding they want to experience a green lover. Human women are more reasonable."

"Nonetheless, I may avoid the soup. If you're willing to defy the chef's wishes, tell me what you rate it, and I'll put the same."

"I haven't decided yet if *I'll* try it." Rylana lifted her tiny bowl of soup to her nose. A tantalizing, rich aroma of herbs and spices she couldn't identify wafted into her nostrils, immediately making her mouth water. And was there a hint of bacon in the soup? That seemed to be one of Jildarin's signature items, and she'd enjoyed every bite he'd offered thus far. "Maybe just a spoonful. To satisfy my curiosity."

"Shall I let the goblin know to prepare himself for atypical human ardor?" Mya smirked.

"It's Rolf, and I'm *not* going to get horny from a spoonful of soup." Since she'd seen the results when others had consumed the dragon spices, Rylana supposed it would be arrogant to believe she couldn't be affected herself. "Not *that* horny, anyway," she amended.

"Do you want me to hold you back if you go after him?"

"Dear gods, yes." Rylana dug into her meal, deciding to save the soup for the end. If dragon spices were like alcohol, they would be less potent on a full stomach.

"What is it, Chef?" Zalani asked when she joined him in the doorway.

Jildarin waved her toward the empty stool. "You will take a break from your serving duties to eat and judge the food. You are only a *half-elf*, so I do not know if your palate will be indicative of the preferences of full-blooded elves, but I do desire a wide range of people to taste my offerings. Perhaps I should also bring Gniknik back, but gnomes deliberately do not allow their kind to apply as judges in the Golden Whisk since they strive to be neutral parties in potentially contentious matters in their city."

"I do hate when cooking contests get contentious," Rylana said.

With a fork in one hand and a spoon in the other, Mya was intently digging into the food and making pleased noises. Busy chewing while her eyes rolled upward and she licked her lips, she didn't respond to Rylana's comment.

Since Rylana was also enjoying her meal, she didn't mind focusing on the food and only nodded and smiled when Zalani sat beside her.

"Chef Jildarin hasn't invited me to opine on anything before," Zalani whispered. "This is an honor, but the dining room is surprisingly busy tonight. I shouldn't leave Rolf and Gniknik alone for long."

As her tastebuds sang, and Jildarin returned to filling orders for the diners out front, Rylana found herself glancing at her soup. It was such a small amount that she couldn't imagine the spices affecting her overmuch. When Rolf had dished up under-the-table to-go orders for people, he'd used much larger containers, and the bowls Rylana had seen it served in for in-house diners had easily been three times the size of her small sample dish.

Halfway through her meal, as Mya and Zalani ate to either side of her, neither speaking other than to smack their lips and issue pleased noises, Rylana risked taking her spoon to the soup. A taste wouldn't hurt, and she had to know why people wanted it so much that they were willing to pay the outrageous goblin tip that Rolf added on when he delivered it.

As soon as the creamy liquid touched her tongue, Rylana understood. Oh, it was so rich, with a unique blend of intensely appealing flavors bathing her tastebuds. She'd never had anything quite like it but immediately loved it. No wonder Jildarin had wanted to introduce the spices to other species. Not only would they delight the palates of everyone who tried them, but they might be able to stop wars and convince people that dragons were to be befriended, not battled.

Before she'd swallowed the first bite, Rylana's spoon returned to the small bowl. She emptied it, then, after hesitating only briefly to wonder if the others would judge her, brought it to her mouth so she could lick it clean.

"That's what I've heard about it," Mya said, having finished her dishes, save for the soup, its creamy contents gleaming appealingly under the light from the nearest lamp.

Rylana had the urge to snatch up the baker's untouched bowl, forego the spoon, and slurp it straight up. Would Mya notice? She'd picked up the charcoal stick to put her ratings on the butcher paper.

Mya looked at her. Guessing her thoughts, she waved in invitation at her bowl.

Rylana glanced over her shoulder to make sure Jildarin wasn't watching—he stood with his back to them, sprinkling salt on a couple of dishes almost ready to go out. She traded her empty bowl for Mya's full one, then forced herself to be civilized and use her spoon. A warm and contented flush filled her as she polished off the second bowl, but why were the servings so small? She could have happily eaten an entire stockpot full.

A clank and shout of alarm came from the dining room. Then a crash sounded as a dish hit the tile floor and broke.

"What was that?" Jildarin frowned and looked toward the hallway. "I have not served any soup tonight, except to my judges. There should not be coital acts in my dining room."

As he strode toward the hallway, Gniknik pushed open the swinging door. "It's really busy out there. Zalani, can you come help?" His serving contraption whirred past his legs and toward the sink. It made distressed gurgling noises, perhaps because a dark gravy smothered one of its sides and coated the wheels.

"There is a problem?" Jildarin asked.

"Just a dropped dish, Chef," Gniknik said. "We're a little overwhelmed."

Zalani rose and slipped past Jildarin. "I'll take care of it."

Jildarin looked at her mostly finished tasting meal. "Return to complete your ratings later."

"I will," Zalani called as she left with Gniknik.

"Have you noticed he orders everyone around instead of making requests?" Rylana licked her spoon, the second bowl, alas, depleted. Maybe her observation should have annoyed her, but she caught herself watching Jildarin more with appreciation than irritation as he returned to his work.

"He's the chef, and this is his kitchen," Mya said. "Also, he's a dragon. Dragons don't make *requests*."

"No, they're uptight and demanding."

Rylana swapped her empty bowl for Zalani's full one. By the time she returned, the soup would be cold, and she might end up wasting it. That would be distressing. Though, as Rylana slurped up the contents of the third bowl, she knew she would cheerfully eat more even if it were cold. She'd never had anything so delicious in her life.

Fortunately, Jildarin was too busy concentrating on his work to notice her overindulgence. Rylana watched him as he moved about the kitchen, powerful and appealing, his strong jaw set with determination.

Mya finished her ratings, then eyed Rylana and the empty bowls. "I'd better return to my bakery and lock up for the night. I'll let you know what I decide about the oven."

"Good," Rylana murmured, her gaze locked on Jildarin.

When Mya walked past, temporarily blocking her view, Rylana frowned and stood, not wanting anything in her way.

"The goblin would be safer," Mya whispered as she left the kitchen.

The goblin? What did that mean?

With a flush of heat and happiness filling her, Rylana walked toward Jildarin. By all the gods in the world, wasn't he handsome? And so strong. The memory of him carrying that oven out the door came to mind. She also recalled him shirtless and frying bacon. How perfect and honed his physique was.

She eased closer to him, such an intense urge to touch him coming over her that all rational thoughts fell out of her mind. As she reached for him, Jildarin turned. Wariness rather than desire flashed in his brilliant emerald eyes.

He caught her wrists before she could grip his shoulders, and he turned her hands over, as if suspecting she might have a dagger hidden under her palm. No, she didn't want to slay him. She wanted to *have* him. His strong hands wrapped around her wrists should have been alarming, but the heat of his flesh against hers was arousing instead.

"Jildarin," Rylana whispered. "I didn't realize... you are so..."

He looked past her shoulder toward the table. "You had more than one sample of soup."

"Yes, I couldn't stop myself from wanting..." Her wrists still grasped in his hands, Rylana leaned forward and kissed him. She had to. She was drawn by his power, his allure, and the *spices*.

Even though she remembered consuming the soups and understood they were responsible for her lust, she couldn't stop the kiss. She needed this. She needed *him*.

For a few heartbeats, Jildarin stood still, letting her lips press against his and allowing her to squirm closer. He seemed surprised and flummoxed about what to do, but he of all people had to understand what was happening. He stepped back and pushed her out to arm's length.

"It was a mistake to serve any of it," Jildarin stated. "But I believed... My spices are like a secret weapon, yes? That is what humans would call it. Their magic makes them potent and appealing to your kind. To *all* kinds. Even dragons cannot consume too much or the power causes us to act… irrationally as well."

"Jildarin…" Rylana couldn't take her gaze from his mouth as he spoke, his lips hypnotic, the rich timbre of his voice drawing her. Why was he keeping her away from him?

Jildarin rotated her toward the door. "This mistake was mine. You will go to the storeroom and sleep until the spices wear off."

"I don't want to *sleep*." Rylana tried to turn back toward him, but he was too strong. He kept his grip gentle, but he pushed her inexorably out of the kitchen. "I want *you*," she said over her shoulder.

"I am aware. By morning, the effects will have worn off and you will return to desiring me dead."

"I *don't* desire that. I never did. You were just a target among the enemy forces, and those forces were trying to kill us."

"Go to the storeroom and sleep," Jildarin said firmly. "In the morning, you will be yourself again."

There was power in his voice, dragon magic that all the tranquility ribbons in the city couldn't diminish, and Rylana's legs moved to obey of their own accord. She walked toward the dark storeroom, but *sleep* was the last thing she wanted. How could she rest now when she was in this state? She needed a release.

She passed through the room and out the back door. If Jildarin would not satisfy her, perhaps another could.

13

OUTSIDE, THE NIGHT AIR WAS CHILLY WITH THE PROMISE OF MORE rain. It helped Rylana to clear her head, and she gulped it in.

"A walk," she decided, starting to recognize that she needed to cool off her heated body. "Maybe a bath in the fountain," she added, only half-joking.

At the least, splashing water on her face might help. She headed to the nearest intersection with a fountain but paused when she drew close. Two cloaked and hooded figures stepped out of the cross street on their way toward the waterfront. They glanced at her, and one slowed down for a longer look. The light from the streetlamp cast illumination for her to see a lock of blond-green hair and a face that she'd come across earlier in the day. It was one of the elves.

The urge to turn and sprint back to the diner swept into Rylana, but they would view that behavior as suspicious. And she didn't want them to have a reason to scrutinize her too closely. Even though she didn't think she'd ever met these particular elves, they might somehow know that she'd been in the war, that she'd been an enemy.

Rylana continued to the fountain, pretending not to notice or care that they'd paused on the other side to confer with each other in soft tones. Feeling constrained by their presence, she only dabbed water on her face instead of splashing it all over her head. Her body was still flushed, and she struggled to get rid of thoughts of running back to Jildarin and dragging him to her blanket. A dragon was too strong to be *dragged* anywhere.

"Human female," one of the elves said, the one who'd looked at her. He pushed back the hood of his cloak, deliberately brushing his hair back to reveal his pointed ears, and stepped close to her.

"Male elf." Rylana faced him, snarky words coming to mind, but she paused, noticing for the first time his striking beauty. Perhaps, if Jildarin wasn't interested in a romantic encounter, another male might be...

The spices, came a warning from the back of her mind. The spices were responsible for these feelings.

"We spotted you earlier in the company of an elf," he said.

"Yes, I was trying to sell her a gnomish commercial oven." Rylana smiled at them to hide her concern for Sylin. "I don't suppose either of *you* might be interested in one? You don't look like the chef types, but I have several available and might even cut a deal for a bulk purchase."

The elves looked at each other.

"No? Well, if you'll excuse me, I'm needed back at the diner. It was recently reviewed in the *Chronicles*, so we're quite busy." Rylana stepped in that direction, but both elves moved to cut her off.

Instinctively, she dropped into a crouch, her hand going to the spot where she *usually* wore a sword, but she'd left her weapons in the storeroom. There was little point in carrying them around when they couldn't be used.

She shifted her grip to the utility knife on her belt, but she didn't draw it. The elves looked young and athletic, and their kind were known for strength and stamina, something she well knew from her sparring matches with Sylin.

"We are looking for the elf that you were seen with today."

The speaker looked at her hand on the hilt of her knife but didn't appear alarmed by it, nor did he draw a blade of his own. Still, there was a coolness to his gaze that brought back memories of confrontations with their kind, of the mercenaries and kingdom soldiers clashing on the battlefield with elven infantry and cavalry. She'd usually stayed back with the other archers and men firing cannons, but she'd ended up face-to-face with a pointy-eared enemy more than once over the years. Each time, she had been lucky to survive. Here, unlike during the war, she didn't have any allies standing at her side.

"I don't know where she went," Rylana said, trying to set aside her unease. One of the city's security pillars loomed on the other side of the fountain. It was unlikely the elves would attack her. "She didn't want to buy an oven," she added.

"I would think not," the other elf murmured, speaking for the first time. "*Baking* isn't what she's known for."

Two hells, these people knew Sylin was an assassin. They probably knew she'd killed her own kind, and they wanted... what? Did the elves intend to kill Sylin because she'd fought on the other side during the war? Even though she was in a city where violence was forbidden?

"Will you step aside, or do I need to yell for the peacekeepers?" Rylana asked, aware of her heart beating faster, the thumps reverberating through her body. The effects of the dragon spices were fading, but she didn't feel entirely herself and worried her reaction speed would be diminished.

"I think this female knows more than she's implying," the first speaker said.

"Undoubtedly. We should escort her to the enclave for questioning." The elf glanced at the pillar but reached for her, regardless.

Rylana sprang back quickly enough to avoid his grasp and drew her knife. "I'm not going with you."

"She is needed at my diner," came Jildarin's voice from the side. "She will return with me."

Wearing his white chef's garb and a cool expression, Jildarin strode into the intersection.

The elves turned without surprise, as if they'd sensed him coming. Maybe they had. Their kind had intrinsic magic and power. Not as much as a dragon possessed but far more than a simple human like Rylana.

"You will not impede her return," Jildarin added, glancing toward Rylana's drawn knife. "She is my bookkeeper and too busy serving me to journey to your enclave."

"Our pardon, Lord Dragon." The elf who'd wanted to take Rylana for questioning bowed low to Jildarin, sweeping his cloak out wide. "She was prevaricating with me, and I had reason to suspect her of withholding information that I seek."

"All humans prevaricate." Jildarin came to stand beside Rylana and face the elves. "It is in their nature."

"Having you come to my defense is a delight," Rylana murmured.

"Yes," Jildarin agreed.

"That is true, Lord Dragon. We will not impede your servant further."

Rylana bristled, her grip involuntarily tightening on her knife. "I'm the *bookkeeper*, not a servant."

"Is it possible, Lord Dragon," the elf said, ignoring her, "that *you* have seen the one whom we seek? A green-haired elven female who moves with the practiced step of a deadly predator?"

"I have seen that one," Jildarin said as Rylana shook her head. "I do not know where she is located at this time." Jildarin cocked his head and considered the elves. "Do you desire a meal? I would offer it for free if you are willing to rate the dishes afterward."

"Rate?" one mouthed, both looking at each other.

"He's in need of elven palates to practice on," Rylana said, though the last thing she wanted was for these two to come back to the diner with them.

"We thank you for your offer, Lord Dragon, but we are not hungry."

The elves bowed to him and walked up the street, passing under the pillar on their way deeper into the city. They *had* been heading toward the waterfront, but something about the exchange was causing them to alter course. They gave long looks back over their shoulders before disappearing from view, and Rylana worried she hadn't seen the last of them. She worried even more for her friend.

"Are you done seeking to mate with me?" Jildarin asked, his gaze on Rylana instead of the elves.

"I..." She wanted to say *yes*, but when she met his striking green eyes, another warm flush swept over her, along with the desire to step closer. "Maybe not entirely."

"You took more soup than you were supposed to," he said with certainty.

"It was really good. I couldn't help myself."

"It *is* good." Jildarin lifted his chin, looking more pleased that he made such fine food than disappointed that she hadn't been able to help herself. "But you did not rate it. Unlike the suitably obedient dwarf baker, you failed to rate *any* of my dishes."

"I got distracted by your allure."

"That is unfortunate."

"You should have shape-shifted into a less handsome form. If you looked like Rolf, I probably wouldn't have kissed you, no matter how horny I was."

"You are certain?" Jildarin asked. "He claims that goblin

females—as well as females of other species—find him irresistible."

"You do know that goblins are even more known for prevaricating than humans, right?"

"Oh, yes. I deem him a dubious resource at best. Come. You will sleep, and in the morning, the spices will have worn off."

"Yes, that would be best," Rylana agreed. "We shouldn't be… I mean, normally, I wouldn't—" She waved at him.

"I am certain," he said dryly, then considered her for a moment instead of leading the way back. "You continue to carry your bow with you on your journey, but you say you are no longer a mercenary."

The way he spoke made it sound like a statement, but he waited, watching her, as if it had been a question and he expected an answer.

"That's right," Rylana said. "The roads outside Tranquility can be dangerous. Besides, I still hunt and target shoot to keep my skills up. I've always found it relaxing. I had a bow before I went south and joined the Moon Daggers."

"You are *certain* you are no longer employed in the capacity of a mercenary? One who might be working for those for whom the war never ended? Those who desire to see dragons killed?"

"I'm certain." Rylana realized he might believe her more likely to answer honestly under the influence of his spiced soup. And maybe it *was* making her more open out of a desire to be close to him, but the answers to these questions wouldn't have changed, regardless. "I lost the stomach for killing and watching comrades die. Long before the treaty and the end of the war, I was ready for it to be over. I only continued to work as a merc because of the captain. We were close."

"You felt loyalty to him."

"And the unit, yes." But especially Mav, Rylana added silently, missing him anew. He would have happily eaten the soup with her, and then they would have explored its side effects together.

"You stayed because of loyalty."

"Loyalty and Mav's gifted tongue and horizontal athleticism." As soon as the words came out, Rylana wished she could retract them. She hadn't intended to explain the details of her relationship with Mav to Jildarin.

He blinked without apparent understanding, so maybe it didn't matter, but then he caught on. "You refer to coitus."

"Yeah. I wasn't just loyal to the captain. I loved him. Oh, not at first. It was many years after I joined the unit, and after I'd worked my way up through the ranks, that we figured out we enjoyed each other's company. Often and vigorously."

"That is what kept you fighting in the war?"

"It was one of the reasons I stayed with the mercenaries, yes."

"Strange. Dragons rarely feel the urge to form a long-term bond with another. We do not mate for recreational interests, only procreational purposes."

How romantic.

"You also mate because of parental pressure though, right?" she asked.

Jildarin squinted at her. "I knew you were spying on my conversation with my brother."

That was another set of words that Rylana wished she could retract. She shouldn't have brought that up and reminded him that he had reasons to mistrust her. Her tongue was flapping with the wind tonight.

"I was looking for an opportune moment to knock and try again to be hired." Rylana shrugged. "And don't worry. I won't speak of what I overheard. I understand parental pressure myself."

Jildarin's eyes remained slitted. She regretted that she'd aroused his suspicion. Especially after he'd seemed open to believing her reason for leaving the mercenaries.

"Captain Maverick died toward the end of the war," Rylana said to finish her story—to explain why she wasn't here because of Jildarin and a desire to kill a dragon. "I tried to help his first officer keep the company together, as there's always work for mercenaries, even when formal wars aren't raging, but it was hard. For both of us, I think. People kept leaving. And I eventually left too, even though it was a difficult choice. As I said, I was loyal to the captain but also to the unit, my comrades. I didn't want people to be hurt because there were fewer archers to cover them in battles." She touched her chest.

"Dragons understand loyalty," Jildarin said, though it sounded grudging. At least he'd stopped squinting at her. "Loyalty to the clan and our culture and ways."

"Yes." She'd seen his kind sacrifice themselves for each other during the war. Some had even seemed to have strong bonds with their elven allies.

"You no longer desire to kill dragons?"

"I'm not sure I ever did."

"No? My scar suggests otherwise." Jildarin sounded more dry than angry, but he continued to watch her, gauging her reactions.

"Maybe my arrow would have lodged in your eye if I'd *truly* desired to kill you."

"Or maybe it was windy, and I turned my head at an opportune time."

Rylana snorted. That *was* what had happened. It had also been a very long-range shot. Usually, she didn't miss. "Maybe so."

Jildarin didn't ask any more questions, but she didn't know if she'd succeeded in convincing him that she wasn't here as part of a ruse and lying in wait for an opportunity to end his life. She sighed, sad that he felt that way, even if she understood perfectly. Tonight, with his soup in her stomach, the thought especially saddened her.

On the way back, she stuck her hands in her pockets since they kept wanting to stray toward him, to grip his arm so she could lean against him. But he didn't want that. And she, when spices weren't flowing through her veins, wouldn't want that either. She still missed Mav. She didn't want romance, and certainly not a one-night stand, with another man. And definitely not a dragon.

Their kind had led the troops in the final battle that had taken Mav down. She shouldn't even be here with one of them. Only a vague longing for home, and a time when she'd known nothing of war and dying, had brought her back to the north. But maybe returning to Tranquility had been a mistake. She hadn't reached out to her family or any old friends; the only familiar faces she'd encountered so far were up to no good.

Rylana wiped moisture from her eyes, not sure if the tears were for her lost mercenary lover or the childhood she couldn't reclaim, but she didn't want anyone to see her cry. It was bad enough the spices had made her vulnerable and foolish, and Jildarin had been there to witness it. To *endure* it. How distasteful the kiss of the one who'd shot him must have been.

"What?" Jildarin blurted, stopping abruptly.

Startled, Rylana also stopped, thinking he'd somehow read her thoughts. No, he was staring at the carriage doors leading to the storeroom. In the short time they'd been gone, someone had come through and painted graffiti on them, giant phallic symbols and a crude dragon head with an X through it. At the bottom, actual words were written: *Dragons can't cook.*

Jildarin's hands snapped into fists, and he growled. He almost roared as rage made his body quiver, and he thrust an accusing finger at the words. To him, they were probably the most offensive part of the sloppy graffiti.

"You can't turn into a dragon out here," Rylana warned, sensing that he was on the verge of it.

He probably wanted to fly through the streets and find the culprit, someone who had *just* done this and couldn't yet have gone far. But he had to know better than she that changing outside of his lair would bring the peacekeepers and their golems, and they'd promised more than a fine if he turned into a dragon in the open city again.

Jildarin remained in his human form, but he threw his head back and roared, his every muscle taut. Maybe Rylana should have backed away since he seemed on the verge of not only losing his temper but changing, and standing next to an irate dragon was suicidal. But, with the spices lingering in her blood, she still found him alluring. Dangerous, yes, but alluring, and she caught herself stepping close and resting a hand on his forearm.

"Whoever did that wants to make you angry," she said. "Maybe they even want you to change and be forced to leave."

Though Jildarin remained tense, his muscled form radiating power, he lowered his head to look at her.

"And you *can* cook. I don't know where you learned how, but your food is amazing. Whoever did that—" Rylana pointed at the maligned doors, "—or hired someone to do that is probably a jealous rival."

Jildarin squinted at the graffiti. "Yes... Yes, I do have rivals. And there are *many* who loathe dragons and want them to leave the city. Even my brother, who is lavish with his tips, has been targeted by similar behavior."

"Ignore your rivals, and keep your calm so you aren't kicked out of Tranquility before the competition. I know you want to win that, not be disqualified before it begins."

"Yes. You are correct." His gaze returned to hers, his emerald eyes fiery with their intensity. Fiery and passionate and...

Rylana released his arm and stepped back before the urge to kiss him could take hold again. His passion was for the Golden Whisk, not for her. Besides, in the morning, once the spices were out of her system, she would remember that she was in mourning for another and not interested in having a relationship with an enemy dragon.

"I will not fall prey to the machinations of my rivals," Jildarin stated, his voice calmer now, though he gave the graffiti another baleful look. "I will practice and continue to hone my skills and be ready for the competition. And I will win it." He looked at her again. "You will attend and watch."

"Is that an invitation or an order? Did I mention how lovely it was of you to let those two elves call me your servant?"

At least, *he* hadn't used that word. His brother would have.

"They will be less likely to disturb you again now that they believe you are mine." Jildarin quirked an eyebrow and walked toward the storeroom.

"I'm the bookkeeper and my own person, thank you very much."

"In the morning, you will rate the dishes you consumed tonight." It was, without a doubt, an order, but he sounded faintly amused as he gave it. And, as he walked inside, he sent a long look over his shoulder toward her. Damn if she didn't find it sexy.

"In the *morning*, I'd better be back to normal." Rylana lamented that she hadn't gotten an opportunity to fully douse herself in the cold water of the fountain.

She looked in that direction, though she didn't intend to return, not with suspicious elves roaming the city. She twitched in surprise when she spotted a golem and two gnomes in peacekeeper uniforms passing through the closest intersection. It appeared to be a normal patrol, but when they looked in the direction of the diner, her instincts told her that someone had ensured the law enforcers would be in the area at the time Jildarin discovered the graffiti. If he'd failed to keep his temper and had turned into a dragon, they would have rushed up, demanding that he leave the city.

Sylin, Rylana decided, wasn't the only one that someone was out to get.

14

By three hours past dawn, Rylana had balanced the books, ordered supplies for the week, located Jildarin's landlord and paid the back rent, and sold another of the surplus ovens. With all that accomplished, she felt justified in slipping into the coffee shop across the street for a break.

She hadn't woken hungover or experienced any ill effects from the dragon spices—if anything she'd felt alert and invigorated—but she *had* been embarrassed by her antics the night before. Had she really flung herself at Jildarin and kissed him? Yes... and she'd wanted to do a lot more than that.

That morning, she'd avoided making eye contact with him, and he, fortunately, hadn't said anything about the night before, other than waving toward the table in the back of the kitchen when she'd passed through. Two of the place settings had been cleared, but her dishes remained by the numbered cloches, the charcoal stick pointedly lying atop the butcher paper. Amused, or maybe *bemused*, that her opinion mattered to him, she'd done her best to remember all the meals and write down ratings. Everything had been delicious so she didn't give any of them less than an eight. She'd thought about pretending the soup hadn't existed, but its cloche *did* have a number, so he'd doubtless expected a rating. When she'd caught him peering over at her while tending a frying pan, she'd written a ten, then underlined it and left three exclamation points. She'd thought about circling it with a heart as well, but that would have reminded him of her foolish behavior. She would prefer if they both forgot about that.

It was difficult though. As she sipped from her cup, enjoying a potent double-shot mocha, Rylana kept thinking of the night before. Even though Jildarin had, before pushing her away, stood unresponsive in the seconds that her lips had been pressed to his, and even though he'd assured her that dragons didn't mate for recreational purposes, her thoughts kept returning to him. Being close to him hadn't been... unpleasant.

"Ridiculous," she murmured.

"Your beverage?" Sylin slid the chair on the opposite side of the table away so that she could stand there and lean her shoulder against the wall.

"No, my mocha is delicious. Those elves from yesterday are looking for you, and I think they know what your occupation in the war was."

"And what it remains." Sylin lifted a finger toward the half-gnome girl waiting tables.

"You didn't take a new job, did you? Not *here*, right? In Tranquility?" Rylana hadn't expected her comrade to swear off assassinations forever—it was what she'd trained her whole adult life to do, after all—but it wouldn't be a wise career to pursue in the city of peace. *Enforced* peace.

"One must remain useful." Sylin smiled enigmatically, then ordered a large coffee and laid a gleaming gold coin on the table.

"I like your friends," the girl told Rylana with enthusiasm, sweeping up the coin and trotting away.

"You got paid already for the job, I'm guessing," Rylana said.

"I did. Though it wasn't my usual type of assignment, I did learn that there's more work for assassins available here than you might think. The inability to challenge adversaries to duels and pursue vigilante justice leaves a lot of people craving satisfaction. Some have financial means."

"I don't need details. I'm retiring from the satisfaction-providing business."

"You're certain? Outside of the city boundaries, you could remove the tranquility ribbon and unleash your bow."

"If I take it out of the city, it'll only be to hunt, maybe to find some unique meat to challenge Jildarin to incorporate into one of his dishes." Rylana smiled at the thought of thunking down a raccoon or squirrel on his cutting board. But would those challenge someone who smoked glowing eels?

Sylin raised her eyebrows. "Is he paying you for your work yet?"

"Only in food. And tips."

"Do bookkeepers receive tips?"

"I haven't yet, but I may if I'm more aggressive about requesting them. Judging by his jingling purse last night, our goblin server does well for himself."

"You at least receive free board, right? I checked the room in the tavern, and you hadn't been by."

"I had to work late last night. It was easier to sleep in the storeroom again." In the storeroom shared with Jildarin, though once he'd turned into his silver dragon form, her thoughts had grown less sex-centered, and she'd fallen asleep wondering who might be trying to get him out of the city. Or maybe out of the cooking competition?

"Dragon adjacent?" Sylin smirked.

"Separated by the piles of crates and ovens."

"Since elves are looking for me, I'm going to be scarce for a while." Sylin waited while her coffee was delivered, with the half-gnome cheerfully introducing herself as Vilma and complimenting her lush green hair, before continuing. "I only came to see if you want to use the room or if I should let the establishment know it's available now." Sylin sipped from the mug, then almost purred a contented, "*Ahhhh,*" as she closed her eyes in appreciation.

"That's the *only* reason you came?"

"The coffee *is* excellent."

"I probably should move my things to the room. Sleeping on a cement floor isn't that comfortable, and Jildarin... Well, he hasn't given me any indication that he wants company in his lair."

"Does he still call you *my enemy* and squint suspiciously at you on an hourly basis?"

"Not *hourly.*" Rylana wished she could say that he was no longer suspicious of her at all, but she remembered him checking her hands for weapons when her intent had been amorous, not murderous. "Someone's after him, too, by the way. He has a reason to be on edge, a bigger reason than the memory of my arrow gouging his temple. Judging by the quality or lack thereof of the graffiti last night, it probably isn't the elves who are after him. I don't think your people could draw something crude if they tried."

"Elves are rarely crude in any art form."

"I'm thinking of trying to help Jildarin by figuring out who wants him out of the city and the Golden Whisk. I doubt he'll tell me the names of his competitors though. Even if he did, I'm not sure how I would investigate them. Show up at their kitchens and ask questions?" Rylana pulled out the folded piece of newspaper with Yerin's review that she'd kept from the day before. She'd meant to share it with Jildarin but had forgotten to during the busyness of the evening. Now, she spread it on the table and tapped it thoughtfully. "I wonder if Yerin would give me a list of the competitors. I told you we were neighbors when I was growing up, right? We weren't exactly friends, but I know his family and where he lives."

Rylana grimaced at the idea of taking the ferry to the west side of the lake and being that close to her family's castle. What if her father saw her? What would she say? And what would he think if she blurted that she hadn't come, after the years without communication of any kind, to see him but to check in with a neighbor?

Rylana rubbed her face. If she intended to stay in Tranquility, sooner or later, she would have to visit him, but she would prefer to put it off until later.

Sylin turned the review around so that she could read it. "It looks like he enjoyed the food. Maybe he would want to keep a fine dragon chef in the city."

"Yeah. Like you pointed out, it says something about Yerin's character that he wrote a good review, right? When you suggested he was honorable, I was skeptical, but maybe he grew into a decent guy."

"I merely said that might be the case, but I don't know him. Nor did my bicycle suffer the affliction that yours did."

"I don't imagine there were many bicycles in the woods with the wolves."

"Very few." Sylin took another sip, made another contented noise, and looked around. "I hope the elves will forget about me soon. I'd intended to stay in Tranquility for a while before moving on, to make sure you're able to settle in, naturally." She picked up one of several cookies that had come with her cup, more than typical, doubtless due to the generous tip.

"Did you become especially interested in staying long enough to ensure I settle in after you discovered this coffee shop?"

"Oh, yes."

They sipped their drinks in silence for a few moments, and Rylana perused the newspaper review for a second time. Sylin alternated between closing her eyes in appreciation as she savored her coffee and peering toward the windows and doors to make sure no enemies were sneaking up on her. Since her hood was down, her dark green hair would stand out to anyone peering in. Even among elves, it was a rare hue. Rylana knew her comrade wore head and face coverings when she worked, so anyone who glimpsed her wouldn't easily identify her, but thought it wouldn't be a bad idea for her to keep her face hidden even when she was sipping coffee.

"He didn't mention any of the ingredients, at least in the review." Rylana recalled that Yerin had been scribbling guesses into his notes when she'd walked up to his table.

"Hm?" Sylin asked.

"At the time, I thought he might be writing down ingredients so that he could include them in his review, but this only talks about tastes and the dining experience. Do you think Yerin might have opted to critique the diner as an excuse to scout the competition for the Golden Whisk?"

"The Golden what?"

"Whisk." Rylana made a vigorous stirring motion. "Didn't I tell you about it? It's the name of the cooking competition. I wonder if Jildarin would have allowed his competitor to dine there if not for Yerin's status as a food critic. He has a temper and is quick to boot people out, though usually for... other reasons."

"Ah." Sylin gazed out the window, looking a little bored with the conversation, but Rylana needed to work through this and figure out who was sending peacekeepers by the diner regularly, especially at a time when graffiti could have prompted Jildarin to disobey the law and turn into a dragon. Besides, it wasn't as if she wanted to ask Sylin any questions about *her* recent activities.

"Of course, Jildarin is very focused when he's at work," Rylana murmured, "and he seems to value honor."

"Dragons tend to do that, yes."

"It might not have occurred to him that a desire to *spy* brought a competitor to visit. I don't even know if he sees Yerin as a threat. Maybe I *should* visit him." Rylana had been considering that already, if for different reasons, but nodded, the idea firming up in her mind. "Do you think he has a place here in town or still lives across the lake on the family estate?" she mused, more to herself than Sylin, who hadn't met Yerin.

"I'm certain I don't know." Sylin's gaze turned thoughtful as she regarded Rylana. "Is there a reason you're working so hard to help this dragon? We've established it's not the pay."

"I know, but..."

But what? Why had Rylana come so quickly to care about Jildarin's fate?

The night before, he'd come out to check on her—to help her with the elves—and that meant something. But she'd been trying to fix the profitability woes of his business from the beginning. Maybe part of it was that she liked a challenge and had felt listless simply traveling the world and seeing the sights. She'd had a lack of purpose since leaving the Moon Daggers. But maybe part of it was...

Sylin raised her eyebrows.

"I did shoot him." Rylana shrugged.

"He was one of the dragons trying to roast our unit. *Shooting* him was the appropriate action."

"Yes, but did you ever think, then or now, that we—the joint kingdoms, I mean—weren't in the right in trying to take the ore from the mountains their kind claimed?"

"The various kingdoms also claimed those mountains. For ages, humans, dwarves, orcs, goblins, and gnomes didn't consider dragons to be intelligent beings, believing them more like animals, so they didn't think anything of entering into the mountains where they lived. It was a long time before the dragons spoke telepathically to them and made their intelligence known. And the elves were barely even seen in the mountains.

They avoided the other races. By the time of the ore extraction and their objections, humans and dwarves and orcs had been settling the area for centuries, and everything was murky." Sylin waved an indifferent hand and looked at a bookcase next to their table.

"I know the history, and I know what motivated the rulers of the kingdoms. That war was about acquiring the resources they wanted for their growing civilizations."

"*Most* wars are about that. Protecting what you have and acquiring what others have."

"It's just that, toward the end, I questioned if we hired onto the wrong side. Captain Maverick was pragmatic and put us where we could make money and win. The way of the mercenary, he called it. And for a long time, that suited me, but after his death... Well, I guess the death of someone close will naturally make you question your own life choices. Where you want to be with yourself and with the world when the end comes." Rylana sipped from her mocha. It had cooled, and she debated ordering a second cup, but she ought to return to work. Or... to the mission she was on the verge of giving herself.

"Such feelings sound inconvenient," Sylin said. "Since I'm not close to anyone, perhaps I'll never experience them."

"You won't question your life if my body turns up floating in the lake?"

"Certainly not."

"Goodness. Who will you have coffee with if I'm gone? I think you'll be lonely, at least."

"There are books here. They're good companions."

"I may be insulted."

"Here's one on psychology." Sylin pointed to a fat tome. "I believe it would tell you that you're trying to fix the dragon's life because you fought his kind in the war and feel guilty about that choice."

In a roundabout way, Rylana had been working through that. Without the help of a psychology book.

"Isn't that all right?" she asked.

"You tell me. You're the one working for bacon and permission to sleep on the floor in his storeroom."

"It's excellent bacon."

"Then perhaps it is all right. Just don't navigate the path of your future based on guilt acquired on roads traveled in the past."

"Is that something you read in a psychology book? And is such literature a strange choice for an assassin?"

"It is not. Since I was raised by wolves, I seek to understand the ways of the two-legs."

"Wolves don't experience guilt, do they?" Rylana asked.

"They do not."

"Lucky creatures." Rylana sighed and leaned back in her chair. "Do you think it's true that dragons only mate for procreation purposes?"

Sylin lowered her cup. "Did I miss my mark about the guilt? Is *lust* why you're doing all this? You hope he'll mate with you?"

"No, of course not. That didn't even cross my mind until, er. I had some of his special soup. Sort of… by accident. I mean, it was so good that I accidentally had more than I should have." Rylana's cheeks warmed at the memory of swiping the servings from her co-diners. "But that was a temporary infatuation. I'm over it."

"You are a strange two-legs."

"Or I'm normal, and *you're* the strange one."

"That is possible." Sylin drained her cup and placed another coin on the table. Before leaving, she added, "You also should not choose your future based on a dragon with a large *zerg* stick."

"I'm *not*, thank you. Also, I haven't *seen* his *zerg* stick." Rylana tried to add *and have no desire to do so,* but the words didn't quite come out. Two hells, maybe the effects of the spices hadn't entirely worn off.

15

After finishing her mocha, Rylana returned to the diner, intending to ask Jildarin if she could leave early and try to find Yerin. The lack of ingredients mentioned in the review didn't *mean* anything and was scant evidence that he was up to something shifty, but if she spoke to him, maybe she could learn more about his motives and also find out who the other competitors in the Golden Whisk were.

It was between meal services, and she found Jildarin not in the kitchen but in the storeroom in the back, talking to his brother. They noticed her approaching from the hallway, so she didn't have an opportunity to spy this time.

"Ah, your new servant." Zilek smirked and extended an arm toward her. "You can command *her* to stay tonight and oversee the distribution of your cherished morsels."

"She has worked here for only a short time. *She* is not who I would leave in charge, should I desire to accompany you to your meeting, which I do not."

"Are you certain? She has a stern aspect about her which

might instill good behavior in your other servants. Some of them are, shall we say, capricious. If not erratic."

"They perform adequately at their serving duties."

"The goblin attempted to wheedle five extra silver coins out of me while inspecting the heft of my purse. Lesser species are terribly emboldened in dealing with dragons in this city."

"Did you give it to him?"

"I did not."

"Check your purse later. You may have."

"I'm aghast at the mere implication, dear brother. *Sternness* is required here." Zilek pointed again at Rylana.

Standing in the hallway, she didn't know whether to feel insulted and indignant, or simply agree. From what she'd seen since starting work here, Zalani was the most reliable of the staff and a more likely candidate to oversee a meal service. As the bookkeeper, Rylana didn't feel qualified. As far as sternness went… Well, she *had* been an officer in the Moon Daggers for years, so maybe she exuded more schoolmarm firmness than feminine whimsy.

When Jildarin only sighed in response, Zilek continued. "Further, it is not a *meeting,* dear brother—what a pedestrian term—but a culinary, cultural event, a delicious one at that. And, as I mentioned, attending the conclave could present you with an opportunity."

"I am not interested in your opportunity."

"What opportunity?" Rylana risked asking, though neither dragon had invited her to participate in the conversation. If Zilek wanted to bring someone to a social gathering where chefs would be present, maybe she could volunteer to attend and sell a few more ovens.

"Zilek is attempting to entice me into going to his monthly *wine club* meeting," Jildarin said, "and there is nothing *culinary* about listless legatees swilling alcohol."

"We don't swill it but sample it, and people from all walks of life may attend, providing someone gives them an invitation and they're capable of bringing the required fine vintages for all to enjoy. The goal is not to become sloshed, as the humans call it, or *trokdon*, as the dwarves say. One desires to have good and intelligent conversation—inasmuch as the lesser species are capable of such—while appreciating and discussing the merits of the offerings."

"Are there chefs there?" Rylana looked toward the tidy row of ovens, a few having been sold but more remaining.

"Oh, not many of the members toil in any capacity anymore, certainly not in a hot and chaotic kitchen. They are generally retired or independently wealthy. Many are, however, attuned to the culinary world, as I informed my brother, and it's possible one might even be a judge at his little contest."

"The judges haven't been announced," Jildarin said, "thus to ensure nobody can send them bribes to sway their vote, which would be fruitless regardless, since the meals will be tasted and rated blindly."

"Ah, but I suspect one might be drawn from this esteemed crowd," Zilek said. "Regardless, should you attend with me, it would give you an opportunity to schmooze with the elites of the city. The gnomish mayor Sedgewick is a frequent attendee. As is the retired dwarven rock-violin virtuoso, Dondark. I've learned through my interactions with them that they've previously been recruited to judge the various cultural contests hosted in Tranquility."

"I will not win the Golden Whisk because I *schmoozed* with influential city dwellers. I will win because my dishes are superior."

"Then simply go to enjoy the wine and take an evening off. You labor in this constrained box all hours of the day every day." Zilek waved toward the walls. "When was the last time you left the city, assumed your native form, and went for a hunt?"

"Not recently, but that would appeal more than a wine meeting."

"It is a conclave," Zilek corrected, "not a simple meeting. But if you'll not attend, let us go for a hunt. I crave the companionship of another dragon, and you need to stretch your wings. I am certain of it."

Jildarin sighed again and looked at Rylana. Maybe she should have left. Neither mayors nor violinists sounded like the kinds of people who would be searching for a good deal on a gnomish commercial oven, so her interest in the meeting—the *conclave*—had faded.

"Perhaps I *will* hunt." Jildarin rotated his shoulders, muscles bunching against the fabric of his shirt. "It *has* been some time, and this work can leave me tense."

"Perhaps it is your rigid obsession that leaves you tense," Zilek suggested. "Should you go south to mate with Mother's female friends, you would doubtless find the act a release, and you would return refreshed."

"*Friends*?" Jildarin asked. "More than one seeks my... me?"

"You should not have been so ferocious and deadly during the war. You know such competence and savagery bestirs the female libido." Zilek looked at Rylana.

Her cheeks flushed as the previous night's memories came to mind. It had been Jildarin's *soup* that had bestirred her libido, not his savagery.

"This is a private conversation," she said. "I'll go record the totals from the breakfast and lunch services in the books. By my calculations, this diner is on the verge of turning a profit for the first time. From the food and service, not only from selling surplus equipment."

As if he knew exactly why she was rushing away, Zilek chuckled. Was it possible Jildarin had spoken to him about her... antics before she'd arrived? Rylana hoped not and grabbed the cashbox from the diner and ducked into the office and opened the accounting book she'd purchased. Only as she sat down did she realize she could still hear the brothers speaking.

"As a dragon, I would see her only as an enemy," Zilek was saying, "especially since she fought against our kind in the war, but when I am in my human form, I find her somewhat... Well, let us just say that her sternness has some appeal. And the outline and contours of her body, yes?"

Rylana's cheeks warmed again as she stared at the page of numbers. He wasn't talking about her having sex appeal, was he?

"I do not know of what you are speaking," Jildarin said.

"Her feminine attributes, my brother."

"Her what?"

"Oh, she is not as strikingly appealing as that female elf who was with her the day she spied upon us, but her face is without blemishes or scars, and her lips are full and her breasts an ample size to draw the eye. As a former soldier, she presumably has a degree of lithe athleticism as well."

Rylana's cheeks did *more* than heat, and she glanced at the door of the small office, wanting to shut it and not hear any more. But there wasn't a window in the little room, so it would be harder to see the pages, and a crate also propped the door open. If she moved it, she would make noise, and the dragons might realize that if they could hear her, she could hear them. Though Zilek probably didn't *care* if his musings were overheard. He wasn't doing anything to keep his voice from carrying.

"The half-elf who serves you is softer with more luscious hair, which is a somewhat intriguing mammalian attribute," Zilek continued, "but I think she might be overly amenable. Even if a dragon doesn't want to be slain by his partner, he does enjoy a challenge. Still, I've considered commanding her to serve me more than steaks. I see from your ongoing blank expression that you've not considered ordering the females around you to do more than carry trays."

"I do not even know what *consideration* is on your mind."

"Why sex, of course. Have you never engaged in it while in the form of another species? It is quite pleasurable, and when it comes to the two-legs, you hardly ever have to worry about their females thrashing about and biting your neck in the throes of passion. Not enough to *kill* you anyway. The last half-elf who entered my bedchamber was prone to nips."

"Why would you want to have coitus while in this form? There can be no offspring produced during such a union. Only the species that are closely related to each other phylogenetically may create young."

"For humans, elves, dwarves, and many of the other two-legs, sex is not always about creating young."

"There is no logical reason to have coitus if that is not the goal."

Zilek chuckled. "Have you not had any urges in this form that suggest *pleasure* might be a logical reason to engage? You must let yourself leave this cave and experience more of the world, my brother."

"You have convinced me that I would enjoy experiencing a hunt. Nothing more."

"That is a start, I suppose."

Footsteps sounded in the hallway, and Rylana grabbed a pen and bent low over the accounting book, pretending she had been too engrossed in the work to hear the second half of the conversation. Jildarin walked past without slowing, and she heard him ask Zalani to watch over the diner, saying he had started dinner preparations and would return in time to finish them.

On his way back toward the storeroom, Jildarin stopped in the doorway to the office and peered in at Rylana. She wrote the totals for the day's services thus far and didn't look at him. But as he remained, she turned warily toward the doorway. Jildarin was looking her up and down with what she read as puzzled consideration. There wasn't anything sexual in the perusal—she had a feeling he was trying to see what Zilek had been talking about—but having his gaze pause at her chest made her think again of the night before.

Jildarin shook his head and flicked a hand in dismissal. "You will continue to sell ovens while I am gone. That has been a lucrative vein. I am pleased that the landlord no longer has a reason to visit and threaten my expulsion." He nodded at her, then disappeared into the storeroom.

That nod of approval pleased her more than it probably should have, but she liked that he was starting to recognize that she had value. While Jildarin was gone, she would take the ferry across the lake to visit Yerin's estate. Even if he wasn't there and she didn't learn anything about Jildarin's competitors, she would pitch an oven to whoever handled the cooking there.

The back doors thudded shut as the dragons departed, and Zalani poked her head into the office.

"Oh, there it is." She pointed at the cashbox. "I wanted to make sure Rolf hadn't figured out a way to abscond with that."

"No. I'll return it after I finish my tally for the day. Zalani, you may want to watch out for Jildarin's brother."

"I always avoid him since he's pompous and full of himself—like all dragons—but why?"

"He thinks you're, uhm, interesting."

"In what way? I didn't think he knew I existed. He certainly doesn't know my name."

"In a bedroom way."

"Oh." Zalani brightened instead of looking appalled. "He's quite handsome, isn't he? I wouldn't mind a romp with him, pomposity aside, but I didn't think— Well, the dragons, even when shifted into human or elven form, always give you the impression that you're so far beneath them that they couldn't *imagine* wanting to have sex."

Rylana thought of Jildarin's stiff aloofness with her the night before. "Yeah."

"And they certainly wouldn't stick around for snuggling afterward if they did deign to unleash their *zerg* sticks in your presence, but I'd be intrigued to have sex with one of them at least once." Zalani scratched her cheek as she looked toward the storeroom, though the dragons had departed. "Maybe I'll wear my low-cut dress the next time Zilek comes by the diner. And accidentally drop a tray in front of him so I have a reason to bend over and pick it up."

"I guess you didn't need my warning to watch out for him," Rylana said. "*He* may need to watch out for you."

"Possibly so." Zalani winked and returned to her duties.

As Rylana closed the book, a crash came from the front of the diner.

"What happened?" Zalani blurted as Gniknik cursed and said in dismay, "My dish collector!"

Rylana hurried to the front, spotting a broken window right away, glass shattered around one of Gniknik's gnomish contraptions. Someone had thrown a large rock with a paper tied around it.

Drawing her utility knife, Rylana ran to the front door to peer outside. A few pedestrians were looking in a window down the street, and an orc with a grin on her broad face straightened after ducking to exit the doorway of the bakery. She strolled away with an oddly shaped cake box and gave no indication that she'd seen whoever had thrown the rock. Farther down the street, a golem walked through an intersection, its stone head swiveling left and right as it searched for trouble.

"Where was it when the rock was being thrown?" Rylana

muttered, thinking of the night before when peacemakers had been *coincidentally* nearby when Jildarin had discovered the graffiti.

Back inside, Zalani and Gniknik were untying the paper from the rock. A note?

"Dragons can't cook," Zalani read. "It is only because you drug your customers that they think your food isn't horrible. Go back to where you came from, and leave the city forever, or your diner will suffer a catastrophic accident." She shook her head and looked at Rylana and Gniknik. "Who do you think did this?"

"Someone cowardly," Rylana said.

"And crude." Gniknik nudged the rock with his toe. "What an unsophisticated means of delivering a message."

"Should we… tell Jildarin about this?" Zalani asked.

"No," Rylana said, then looked in the direction of the lake. "I'm going to take care of it for him."

"Is hunting down rock hurlers among your duties as a bookkeeper?" Zalani asked.

"No, but it's… somewhat in line with my previous duties."

Rylana nodded firmly and grabbed her belongings. She couldn't put off a visit to the west side of the lake any longer. She had to get a list of Jildarin's rivals and find out who was trying to get him kicked out of the competition.

16

As THE WHEEL AT THE BACK OF THE STEAM-POWERED FERRY churned, Rylana leaned against one of the side railings in a passenger area that was separate from the horse-drawn wagons and magic- and steam-powered carriages and lorries loaded for the trip. Sylin stood at her side, her hood up and her hair pulled back so that its vibrant forest-green coloring wouldn't be visible unless someone peered closely at her. Rylana had chanced across her coming out of the coffee shop and invited her along. Hopefully, the elves looking for Sylin wouldn't realize what a magnetic pull that place had on her, or she would be easy to find.

The sun brightened the pale-blue sky, and, with only a slight breeze whispering across the lake, the water was calm, the movement of the ferry barely noticeable. Rylana could make out Lucky Island and the boardwalk stretching to shore and noted they were past the point that Jildarin had said marked a spot where a dragon might fly without setting off the city's security pillars. She caught herself looking at the sky beyond the end of the lake, wondering if he and his brother had gone in that direction to hunt.

"At what point during this journey will you give me details

about the job you promised? Or is *this* it?" Sylin waved at the ferry deck.

"I might very well have been moved to pay someone to come along for moral support," Rylana said, "but, if you'll recall, all I said when I invited you along was that if this trip didn't lead to the answers I'm hoping for, I might need to hire you."

"So, it was not a promise of work."

"No. I was surprised you jumped in eagerness to accompany me."

"The jumping had more to do with all the cups of fresh coffee that the waitress brought for me to sample. They have quite the stimulatory effect, something you'd be familiar with if you didn't dilute yours so thoroughly with milk and chocolate." Sylin sneered.

"Mochas and lattes sufficiently stimulate me. There's someone leaving threatening messages at the diner, telling Jildarin to leave or else."

"Or else what? Even *I* wouldn't attempt to *else* a dragon. Not without a lot of allies."

"The last message said a calamity would befall the diner, not Jildarin specifically. But, having grown up in Tranquility, I've seen that people can be emboldened to a foolish extent by the knowledge that the law protects them from violent repercussions."

"Ah, yes. We discussed that before. They're like dogs barking at passersby from behind a fence."

"Exactly. When I first went south and joined the mercenaries, I was surprised by how polite everyone was around people who are armed and trained. As to the potential job... if I can't ferret out what I want to learn, I may need someone to stake out the diner and capture whoever is leaving graffiti and lobbing rocks through the windows."

"Capture or kill?"

"*Death* would be a harsh punishment for someone painting a *zerg* stick on a door, don't you think?"

"When I accept jobs, I don't make ethical or moral judgments about the choices of those who hire me. I only count the coin to make sure it's sufficient for the level of personal risk involved."

"You're a practical elf."

"Always."

"I don't need an assassin," Rylana said. "Just someone tough with good eyes who doesn't mind lurking for hours on a rooftop to observe an area."

"I charge an hourly rate for lurking. And I require the fee up front, especially from those who work for an employer who pays only in soup and bacon."

"I'll talk to Jildarin about arranging payment from the diner's cashbox. Or he can pay *you* in food. He actually wanted your palate last night to sample some of his dishes. I understand there may be elves among the judges for his contest."

"Remind me not to come to watch it, then."

"Were you planning to? One doesn't think of assassins as typical audience members for a cooking competition."

"The uniqueness of watching a dragon chef might be enough to draw one. Does he flambé all his dishes?"

"I haven't seen him flambé anything. Wait, that's not true. I've noticed that the burner isn't always *on* when he's cooking, and, at last night's meal, there was seared fish."

"*How* seared?"

"Just on the outside. The inside was only lightly cooked."

"Huh. That's more finesse than I would expect from a dragon chef."

"There was also a delicate custard dessert with a sugary top that was crystallized by heat." For the first time, it occurred to Rylana to wonder if the peacekeepers knew dragons could create fire while in their human forms. Probably. They exuded magic even when shape-shifted.

"Delicate is not a word one usually applies to dragons."

"You sure you don't want to come to the cooking competition to watch him work? It could be fascinating. He invited me. Well, no. He *commanded* me to come."

"Are you his employee or his servant?"

"His brother considers me a servant. And Jildarin..." Rylana scratched her jaw, not sure what exactly Jildarin considered her. He was calling her *my enemy* less frequently, but he hadn't stopped altogether. "He has a commanding presence," she finished with.

"That's a safe way to describe a dragon. More apt than *delicate*, I'm sure."

"The *dessert* he made was delicate. That's all."

Rylana turned toward the bow to regard the western shoreline, her family's castle visible in stark detail as the ferry drew closer. Numerous private docks jutted from the beaches and points, but there was only one public dock, a wide gravel road heading inland from it. Neither the road nor the Avandar estate had changed much in the years she'd been gone, but some of the surrounding properties had been built up with additions or had sprouted new boathouses and gazebos.

"Yerin's family lives up on the same bluff as my father's castle, but it's not quite visible because of the trees." Rylana pointed. "It's behind and down the road a bit from Avandar Estate."

"You're going to see the food critic? To ask about the lack of specificity in his review regarding ingredients?" Sylin didn't sound excited by the prospect.

"I'm planning to talk him, yes."

"I shouldn't have been so eager to come along."

"As you pointed out, all the coffee you consumed compelled eagerness."

"True. I'd also hoped for adventure."

"It's possible we'll find that."

"This area looks sedate." Sylin eyed the ritzy estates as the ferry docked, crewmen tying it up with ropes. Someone waved for the pedestrians to disembark before the wagons and carriages. "There probably aren't armed elves strolling about, looking for me."

"I can't tell if that's a positive or a negative for you."

"Well, if said elves *found* me, they would be easier to deal with over here, where there aren't peacekeepers swarming the roads like ants assailing a fallen cookie."

"Tranquility's laws are enforced all along the waterfront over here too." As they walked off the ferry, Rylana pointed to a pillar half-hidden by tree leaves.

"Ah. I may not be able to stay long-term in this city."

"Because of the enforced peace?"

"It's kind of boring, isn't it?"

"Maybe you could take up a new hobby. Do you want me to ask if Jildarin accepts apprentices?" Rylana led the way up the road, walking to the side to avoid the wagons and carriages heading inland from the ferry. At the top of the bluff, the road branched to travel north and south along the lake, or one could continue inland toward the mountains.

"I do not," Sylin said. "And is he even *qualified* to have an apprentice?"

"The flavors I've tasted thus far assure me that he is."

"How did a dragon learn to cook? Don't most of them eat the raw meat of whatever animal they killed two minutes earlier? That's what I've observed when I've seen them hunting in the wild."

"I'm not sure where he learned." Rylana turned down the road that would lead to Yerin's estate—and also past her family's land. A horse-drawn carriage clopped by, one of several heading in the same direction. Rylana eyed the route ahead warily, having no idea what she would say if she ran into her father or any neighbors who remembered and recognized her.

Or *would* anyone look twice at her? It had been so long, and she'd had long hair when she'd left. Even people who'd known her as a girl might not recognize her at first glance.

Sylin followed her gaze to the castle in the middle of the grassy lawn, a low stone wall with wrought-iron bars on top of it providing separation from the road and the properties to either side. A weathered copper plaque identifying the property as AVANDAR MANOR was mounted by the gate, the patina more advanced than when she'd left.

Rylana spotted someone walking between the castle and a wooden stable and veered to the far side of the road. It wasn't anyone she recognized, but she didn't want to be seen. One day, if she remained in Tranquility, she would visit her father and brother, to say hello and ask them how they were doing, but she dreaded the idea. She would have to explain the decisions she'd made what seemed like a lifetime ago. Assuming they cared enough to ask about her decisions. Her father might still be disappointed that she hadn't, after all the money he'd spent on tutors for her, gone into the family business. That had probably offended him more than the fact that she had departed without leaving more than a terse letter. She hoped things were going well and that her brother hadn't also disappointed him.

"That's your castle?" Sylin asked, no doubt having read the sign.

"It's where I grew up, yes. I don't claim any ownership of it."

"It's even more grandiose and pompous than I imagined."

"Castles can't be pompous."

"Please. That place oozes pomposity from its leering, self-important gargoyles to the oversized towers to that fountain—it's almost as big as the gatehouse. And there are stained-glass inserts in the machicolations. Those clearly aren't functional anymore."

"Thanks to the golems and pillars, the estates along the lake rarely need to fend off nomadic hordes of orcs, ogres, trolls, and barbarians anymore."

"Is there a throne?"

"No. This wasn't ever the seat of a *king*. My father does have a big cushy chair in his office that's made from the hide of a spotted cow. I got in trouble for spilling grape juice on it as a kid."

"Did you have to clean it, or did a servant pat you on the head and handle it?" Sylin asked.

"I told you we didn't have servants. My mother gave me a bottle of vinegar and told me to blot, not scrub, until the evidence went away." Rylana didn't remember anything else from that long-ago day, but she did recall the strong scent of the vinegar that had hung in the air as she'd blotted furiously, trying to get the stain out before her father returned home from a business trip.

"The nice thing about living in a forest is nobody cares if you stain the trees."

"The wolves weren't offended by grape-juice spills in their den?"

"They neglected to supply me with such treats. I wasn't as spoiled as you." Sylin smirked.

"But they also didn't pressure you to go into the family business, I'll bet." Rylana pointed ahead to a manor sprawling along the opposite side of the road. Even though it wasn't on the shoreline with a beach of its own, the elevated terrain gave it a view of the lake. A surprising number of carriages were parked along the wide circular drive, and people were heading through the front doors or around the home toward the back. The smoke of a bonfire wafted from that direction. Was Yerin's family hosting a party? There weren't any notable holidays this week, but maybe they were celebrating the arrival of good spring weather.

"When you're a wolf, the family business is hunting," Sylin

said. "The *pack* business. I didn't mind being a part of that since I enjoyed eating."

One of the carriages that had been on the ferry arrived, the horses pulling it into the driveway to park at the end of the queue. Once it stopped, the door opened, and a man and woman in elegant clothing stepped out. A butler came out to greet them, accepting a gift in a ribbon-tied box and leading them toward the front door.

The butler glanced toward Sylin and Rylana and looked like he might impede them if they tried to step onto the estate, but the newcomers spoke, distracting him.

"Will we be able to get into the shindig without force?" Sylin looked at Rylana, as if she might pull ornate invitations written with fancy calligraphy from an inside pocket.

"Let's hope so." Rylana hadn't expected there to *be* a shindig. "There are rules about using force against people you played with when you were children."

"You wouldn't put the butler in that category, I assume. Or is he also a childhood chum who once displayed aggressive tendencies toward your bicycle?"

"I've never seen him before."

"Force could be acceptable then." Sylin cracked her knuckles.

"Let's first *ask* if we can go in." The breeze shifted, and Rylana caught a whiff of seasoned meat roasting. "That smells wonderful."

"Yes."

By the time they were climbing the broad marble steps toward the front doors, the butler had ushered the couple inside and returned. He frowned at their approach, his gaze taking in their unassuming travel clothing and faces that hadn't seen makeup brushes in a long time. Rylana didn't know if Sylin had *ever* worn makeup, not that her beauty needed any enhancing.

"You do not have invitations," the butler stated, more certainty than a question.

"No, but we're not looking to go to the party. I'm hoping to speak with Yerin." Rylana thought about giving her family name, which would probably result in her being invited in, but it would doubtless also result in someone mentioning to her father that she'd been by. "I'm a fan of his work as a food critic. He published a write-up recently in the *Chronicles* about the Dragon Diner, and, while it spoke highly of some of the menu items, he didn't mention the ingredients in any of the dishes. There's a certain soup, in particular, that I was hoping to learn more about. Is it possible he would come out to discuss it?"

If Yerin was as passionate about food as Rylana believed, an invitation to talk on the subject might appeal to him. Unfortunately, the butler gazed at her without expression, then closed the door in their faces. Rylana had a feeling the message wouldn't get to Yerin.

"Are you *sure* force wouldn't be acceptable?" Sylin asked.

"Force on the door? Your elven blood might give you the strength to knock it down. It looks solid though."

"My years of assiduous training would be of more assistance than my blood."

"If you say so." Rylana, who wouldn't have minded a little elven blood of her own, knocked on the stout oak. Maybe she would mention her family name, after all. But the butler didn't return to give her a second chance. "Rude."

17

"We could go around the house to the backyard," Sylin offered when the butler didn't return. "There's not a gate, a bramble patch, a dog with long fangs, or any of the other typical deterrents."

"True."

And the scents of roasting meat were coming from that direction. Maybe Yerin was back there, attending to a rotisserie spit over a fire.

They padded across the well-trimmed lawn, rounded a great stone chimney, and walked into the backyard and onto flagstone pavers with moss growing between them. The paver patio stretched across the length of the back of the manor, and dozens of people stood and visited while holding small plates and tankards or wineglasses. Most were human, but a few dwarves and gnomes dotted the gathering. No elves, fortunately, for Sylin's sake.

A large fire did indeed burn in a rectangular stone pit with a full pig roasting over it, a yawning servant rotating it. Beside him stood Yerin, basting the meat with a large brush. Before Rylana could wave to draw his attention, he frowned into his saucepan, shook his head vigorously, then strode toward a back door. He went inside without noticing them.

"At least we know he's home," Rylana said.

"As is that roasting pig." Sylin's nose lifted into the air. "Perhaps we should visit it while we wait for him to return."

"Visit it with a knife and fork?"

"Naturally."

More interested in her mission than the food, Rylana headed for the same door that Yerin had used. Sylin followed but also plucked up a small plate and wineglass that someone had abandoned, a few morsels remaining.

"You might want to put down your hood if you're going to pretend to be a guest," Rylana suggested, though she didn't know if that was Sylin's plan or if she only meant to consume the leftovers. After all, *she* wasn't being paid in free food from the diner. "It's a nice spring day," Rylana added, "and nobody else is skulking about in assassin's garb."

"In this crowd, my pointed ears might stand out more than a hood."

"Nah, elves often get invited to parties hosted by the rich. Their innate regal elegance makes them ideal to add a degree of pomposity."

"I don't necessarily disagree with that description of my people, but I'll point out that your family's castle is more pompous than the most grandiose elven enclave."

"Maybe so, but elves carry their pomposity with them. Much like dragons."

"That must be what drew our kinds to fight together during the war. Maybe it had nothing to do with protecting resources."

"I believe scientific experiments have proved that pomposity attracts like."

As Rylana neared the door, a woman in a black-and-white

uniform stepped outside. She carried a tray laden with more of the small dishes, featuring delicious-looking trolled eggs, glazed ham curls, caviar-smeared crackers, and other appetizers. Though the woman barely glanced their way, Rylana turned away, feigning interest in a bronze rain chain dangling from a gutter. Sylin's gaze drifted back toward the roast.

The woman continued past without taking notice of them. As Rylana was about to turn again toward the door, she spotted someone familiar maneuvering through the crowd.

"Two hells."

Sylin followed her gaze. "What?"

"That's Vormalt. What is *he* doing here?" Rylana watched him browse from trays as he chatted with people near the spit. Meanwhile, she pressed herself against the cool stone wall of the house, willing shadows to hide her, but the sunny day left few of them.

"Eating," Sylin said.

"No, he's ruining my plans." Rylana started to say more, but Vormalt turned in their direction, and she darted through the door.

Sylin glided inside after her, and they almost ran into another uniformed servant with a tray.

"May I help you, my lady?" the woman asked.

"I need to use the lavatory," Rylana blurted, barely keeping herself from glancing out the door to check whether Vormalt had seen her. She'd been worried about running into her family up here. She hadn't thought *he* would be lurking in the area.

"The guest toilet is down that hall. Make sure you don't go into the kitchen. Lord Yerin is working on his masterpiece. It'll be unveiled later, but he doesn't want anyone to interrupt him—or see the dish before it's ready."

"He's a special sort, isn't he?"

"Oh, yes, my lady." The servant winked and stepped outside with a tray. "Oh, good afternoon, Lord Vormalt."

"Two hells," Rylana cursed again and hurried down the hall. He must have seen her and come to find out what she was up to. What would she say?

She opened the first door she came to, not the lavatory but a closet with mops and brooms inside, as well as shelves stuffed with blankets and linens. There wasn't much room, but she squeezed in and squished herself against the wall to make space for Sylin to slip in with her before shutting the door most of the way. There weren't any windows, and little light from the hallway made it inside. Rylana pressed her eye to the gap in the door.

"I would offer to dispatch your nemesis for you," Sylin said quietly, her shoulder jammed against Rylana's, "but I know you can't afford my services."

"You don't offer a special rate for friends and family?"

"Assassins don't *have* friends, and you know I don't have family."

"We're hunkered in a tiny closet together, and you don't consider me a friend?"

"At the moment, I consider you a pest. Is that your elbow jutting into my ribs, or is the broom handle being forward?"

"Sh."

Vormalt had come inside. Without waiting for guidance from the staff, he strode down the hall.

Rylana braced herself for him to fling open the closet door. Instead, he walked past without glancing at it and turned into a room farther down on the opposite side of the hall.

"That pig smells wonderful, Yerin," he said, his voice drifting back to Rylana. "Will you enter it in the contest?"

The return voice was more muffled, but she made out an indignant, "The Golden Whisk is far more than a *contest*. And you don't *enter* items that you craft ahead of time. You have to perform on the spot, under pressure, with the audience and judges looking on and the sand in the hourglass running out."

The men moved too far from the hallway for Rylana to hear the following words.

"It seems Yerin is practicing too." She opened the door a little wider, wanting to get close enough to eavesdrop, but a servant stepped into the hallway with freshly laden trays.

Rylana scooted back, her hip bumping Sylin, and she almost tripped over a mop bucket on the floor. Fortunately, she didn't make any noise, and the servant passed without checking the closet.

"You're going to have to reveal yourself eventually if you want to speak with him," Sylin pointed out. "Wasn't that your goal?"

"Yes, but if I could spy, I might learn even more."

Too bad both men would recognize her. It wasn't as if she could pull one of the servants into the lavatory, tie her up, and steal her uniform. And Sylin… Even if Yerin was focused on his work, he was bound to notice if one of the servers abruptly had pointed ears and green hair.

Another of the staff returned, walking up the hallway with an empty tray.

"Do you want me to make a diversion that will keep these servers occupied?" Sylin asked.

"Yes. Do you have an idea how?"

"I'm a repository of ideas. Also, I'm eager to escape this cramped closet." Without explaining further, Sylin squeezed past and headed for the door they'd come through.

Rylana doubted they would be able to remain undiscovered for long, but it wasn't as if the staff were carrying crossbows and would slay intruders. At the most, she would be escorted out.

After leaving the closet, Rylana crept toward the kitchen. There wasn't a door, and warmth and appealing scents floated out, along with the murmurs of voices.

She peeked inside, spotting Yerin in a white chef's coat similar to the one Jildarin sometimes wore. Vormalt stood beside him, his arms folded over his chest. They faced one of two hearths burning cheerfully in the back of the kitchen, each with pots hanging over the embers. A large woodstove rested near the stone wall between the hearths, and Yerin was stirring something in one of several saucepans on top of it.

Near the entrance to the kitchen, Rylana spotted a half-closed door to a pantry, shelves of glass and ceramic jars visible inside behind hanging pieces of cured meat. She might be able to hide in there to keep from being noticed for longer, but then she could end up trapped. Or someone would look in, and she would have to explain that she was looking for the lavatory among the spices and salamis.

"I'm perfecting my dishes," Yerin said, apparently answering something Vormalt had asked before Rylana came in, "not worrying about the guest list."

"Did you even *invite* Lord Avandar?" Vormalt asked.

Rylana gaped at their backs. That was her father.

"Yes, I had someone deliver an invitation two days ago."

"Did he say he would come? Rylana's brother and his family are out of town. If Avandar leaves the premises, that would be an ideal time for me to visit unannounced and take advantage of the fact that they don't maintain much in the way of staff. There are the magical security wards and such, but I finally found out who put in the system and paid her to draw me a map with instructions on bypassing everything."

"Your plans for illegal trespass are less fascinating to me than you'd think," Yerin said as Rylana kept gaping. Did Vormalt want to sneak in and *steal* something from her father's castle? What and why?

"Your plans to win a stupid cooking contest aren't that fascinating either," Vormalt said.

The back door must have opened because the sounds of voices

in the backyard drifted inside. Was one of the staff coming in with another tray?

Rylana hesitated, wanting to hear what else the men said—as much about *illegal trespass* into her father's castle as the cooking competition. She ducked low, beneath the level of the butcher block countertop on one of three islands in the kitchen, and hurried to the pantry, barely bumping the door as she slipped inside.

"Hand me that spoon," Yerin said. "Then go away. Or go loiter with the butler to see if Lord Avandar comes."

"Your butler *would* be better company. Haven't you already practiced enough dishes to ensure you'll win?"

"I'll definitely beat Horts, Dagmire, the elf chef, and that weird lady who, rumors say, is a jaguar shifter from the south. But that dragon… He's using magic in his dishes. I'm certain of it."

"Is that allowed?"

"It's not *not* allowed, but dragons are inherently magical, so it's hardly fair that they be allowed to compete."

"Aren't elves inherently magical too?" Vormalt asked. "And gnomes and dwarves, for that matter?"

"*Yes*. But not *dragon* magical."

"I see you've a well thought out and rational argument on why he shouldn't be competing."

"Quit pestering me, Vormalt. I don't know if my neighbor is coming or not." Yerin lowered his voice, sounding more like he was shifting to absent muttering than anything directed at Vormalt. "Magic isn't usually anything that affects the taste of food, so the judges don't worry about it much, but it's not fair. I've heard of a few species—elves, in particular—that create alchemical concoctions to enhance people's emotions and *feelings* about ingredients and use them in their food, but that's not what the dragon is doing. I know it. I could *tell* by tasting his food. People have been talking about special dragon spices. I don't know much about those specifically, like where they come from or if he could get more if his stash mysteriously disappeared..."

"Sneaking into a dragon's diner to steal ingredients sounds even less wise than sneaking into a lord's library."

The library? Yes, Vormalt had mentioned that before, hadn't he? Apparently, it hadn't been her company or the *view* that had kept the castle in his mind for seventeen years.

"I agree," Yerin said. "But I'm going to get him out of the competition. One way or another. I'm *not* going to lose the Golden Whisk, not again. I still can't believe that bumbling gnome won last year. It was completely unfair. There was a gnome judge when there shouldn't have been, just because the dwarf got sick and pulled out, and I'm *sure* she was predisposed to favor dishes made to appeal to the tastebuds of their kind. I'm *not* going to lose again. I'm tired of my father thinking— Look, if you're going to hover, you need to help out. Get me a jar of blackberry jam, will you?"

"Where is it?"

"The pantry."

Rylana swore under her breath and peered through the crack, but Vormalt was already heading toward her. She grabbed one of the salamis and hefted it with a vague notion of clubbing Vormalt. Maybe if she knocked him on his ass quickly enough, he wouldn't see who was responsible...

As he reached for the doorknob, a scream came from the backyard. Alarmed shouts followed.

Salami clenched in her hands, Rylana didn't know whether to hope Sylin had lit the back of the house on fire or not.

"What is it?" Vormalt paused, his hand inches from the knob.

"Fire!" came a cry from outside.

Someone else shouted, "The pig!"

"My pig?" Yerin charged around an island and toward the exit. "What's happening to my pig?"

He and Vormalt ran out of the kitchen and toward the back

door. Rylana slipped out of the pantry and went in the opposite direction, trotting through numerous rooms to reach the foyer and the front door. The butler and two other staff were peering out a back window and didn't notice her ease outside. She jogged for the road, trusting that Sylin would catch up with her.

Plumes of smoke rose from the backyard, and shouts continued, calls for buckets of water. Rylana might have felt guilty about inadvertently causing the chaos, but after listening to Yerin, she wagered he was behind the attempts to get Jildarin to change into his dragon form and be kicked out of the city. The problem was that she didn't have any idea how she could prove that.

Sylin stepped out of a hedgerow in front of the property next door, and Rylana jumped. Her elven comrade's hood remained up, but a smudge of soot was visible on her cheek.

"Thank you for your assistance with the distraction," Rylana said, wondering how Sylin had started a fire—or caused the existing fire under the pig to spontaneously quadruple in size—without anyone noticing.

"You are welcome."

"You're a good friend," Rylana said as they walked up the road toward the ferry. "Even if you don't consider *me* one."

"Assassins can't allow themselves to get close to others, lest enemies manipulate them by their emotional attachments."

"You don't think we were close when we were smashed into that closet together? The hilt of your knife was jabbing into my kidney."

"Not emotionally close, no. Feelings weren't involved."

"Are you sure? My kidney had some feelings. I—" Rylana stopped as the gate to her family's property rolled open.

She glanced left and right, but there were no convenient hedgerows to leap behind along this section of the street. She almost whirled to sprint back toward Yerin's estate, but the plumes of smoke still wafting from behind his manor convinced her that returning would be a bad idea. Besides, her father stepped into the street, and it was too late to escape notice.

He halted and stared at her, back rigid and nothing inviting about his pose. Rylana didn't know what to do but stare back at him, noting that his formerly brown hair was gray, and he now wore it short, cut to meld into a well-trimmed beard that lined his jaw under his stern lips and a tidy mustache. His cool brown eyes regarded Rylana with mild surprise but not utter surprise. Right away, she guessed that Vormalt or another acquaintance had reported her presence in the city to him.

"He's stiffer than an alpha wolf with its hackles up," Sylin murmured too softly for him to hear.

"What would one of your pack do if it chanced across a family member it hadn't seen in years?" Rylana murmured back.

"Go up and sniff butts."

"I... probably won't try that." Rylana raised her voice. "Uhm, hello, Father."

"Good afternoon, Rylana." Despite his rigid stance, his tone was polite, polite but without any warmth. He'd never been effusive with affection, even with Mother when she'd still lived, so that wasn't surprising.

"You look well." Rylana cringed at the awkwardness of her words. "I came to..." To what? She hadn't come to see him at all and had hoped to avoid this. "Ah, do you remember Vernest Vormalt?"

"He's returned to Tranquility periodically over the years since leaving my employment. Each time, he's attempted to gain access to our estate for reasons he won't disclose."

"So you *do* remember him."

"Yes."

"Well, he's plotting to get you out of the castle so he can check out the library for some reason. If you're heading to the Molingvar estate because you were invited to sample Yerin's food, you might want to change your plans." Rylana looked back over her shoulder at the smoke being blown across the street and toward the lake.

"I see." Father didn't appear alarmed by the smoke and merely shifted his gaze to Sylin.

"Oh, sorry," Rylana said. "This is my friend—well, not an emotionally close friend who has *feelings* for me—Sylin of Darken Forest in the south."

"A mercenary?" For the first time, there was judgment in Father's voice, the politeness evaporating.

"Yeah."

"As you are, from what I've heard over the years. I admit I didn't expect to see you again. I assumed you would be killed."

"That did nearly happen a few times. Aren't you relieved I'm still alive?" Rylana smiled and spread her arms, though *relieved* was the last thing her father appeared to be. His lips pinched together, and he didn't reply. Was he still irritated, after all these years, that she hadn't gone into the family business?

"What do you want?" he asked. "Are you here for money?"

"No, I'm trying to help a dragon win a cooking contest."

His jaw descended a few millimeters. Whatever he'd expected from her, that wasn't it.

"We need to get back to that, don't we?" Sylin asked.

"Yes. Yes, immediately. Goodbye, Father!"

Rylana didn't know if assisting a dragon was a socially acceptable reason to hasten away, but she did anyway, and she didn't look back.

18

Twilight was sinking over the mundane and magical lights of Tranquility as the ferry returned Rylana and Sylin to the city. They headed straight for the diner, Rylana's mood somber. She tried not to feel disappointed that her father hadn't been glad to see her—or welcoming in the least. Such emotions wouldn't be logical. After all, she hadn't been glad to see him either; she'd planned to avoid him altogether for as long as possible. Not because she didn't care but because she'd expected him to be… exactly as he had been. Distant. Aloof. Still disappointed in what she'd become. Not only that, but he'd accused her of showing up for money. That rankled more than the rest.

"Hm," Sylin said, her gaze toward the diner as they turned onto Acorn Street.

A giggling couple stumbled out the front door with their arms around each other's waists. Several teenage boys were peering in the window.

"What now?" Rylana muttered, increasing her pace.

Had Jildarin returned from his hunt yet? She didn't know, but something told her that he hadn't.

One of the boys snickered and elbowed a buddy. Another blurted that he had to leave and ran into the alley.

The door opened again, and, as another amorous couple exited, moans, groans, and an enthusiastic cry of, "Yes!" wafted out of the dining room.

"I thought Jildarin was figuring out how to tone *down* the dragon spices." Rylana shooed away the boys and walked inside.

Right away, she flung her arm up, not to block a weapon but to block the view of all the bared flesh on display on vigorously moving bodies. How in either hell was that man pumping his waist like that while hanging from a candelabra? He had to be half-elven. With the grip strength of a coconut crab.

One of the moans coming from the back corner was familiar—and not sexual. Gniknik knelt on the floor, cradling one of his ambulatory contraptions. It looked like someone had stepped on it—or maybe kicked it across the diner in the throes of passion. That had happened to more than one empty bowl. Almost every booth was taken by couples—and there was an athletic trio standing up and making creative use of the walls and sconces in the hallways.

Rylana looked around for Zalani—hadn't Jildarin left *her* in charge?—but wasn't surprised when she spotted Rolf behind the counter, dropping silver coins into his bulging purse instead of the cashbox.

"Your life has gotten exceedingly strange since you started working here," Sylin observed.

Shaking her head, Rylana stomped up to Rolf and planted herself in front of him. "What happened?"

Rolf spread his arms, his white eyebrows rising in innocence. "It was an accident."

"An accident," Rylana said in a flat tone, eyeing the bag of coins. It looked heavy. Were some of those *gold*?

"Yes, indeed. When I went to ladle up plates and bowls in the kitchen, some of the dragon spices fell into the soup pot."

"They *fell* in?"

"Yes. I believe the breeze created by my passing caused the jars to tip and tumble over."

"I do hate it when my movements result in an overly aggressive breeze." Sylin joined them, dodging the groping hands of a couple that wanted to include her in their horizontal encounter.

"You're a goblin, not a dragon flapping its wings. You intentionally did this." Rylana snatched the bag of coins from Rolf's hands.

"That's mine!" he blurted and lunged for it, but Sylin caught his wrist in the air, squeezing enough to make him wince and halt the movement.

"If what you said is true," Rylana said, "and this is from the copious number of diners who came in for meals tonight, then the coins belong in the cashbox."

"Only *some* is from the meals. The rest is from, uhm." Rolf looked around for support.

Gniknik walked over with his maligned contraption gathered in his arms, a bent spring dangling sadly. "He's charging people for space in the back to have sex."

"There are people in the back? In Jildarin's *lair*?" Rylana gaped at Rolf. "Are you crazy?"

"Horny people with their brains diddled by dragon spices will pay exorbitant amounts for private nooks," Rolf said.

A moan came from a couple thrashing in a booth. Rylana rolled her eyes and looked away.

"And public nooks," Sylin said, *her* eyes crinkling.

Rolf tried to reach for his purse again, but Sylin tightened her grip on his arm. He crumpled dramatically—*melodramatically*—to his knees.

"Your heavy is maiming me," he blurted.

"My heavy, please," Rylana said. "Sylin is an elf. She would blow away in a stiff wind."

"Or the breeze caused by a goblin's passing." Sylin looked far more amused than affronted by the situation in the diner. Because *she* didn't work there.

Jildarin would be furious if he walked in to find this. He might change into a dragon on the spot. If Rolf hadn't looked so guilty, Rylana would have guessed this was another plot instigated by Yerin to get Jildarin in trouble with the authorities.

"I'm a goodly goblin increasing the revenues to the diner." Rolf tried unsuccessfully to extract his wrist from Sylin's grip. She might not be heavy, but she *was* strong. "I don't deserve maiming."

"Look," Rylana said, "if you help me get all these people out of here before Jildarin comes back, I'll have the diner's cashbox *split* what's in this bag with you."

"But I earned it all."

"You didn't *earn* it. You exploited people by drugging them. We *should* give it back." Rylana looked around, wondering if any of the couples had the wherewithal to even know how much they'd paid. She well remembered that the dragon spices affected one's mind as well as one's libido.

"Half is fair." Rolf pushed himself to his feet.

Zalani stepped out of the kitchen with her face flushed, her hair down, and her dress rumpled with a few buttons unfastened. She gripped the hand of a burly man who probably had orc blood but managed to have a broad, handsome face regardless, and they walked toward the dining room. He wore a pleased grin. When Zalani spotted Rylana, she halted and pointed her companion toward the back exit, then made shooing motions. Still grinning, he bowed to her and headed that way.

"Did you have the soup?" Rylana guessed.

"Uhm, let's say yes." Did Zalani's cheeks redden even more as she glanced at Rolf? "Do you know when Jildarin is returning?"

"Any minute," Rylana said, though she had no idea. Maybe his hunt would keep him out all night. Or maybe he would let his brother talk him into the wine gathering afterward.

"He won't be happy about this, will he?" Zalani looked around the dining room with wide eyes—maybe it hadn't been as busy and chaotic when she'd slipped away for *her* rendezvous. "I shouldn't have..."

"Not during work hours, no." Rylana couldn't manage more censure than that. After all, she'd also succumbed to the soup's allure when she'd been told better. "We need to get these people out of here, and clean up the mess they have to be making in the storeroom."

In Jildarin's *lair*. She winced.

The cry of someone's climax came from a corner, and Rylana glanced toward the front window, half-expecting to spot Jildarin striding toward the door. But only the teenage boys were back out there with their noses pressed to the glass.

"You and Rolf and Gniknik, get all those people out of the hallway, kitchen, and storeroom. Tell them Jildarin is coming, and he'll be in his dragon form. And furious. Then clean up the best you can." Rylana rolled up her sleeves. "Sylin, will you help me roust the people out here?"

"Did you say roust or rouse? Because the latter is sufficiently handled, I believe." Sylin still looked amused. Of course. *She* didn't care about helping and winning the trust of the dragon owner.

"You know what I said. Come on."

"I'm not grabbing any naked body parts," Sylin warned but did follow Rylana toward a couple that had finished and dozed off under a table.

"Do you only assassinate fully dressed people?"

"Ideally. Even if they're nude, I don't usually have to grab anything to do my work."

Shaking her head, Rylana pulled a sleeping man out by his

boots. Sylin hefted the woman over her shoulder, her elven strength coming in handy. Rylana had to drag her load across the floor and into the street.

"You boys, go home," Rylana told the peepers. "The boss is on his way back."

"The dragon?" One of the taller boys lifted his chin. "He can't change in town. I'm not afraid of him."

"I'm a little afraid of him," one of the others whispered.

"I think I see him flying toward the southern edge of the city now." Rylana pointed down the street, though she didn't see anything in the dark sky.

Most of the boys swore and sprinted into the alley. The one who wasn't afraid hesitated, realized he was alone, and then slunk off in another direction. Sylin laid the sleeping woman down against the wall, eliciting a groan.

"The ones who are still engaged won't be as easy to evict," she warned.

"We'll do it anyway."

"Does this really fall under the purview of a bookkeeper?"

"It does tonight."

Back inside, Rolf and Gniknik were maneuvering a snoring woman onto a long flat board with wheels. Some contraption the gnome had made to carry cargo? Rolf pointed at her chest when it jiggled, jostled by the movement. Gniknik slapped his hand out of the air and told him to grab her by the shoulders. They used the wheeled device to push the woman out the door. Zalani, who was throwing a bucket of water on a couple still engaged, had to step aside so they could pass.

An irate man lunged for her. Rylana stepped in, caught his arm, and twisted it behind his back, forcing his nose against the wall.

"No attacking the staff," she said. "Take your lady friend, and go home."

His shoulder muscles bunched, and he tried to escape, but Rylana's years as a mercenary had left her capable of keeping a man pinned—especially one whose thinking and reflexes were slowed by dragon spices.

"Let's go, Jowlark." His companion took his free arm and nodded to Rylana that she would take him away.

She released the man, but as she headed toward another couple, a hint of smoke reached her nose.

"Do you smell that? Is something on fire in the kitchen?" Rylana waved for Sylin to keep dragging people into the street and jogged to check.

Flames burned heartily in the pantry as someone skulked away from it. A goblin in a cloak. For a confused moment, Rylana thought it was Rolf, but he was out front helping Gniknik.

"Fire!" the goblin blurted when he saw her.

He pointed at the pantry and tried to run out the door. Rylana intercepted him, suspecting he'd started it.

"Who are you?" she demanded, then called, "Zalani, bring your water bucket!"

That wouldn't be enough. The flames were spreading, and Rylana grimaced, almost releasing the goblin when he struggled for freedom.

"I'm nobody," he squeaked, flailing and trying to escape her grip. His head came down, and he bit her arm.

Rylana snarled and pushed him against the wall beside the doorway as Zalani ran in. "Who hired you?"

"Nobody!"

"You're *nobody*, and *nobody* hired you?"

"Yes!"

"Fire!" someone called from the storeroom.

"Another one?" Rylana patted down the goblin, finding pockets with matches in them. She also pulled out a sack with what felt like sand inside. "What's this?"

"Nothing! Let me go. I'm innocent!"

"As innocent as Rolf, I'm sure."

Gniknik ran past in the hallway. "The whole building is on fire! Everyone out!"

"I need help, Rylana!" Zalani blurted, filling a pot and throwing water into the pantry.

The second time the goblin bit Rylana, his teeth grinding through her sleeve to tear into flesh, she yelped in pain and released him. She almost lunged after him, but the gong of a pillar sounding reached her ears. Peacekeepers might run inside at any moment, and she didn't want to be caught pummeling someone. Besides, the fires were a greater concern at the moment. She did, however, stuff the sack of powder into her pocket before leaping to the sink to grab and fill a stockpot.

Meanwhile, the remaining amorous couples realized their danger and raced for the front door. Smoke hazed the air and made Rylana's eyes water, but at least the dining room wasn't on fire yet.

"What is happening?" came a booming voice from the storeroom.

Jildarin.

"Two hells," Rylana blurted, distressed that she hadn't been able to fix the mess before he'd returned.

"He can help!" Zalani cried as she threw more water onto burning pantry shelves and flames licking an overhead beam.

Thumps, cracks, and shouts came from throughout the building. Feeling overwhelmed, Rylana filled and threw pot after pot onto the flames in the pantry. Fortunately, they'd caught the fire before it had spread into the kitchen, but she could tell from the amount of smoke in the hallway that greater flames had to be burning in the storeroom.

Jildarin roared. He still sounded human—barely.

"The peacekeepers are here!" came Gniknik's yell from the dining room. It sounded as much a warning as a cry of relief.

"Give them buckets!" Rylana yelled.

Convinced the pantry fire wasn't in danger of rekindling, Rylana backed out. She feared the ingredients stored within were all ruined, but she had Rolf's bag full of ill-gotten coins. Maybe it would be enough to repurchase groceries. As far as fixing the fire damage... She had no idea what that would cost but grimaced and wished she'd managed to keep hold of the goblin for the peacekeepers to question. All she had was the sack of sand or whatever he'd been carrying around with the matches.

Carrying another pot of water in hand, Rylana headed into the hallway and turned toward the storeroom. The smoke was thicker in that direction, and she couldn't tell if the fire was out. That part of the building wasn't plumbed with water.

As she drew closer, the air wasn't as hot as she expected. If anything, a great chill swept through the storeroom, stirring the smoke and raising gooseflesh on her arms. It was as if someone had opened the carriage doors as an arctic storm swept in from the north.

Two gnomish peacekeepers coughing and wiping at their eyes came down the hallway from the dining room to follow her.

"What's happening here?" one asked.

"A goblin started fires." Rylana tried to wave smoke away as she entered the storeroom. "If you go outside, you might be able to find him before he gets away."

Unlikely. The goblin had taken off at top speed when she'd released him, but she worried that the peacekeepers would find a way to blame Jildarin for this, so she wanted to get rid of them. What if he, enraged by the assault on his diner, changed into his dragon form?

Rylana almost ran into not one but *two* silver-scaled dragons crammed into the storeroom, smoldering crates and burlap sacks of grains knocked to the walls. The icy air she'd felt emanated from the one with darker scales. Was that Zilek?

The dragon beside him was familiar—she recognized Jildarin even before his head swung toward them, emerald eyes locking onto her and the peacekeepers. Magic emanated from the dragons, but she couldn't tell what it was doing, only that the flames, already far fewer than she'd imagined, were winking out.

"They've changed!" one gnome blurted. "Get the golems. Get—"

"They're in their lair," Rylana called over the peacekeepers.

"This isn't *both* of their lairs."

"Yes, it is," she said. "They're, uhm, together." Rylana grabbed one of the gnomes by the arm and pointed toward the carriage doors. They had indeed been thrown open. "Go find the goblin that started the fires. That's the *real* crime."

Jildarin's eyes grew cool as he lowered his head closer to the gnome that had yelled. The peacekeeper may have realized he was in a dragon's lair, possibly *irking* said dragon, and that the golems that might have helped him were still out in the street.

"It was a goblin, you say?" he asked, his voice squeaky as Jildarin's maw parted to reveal his fangs.

"In a cloak, yes." Again, Rylana pointed at the doors.

This time, both gnomes darted around the dragons, finding room where taller beings couldn't have, and fled into the street out back.

Sylin came up to stand beside Rylana, not appearing alarmed by the two hulking dragons. Another wave of icy air flowed from the darker silver dragon, and the last of the flames disappeared. Rylana stared glumly around at the damage. Crates and barrels had burned, leaving soot on everything, and a strange layer of frost had crystalized over the char. Only the gnomish ovens remained in good shape, though ash dulled even their magical gleam.

The lighter silver dragon's form blurred, and Jildarin soon stood in front of Rylana in human form. He glowered at her, ignored Sylin, and also glowered at Zalani, Gniknik, and Rolf, who had gathered in the hallway, peering warily into the storeroom.

"What happened?" Jildarin demanded, his hands clenched into fists, frustration and anger roiling off him. "Who was responsible? I was only gone for a few hours." He squinted at Rylana, then squinted harder at Rolf.

Rolf stepped behind Zalani.

When Jildarin's cold gaze swung back toward Rylana, she almost blurted that it had all been Rolf's fault, but his shenanigans hadn't had anything to do with the fire, other than it had caused the staff to be distracted. Even if he legitimately *could* be blamed, she had never been one to tattle.

The dark silver dragon shifted into the familiar form of Jildarin's brother, Zilek. He gazed about, appearing more bemused than angry. Of course, it wasn't *his* dream that someone had tried to burn down.

"A goblin sneaked in and started a fire," Rylana said when nobody else answered Jildarin, other than to look guiltily at each other. "*Fires*. There was one in the kitchen too. The goblin got away before I could get any information out of him, but I have a suspicion that whoever was behind the other assaults on the diner may have hired him."

She debated whether to add that she had a suspect, but Jildarin blurted, "The kitchen?" with fresh alarm, his head snapping in that direction. "Why didn't anyone stop a suspicious goblin from coming inside the diner? And into my *kitchen*?"

Without waiting for an answer, Jildarin raced into the hallway, the staff parting to get out of his way.

"It was a busy night," Zalani called after him with a grimace.

Rylana started after Jildarin, but Sylin caught her shoulder.

"Maybe you should let him cool down before following after," she suggested. "He looks as likely to kill friends as foes right now, and you're... Well, that look he gave you says he's more likely to put you in one of those categories than the other."

A roar of fury came from the kitchen.

"He's seen the pantry," Rylana said, debating whether to go and try to explain or to obey Sylin's suggestion. It seemed cowardly to hide, but...

A thunderous crash came from the kitchen.

"He would be in a less dour mood if he'd mated this evening," Zilek said blandly.

"I thought you two went hunting," Rylana said.

"It was a special *kind* of hunting." Zilek winked, then waved toward the hallway. "I'm going to the wine conclave before all the best vintages are gone. Tell my brother that he can express his gratitude for my assistance in here later."

"The dragons that choose to reside in this city are a touch eccentric," Sylin observed.

"I would think they'd have to be to deign to mingle with our lowly kinds," Rylana said.

Sylin rested a hand on her chest and mouthed, "*Lowly*?" with her eyebrows up. "Elves are considered genteel and sophisticated and respected by all the races. Dragons often appreciate our companionship."

"Didn't you cut off one's tail during a skirmish in the war?"

"Just the tip. Dragon tails are quite thick, and their owners rarely sit still for a thorough maiming."

"I'm sure it was a genteel cut." Rylana headed to the kitchen, bracing herself for Jildarin's anger.

But when she stepped inside, the scent of smoke hanging heavily in the air, he was slumped against the pantry doorframe. Several shelves had burned, broken glass jars and bottles littered the floor, and dented tins lay in the middle of it all, everything from raisins to garlic to dried herbs spilled out and charred.

From behind, Jildarin looked more defeated than angry. That slump was uncharacteristic; he always seemed tireless and so determined to fulfill his quest to win the Golden Whisk that minor irritations couldn't derail him.

"We can get everything cleaned up," Rylana offered when Jildarin didn't turn to look at her but continued to stare dejectedly into the pantry. Soot coated the walls of the entire kitchen, but his focus was on the mess in there. "I'll help," she added. "And I *know* Rolf will help."

If he wanted his half of the coins, he would.

"If you can give me a list of what was destroyed in the pantry, I'll shop for fresh ingredients at the market in the morning. The diner was actually rather, uhm, busy before the fire started, and we should have the coin to replenish everything in there. I'm not sure what was destroyed in the storeroom, but..." Rylana trailed off when Jildarin turned, his head shaking as he met her gaze.

"The dragon spices were in here." He pointed to a couple of broken ceramic canisters among the mess, their contents dumped out and charred and mixed with everything else. "You can't get more from the market. I'll have to fly to the southern hunting grounds of my people, where the mosses and fungi grow in the ancient caves of our homeland, and collect more. Then they must be dried and properly preserved and ground." He shook his head again. "But the competition is in two days. There's not time."

Ah. And they were the secret ingredient he'd been perfecting, trying to mix enough into his dishes to make them deliciously irresistible without the side effect of randiness.

"You can win without them," Rylana said. "All of your food is good. I know you don't put dragon spices on the bacon."

"At the Golden Whisk, *good* won't be enough. The chefs who will compete are masters at their craft, many with decades of experience, including years spent studying at culinary academies. And I... I learned to cook from an elf in the forest."

Since she'd met him, Jildarin had seemed supremely confident of his skills and ability to win the contest, but his shoulders remained slumped as he walked slowly out of the kitchen. "I cannot win without the spices, and I cannot get more in time."

As he continued toward the front door of the diner, Rolf stepped into the kitchen.

"All of the lovers are gone." He looked expectantly at the purse in Rylana's hand.

"More because of the fires than your hard work at booting them out," she said, but they'd made a deal, so she doled out half the coins. "I don't suppose you saw and recognized the goblin who did this?" She waved at the destroyed pantry.

"I did see him. He's one of the dock goblins that loiter around on the waterfront. They get work loading and unloading cargo or whatever people will pay for. As soon as they make a bit, they go spend it on booze and gambling." Rolf sniffed with disdain.

"What do you spend your money on?"

"I have two wives and eleven kids."

Rylana blinked. "Really?"

She didn't trust much of what came out of Rolf's mouth, but Gniknik was passing in the hall and said, "Rolf is known among his people for being virile. There's a twelfth baby on the way, isn't there?"

"This summer, yes."

Rylana gave the goblin a couple more coins. She might have returned the entire purse to him, but he'd made those coins by drugging the customers. Besides, even mundane spices were expensive. It would take a lot to restock the pantry.

Not complaining, Rolf bowed to her and departed. Rylana went out front to help Zalani start cleaning, but she'd paused with her broom in hand to look out the window.

"Is he going to be all right?" Zalani asked. "He's just standing there, letting rain fall on him."

"Jildarin?" Rylana joined her at the window.

"Yes. Maybe you should go cheer him up. My rent is coming due soon. I need the chef to keep working so customers will come and tip me."

Rylana looked around at the dining room, at soot on the walls and ashes coating the floor. The air stank of smoke, and she worried it would take more than a broom to return the Dragon Diner to an appealing place to eat.

"What makes you think *I* can cheer him up?" Rylana hadn't had any luck bolstering Jildarin in the kitchen.

"He thinks Rolf and Gniknik are twits and that I'm a slut."

"He told you that?"

"No—I doubt he knows the word—but he looks disapprovingly at me whenever I go home with a man, no matter *how* handsome and charming he is, and thinks I shouldn't flirt with customers. It's not my fault that I *like* flirting. And men. Besides, they tip a lot better when you bolster their egos a bit."

"Well, I'm the one who gave him the scar on his temple," Rylana reminded her. "I doubt I can cheer him up. He considers me an enemy."

"Then you're the *perfect* person." Zalani smiled and pushed her toward the door. "Enemies are the only ones you can trust to be honest with you. Go talk to him. For the sake of Rolf's children and my rent money."

Rylana had no idea what else she could say to Jildarin but walked outside to try. It would be a shame if he gave up on the contest and Yerin won.

19

WHEN RYLANA STEPPED OUT OF THE DINER, JILDARIN HAD disappeared. One of the peacekeepers must have turned off the alarm gongs that emanated from the nearby pillars, because the night had grown quiet.

Shutters drawn, the bakery as well as most other stores on the street were closed for the day, but soft yellow light emanated from the coffee shop, and people were visible through the window. Outside, mist fell, wreathing the streetlamps, and a few hooded pedestrians hurried along their routes.

"It'll be hard to chat with Jildarin if I can't find him." Rylana headed for the alley, though she doubted he was lurking there. Might he have headed out of the city for another hunt? Or to do... whatever his brother had been alluding to earlier? *Mating*? "Maybe he went to the wine party," she murmured.

When she peeked around the corner to the alley, she didn't see anyone, but her instincts warned her of a threat behind her. She spun about, reaching instinctively for the sword that wasn't at her waist, but she wasn't quick enough. A strong arm pulled her against a hard chest, and a hand clamped over her mouth.

Fear swept through her as well as a sense of indignation and betrayal that she would be attacked in Tranquility. Where had those cursed peacekeepers gone?

"You seek to take advantage of my distraction and slay me?" Jildarin asked.

"What? No," Rylana tried to say, but his hand muffled her words. She stomped on his foot and drove an elbow backward, the discussion with Zalani about him still considering her an enemy springing to mind.

She landed her blows, but he endured them without releasing her.

"No," he murmured to himself. "You were attempting to assist my diner when I arrived."

She nodded. Yes, she had been.

"And you have sold my stoves."

Another nod.

Jildarin released her and stepped back. "You are a strange enemy."

"Because I'm not *trying* to be your enemy." Rylana turned to face him. She'd thought—*hoped*—he was past being suspicious of her, but having an arsonist target the diner had probably set him on edge again. "The war is over."

"Long before the war, humans considered dragons enemies."

"I'd never met a dragon before the war. I rarely considered them at all."

He blinked a couple of times, as if he couldn't imagine someone *not* considering dragons.

"There weren't any in Tranquility before you and your brother arrived." There at least hadn't been any in her youth. Rylana didn't know if any had visited in the more distant past. "I don't think *I'm* the strange one here."

Jildarin gazed at her, and she expected a rebuttal, but what he said was, "You are perhaps not the *only* strange one."

"I'll agree with that. Do you want to get a cup of coffee?" Rylana pointed up the street to the shop.

"What?"

"It's a caffeinated beverage, so it might stimulate you, but... someone lit your diner on fire. You weren't going to sleep tonight anyway." Since she, as a good worker—and *not* his enemy—felt compelled to go back and help clean after this, she didn't expect she would be able to sleep for quite a while either.

"I have tasted it before."

Right. She remembered that he'd called it *flavored water* and Sylin had been affronted.

"And you didn't like it?" Rylana asked. "Have you tried a latte or a mocha? I didn't think I liked coffee either until I had it mixed with milk and sugar. Those ingredients improve a lot of things."

His lip twitched with distaste. "The half-elf suggested I make bacon coated with maple syrup, sugar, and other sweet offerings because the two-legs enjoy such things. To drench delicious meat in sweet substances sounded loathsome to me, but it has proven popular. Especially the bacon glazed with blueberry jam and other fruits. I am attempting to adapt my cooking to the palates of my clients." That admission didn't keep him from twitching his lip again.

"Humans don't mind sweets mixed with savory. Or with bitter, as in the case of coffee. Why don't you let me buy you a latte, and you can try it? They don't *have* to add sugar. Do you like milk?"

"Milk is a peculiar thing for adults to consume since it is produced as part of the mammalian birthing and weaning cycle, but its viscosity, fat content, and taste are not entirely unappealing."

"Yeah, I'm a fan too." Rylana presumed to take his hand, the very hand that had been smashed to her mouth, and started toward the coffee shop.

Jildarin walked with her but warned, "You will not attempt to poison my beverage."

"I will not, no. A moment ago, I thought you were starting to realize that I want to help you, not kill you."

"It is strange for any two-legs except an elf to desire to help a dragon."

"Yes, but we just established my strangeness."

"That is true. Poison came to mind because I noticed a bulging pouch of something malleable, likely a powder, against my thigh when I pulled you into me."

"Oh. I forgot about that." Rylana stopped under a streetlamp, released Jildarin's hand, and pulled out the sack. "I don't know what's inside. I suppose it *could* be poison, but there's a lot of it." She lifted it to demonstrate its heft. "My elven friend is far more knowledgeable on the subject than I, but I think poisons tend to be hard to come by and purchased by the dram rather than the pound."

"Whatever is inside is magical." As Jildarin eyed the pouch, some of his perennial suspicion returned to his gaze.

"Is it? I took it from the goblin who started the fires. Maybe it's something magical mixed with black powder. If so, we're lucky he didn't blow up the entire diner."

"He did enough damage," Jildarin said glumly, doubtless thinking of his ruined dragon spices.

When Rylana untied the knot in a ribbon holding the pouch shut, Jildarin stepped back.

"I do not know what the magic signifies," he said, "but my instincts warn me to be wary."

"Funny, my instincts always warn me to be wary of *you*."

"It is wise for the lesser species to be cautious around dragons. Even other dragons are wary among our own kind."

There wasn't enough light to see much when Rylana peeked into the pouch. She sniffed the substance inside. It didn't smell like black powder or strongly of anything. She risked pinching out some of the granular substance and spreading it on her palm to study under the light. It was closer to sand than a powder and a dull gray-green in color. She opened the access panel on the side of the streetlamp and tossed a pinch of the substance into the flame, then jumped back in case it exploded.

It didn't, but it did *flash*, and a silver ring of light floated like a halo in the air around the flame for a moment before disappearing.

"Magical," Jildarin stated with a nod.

"Yes, but to what end?"

"I do not know."

After tying the pouch shut again, Rylana tucked it away. "I'll try to find out later. An alchemist might be able to tell."

"Yes."

"Let's get that coffee." She extended a hand toward the shop.

The door opened before they reached it, the blue-haired half-gnome who had waited on Rylana before inviting them in. Vilma, wasn't it?

"Greetings, greetings." She nodded at Rylana, then looked curiously at Jildarin as she guided them to a table.

During her previous visits, Rylana hadn't received such prompt treatment. Maybe the coffee shop had a different policy in the evenings. Or maybe, since she'd brought two comrades by who'd proven generous tippers, she was now rated as a V.I.P. guest. Indeed, another server was rubbing her side, like Vilma might have elbowed her to reach the door first. Rylana doubted Jildarin would be as grand a tipper. Dragons, after all, were notoriously stingy about giving up portions of their treasure.

Vilma seated them in a cozy corner near a fireplace with a partial view of the kitchen where a magical gnomish espresso machine hissed as it heated and foamed milk. Most of the tables were occupied, with the usual middle-aged or older clientele replaced by university students with stacks of books surrounded by coffee cups in various stages of depletion. A gnome with a pad of paper knelt before the roasting equipment, either drawing a schematic or simply sketching the machinery like a human or elf would paint a landscape piece.

"What can I get you?" Vilma asked over the sounds of an argument in the kitchen.

"I *told* you the recipes would have to be adjusted," one voice wafted out. That sounded like Tezilly. "The oven is far more *magical* than normal ones. That will affect the baking process."

"You can't possibly believe that a dragon sleeping next to this oven for a few weeks means the cookie recipe needs adjustments." And that crabbier-sounding voice belonged to Brella.

"Dragon emanations are *known* to cause things around them to turn magical. It says so in the book."

"It's talking about the rock formations in their caves, not gnomish commercial ovens."

"*All* things."

"It's fine," Vilma assured Rylana and Jildarin when they hesitated to place their order. "Those two argue about everything. And the sprinkles are hardly glowing at all with the latest batch. Some customers might even *like* a little sparkle in their baked goods. What can I get you?"

"My enemy assures me that I will enjoy the flavored water with milk," Jildarin stated.

"My enemy?" Vilma mouthed.

"I didn't *assure* you that you would like a latte," Rylana said. "I just said you might."

"We have a new mocha sampler with four small cups using different roasts and different cocoas," Vilma offered.

"I'll take that," Rylana said. "Jildarin will have a latte. Without sugar."

"Hm," he said, almost a growl.

"Jildarin... the dragon?" Vilma took a step back.

"The dragon *chef*," Rylana said. "He's quite talented. Have you been to the diner?"

"No, I've heard... things. And earlier..." Vilma looked toward the window and made a face.

She must have seen some of the amorous couples stumbling out with clothing askew—or missing.

"The food is very good," Rylana promised.

"I'll get your drinks." Vilma hurried away. Maybe she'd figured out that Jildarin was unlikely to leave gold coins.

"What happened at the diner while I was gone *besides* the fire?" Jildarin asked.

"I wasn't there the whole time, so I'm not entirely sure." Rylana was reluctant to tattle on Rolf, especially since his ill-gotten coins would help replenish the pantry.

"Under the pervasive scent of smoke—smoke that will linger for ages and befoul the taste and appreciation of my meals—I detected the myriad musky odors of sex."

"Huh."

"*Many* people were engaged in coitus. Not only in the diner but in my *lair*." Jildarin shuddered. "I *sleep* back there."

Rylana thought about suggesting that, if he could tell all that by scent, he ought to join the canine-handler division of the peacekeepers. He could find missing treasures lost to pixies and other thieves as easily as the trained hounds did.

"That should not have happened," Jildarin continued. "I've lessened the amount of spice employed in my soup. Lately, it hasn't been having that effect." His eyes narrowed. "Did one of the staff meddle with the pot that I left simmering?"

"I heard a rumor that someone bumped a jar, causing more spices to fall in."

"Rolf. To what end does he desire my patrons to have coitus?"

"Profit."

Vilma arrived with a tray, a regular-sized steaming cup for Jildarin and four tiny espresso cups for Rylana. She set them in a row with little cards that shared tasting notes and information about the regions and history of the chocolates used in the mochas. Rylana smiled happily, enjoying the luxurious drinking experience. After years of being a mercenary and being lucky if the supply wagons brought coffee beans of any sort, this almost made up for the fact that her father hadn't been happy to see her, the diner was under siege, and Vormalt was up to who knew what.

Once Vilma left, Jildarin picked up his cup with both hands. He examined the latte from all angles, sniffed it, then set it back down.

Rylana closed her eyes as she sipped from one of her cups—ah, the rich, almost buttery texture of that mocha delighted her tongue. She decided she wouldn't try to coerce Jildarin to drink, but would simply enjoy her own. He might think she'd arranged to have his cup poisoned if she tried too hard to get him to sip. Besides, she'd brought him here to bolster him—and ensure that he returned to the diner—not turn him into a coffee connoisseur.

When she opened her eyes to deliver a compliment, she found him looking at her, his eyes narrowed.

"Are you silently judging me for relishing my flavored water?" she asked.

"Your *four* flavored waters."

"Yes." Rylana sipped from a second cup. "They're delicious. I'll bet this would go well with one of your sweeter bacons. A delightful breakfast dessert experience." She finished the thought with a drawn-out *mmmm.*

"I suppose one who spends time crafting fine foods does like seeing that people enjoy them," Jildarin said.

"So, you're not judging me?"

"Hm." He eyed the cups, probably not considering a barista a chef or the mochas fine foods.

At least he hadn't insulted Rylana. That made it easier to continue with her bolstering mission.

"Silent judgments aside, you are a wonderful chef, Jildarin," she said. "You should enter the contest even without your spices. I'm sure you would do well."

"Why do you care if I enter it or not?"

"I want to see you succeed."

"Why?"

"Your charisma, wit, and dashing smile have made me fall passionately in love with you."

"I do not smile."

"I know. I was being sarcastic." So much for her bolstering attempts. Rylana groped for a reason he would believe.

Why *did* she care? Maybe Sylin was right, and she felt guilty. Not only about shooting him but about the role of the mercenaries in the war as a whole. Maybe she was trying to make up for the past. Or maybe, after leaving the career she'd had for more than fifteen years, she needed a mission. *Purpose.* She could be feeling some of the same ennui at traveling listlessly as Sylin.

"You are my enemy and do not love me," Jildarin said, "but I believe you *are* attracted to me."

"You think so?"

"If not, after you imbibed so many servings of my soup, you would have directed your lust toward another."

"Rolf and Gniknik were the only other males around. You could have shape-shifted into a fungus-covered log and had more appeal than they have. Than Rolf anyway. Gniknik is kind of cute, I suppose, but not in a sexual way, at least not to me." Rylana sipped her drink. "I don't think any assumptions can be made based on what a woman does while under the influence of your spices. I also thought the elves that wanted to drag me to their enclave for questioning were hot."

"To sexually pursue one would have been unwise."

"Oh, I know."

"A surprising number of humans did so during the war, finding elves alluring," Jildarin said. "The elves sometimes used that to their advantage and gained intelligence from those who sought them out."

"I heard of such things, yes. We were warned often against having liaisons with the enemy."

Jildarin considered the latte again, then lifted it for a sip. He made a face afterward and set it down, but then he squinted thoughtfully at it. "I've heard of recipes that employ coffee as an ingredient."

"You should make them promptly. I would be a fan."

"I prefer to develop my *own* recipes, but sometimes I find existing ones to be inspiring."

"I remember having coffee cake as a kid that had actual powdered coffee in the cinnamon streusel. It was fabulous."

"A favorite treat of dragon young is the marrow of the giant foxtail ungulate."

"I'm sure they share a similar flavor profile. You'll keep the diner open, won't you? The staff has concerns, but we can fix it up. You can't let a rival drive you out of business. By my calculations, you're starting to turn a profit—or will be if we can keep arsonists from destroying your inventory."

Jildarin sipped the drink again. "My brother is the reason I left the diner before the dinner hour. You will tally the costs of the fire damage, prepare an invoice, and I will send it to him. He has far more funds than I, and he *deserves* to pay after his treacherous behavior."

"What did he do?" Rylana thought again about Zilek's comment on *mating*.

When Jildarin took a few more sips without pausing to answer, Rylana assumed he wouldn't. Maybe it was a private matter. But he thunked the cup down, his milk foam quivering, and spoke with exasperation, whatever irritation he felt bubbling over.

"One of my mother's female friends was waiting in the woods, seeking to mate with me, and he attempted to *trick* me into doing so. She was going to shape-shift into an elf, thinking that I would, in this human form, find that alluring, and be at the wine meeting that he first attempted to lure me to. When that did not work, he enticed me with the promise of a hunt. I *enjoy* hunting, the exhilaration of seeking out prey and flying at great speed over and under and around obstacles as it flees. I even enjoy hunting with my kin, though Zilek has perturbed me often enough of late that I may not go with him again. Instead of seeking prey, he led me toward Sophoneliza."

"Is that... a female dragon? Or the name of an innovative new alchemy formula?"

"It is—*she* is—my mother's acquaintance who seeks to reproduce soon and desires my sperm. I do not wish to be manipulated into mating." He looked up from his latte to turn his exasperated gaze on her.

"I've gathered that." Her cheeks warmed when she remembered kissing him. But that hadn't been her fault, damn it. He shouldn't have given her any of that soup. It wasn't as if she would have sprung upon him if she hadn't been drugged—*spiced*. Even if his gaze was a touch smoldering when he looked at her over the rim of his cup.

Rylana looked away. He was right. She *was* attracted to him. When had that happened?

"Are elves your type?" she asked, to distract him from the memory of that experience—and maybe herself as well.

"My what?"

"Are they what, er, *who* you're attracted to when you're in this form? I assume that when you're a dragon, you're attracted to your own kind."

"Certainly."

"But, as we discussed earlier, humans and elves had been known to... you know. *Most* of the intelligent two-legged species are closely enough related genetically that they can produce offspring."

"I had an elven companion during the war, so perhaps that is why my brother believed a female with pointed ears might interest me, but my companion was *male.* We never had coitus. He rode on my back and fired arrows at the enemy when we flew into battle."

"I saw some elves and dragons do that." Rylana grimaced at the memory of such pairs flying past, the dragons breathing fire while the elves loosed arrows. Those teams had been devastating to the ground-bound human, dwarf, and orc militias.

"We fought together for many years before his passing during the last months of the war." Jildarin looked toward the hiss of the espresso machine. "He is the one who made me realize that food could be much more than raw meat from a fresh kill. In addition to being a fine archer and sword master, he was a chef among his people."

"Ah." Rylana had wondered how Jildarin had ended up with his culinary passion and where he'd learned what he knew.

"When we were not in battle, we foraged together for ingredients and made unique dishes. Considering we often had only a campfire and a pot, he came up with surprisingly exquisite concoctions." Jildarin sighed at whatever memories came to mind.

Since Rylana had also lost good companions over the years of being a mercenary, she understood perfectly well.

"He is the one who said I had a knack for combining ingredients," Jildarin said, his gaze still toward the espresso machine and the steam wafting from it, though he was probably looking into the past instead of seeing it. "He even suggested... We talked of visiting Tranquility together once the fighting was over. He spoke of the many and varied cuisines and fine diners here. We planned to taste from the menus and critique the offerings." Jildarin, who'd said he didn't smile, smiled ever so faintly, but it soon faded. "He was killed three months before the war's end."

"I'm sorry that you lost a good friend."

He barely seemed to hear her, but he murmured, "Yes."

"I'll bet he would want you to keep cooking—and to go to that contest and win it."

Jildarin rumbled something that could have been agreement, disagreement, or just a thoughtful *hm*. Then he got up and walked out of the coffee shop.

Rylana didn't know if she'd succeeded in talking him into staying in the competition or not, but it was at least promising that he wanted to invoice his brother for the repair costs of his diner. One only repaired something that one planned to continue to use.

20

The Tower Square Market was the largest in the city with a mix of permanent wooden booths around the exterior and tents and wagons making haphazard rows in the interior. Intelligent beings from many species visited it to find the common and the rare, even those who didn't get along well enough with others to live full-time in Tranquility. As she passed through, Rylana had to dodge everyone from ogres to trolls to gnomes to horses and donkeys pulling carts. A wyvern even flew in to land next to a tent selling rare meats.

With a pillar at every corner of the square and the omnipresent peacekeepers in the crowd with their golem enforcers, none of the visitors started fights. Even so, Rylana kept a hand on the pouch of magical sand, always wary about pickpockets.

Determined to learn what the goblin arsonist had been prepared to deploy, she walked toward a corner where herbalists sold their wares and alchemists mixed custom formulas for people. She diverted around a fountain to avoid a pair of female elves, though the half-filled baskets hooked over their arms suggested they were there to shop, not hunt down pointy-eared assassins.

A taller-than-average gnome peacekeeper walked through the crowd with two floppy-eared hounds on leashes, their noses twitching and their tails wagging as they sampled the air. One paused to sniff at Rylana's pocket. Since they were trained to find magical items, she drew out the pouch, curious to see if whatever reaction they had could provide a clue about the contents. One sniffed it briefly, then turned its nose toward her pocket again and licked it. Oh, was that a grease spatter? She'd had some of Jildarin's bacon for breakfast that morning.

"Sorry, ma'am," the gnome said and clucked at the dogs to move them along.

"Whatever this is, it must not be *that* interesting." Rylana eyed the bag again, then walked up to the first alchemist's stand she spotted.

An elf stepped into view, a beaker in one hand and measuring utensils in the other. Rylana almost veered away. But the silver-and-green-haired male had sharp eyes and spotted her and her pouch immediately and waved for her to come closer. He wore an apron, the pockets bulging with tools, and didn't look that menacing, so she approached.

His gaze skimmed the crowd behind her. As if he expected someone else to be with her? Sylin?

"Hello." Rylana told herself it was unlikely that *all* the elves in the city were looking for her comrade. "How much do you charge to identify a substance?" She set the pouch on the counter.

"It depends on how long it takes to run the tests to do so. If you've brought nothing more than a bag of nutmeg or sand, I could identify it quickly."

"I'd like to think *I* could identify such substances."

"Humans aren't very apt at using their senses."

Since she needed his help, Rylana made herself smile instead of baring her teeth. "So, you've an hourly rate? Of what?"

"Two gold."

"That's steep."

"There are others you may seek out if you desire mediocre service. As an elf, I have keen senses, extensive knowledge, and decades of experience, thus ensuring a high rate is fair." He looked past her shoulder again. "You have come to the market alone?"

"Yeah, I don't like chitchat to get in the way of my shopping experience." Rylana didn't mention that Sylin didn't care for crowded places and wouldn't come to a market unless it was an emergency. So far, Rylana didn't know for certain that the elf was looking for Sylin.

"I see." The alchemist opened the pouch, dipped a measuring spoon in to extract a sample of the granular substance, and spread it on a square of paper. He sniffed it, eyed it, then rubbed it between his fingers. "It is magical."

"Yes."

"Where did you acquire it?"

"A goblin arsonist."

His eyebrows rose, and he picked up the pouch, turning it all around. There wasn't a label or mark that might have suggested its origins; Rylana had already checked.

"I can run tests on this sample if you wish." The elf waved at equipment on a counter behind him. "But a goblin alchemist might recognize it immediately if it is something their kind makes."

"*Are* there goblin alchemists? I thought their people are mostly herbalists and foragers who sell what they find to the alchemists of other species."

"There are some with a passion for making concoctions that give their kind advantages—or at least make them less *disadvantaged*—when dealing with taller and stronger species."

"Are there any in the market?"

"Hegimok sometimes brings a wagon and parks down there." The elf pointed. "If you leave this sample with me, I will also test it. Even learned goblins aren't the most reliable of resources."

"Can you figure out what it is in an hour?" Rylana wasn't swimming in gold coins, especially since she'd spent all of Rolf's earnings on pantry supplies that morning. The money hadn't gone as far as she'd hoped. She hadn't even done an inventory of what in the storeroom had been destroyed yet.

"Impossible to say." The alchemist took the paper with the sample and turned toward his equipment, but he paused to look back over his shoulder. "Were you to inform me of the location of the dark-green-haired elf assassin, I might do the work for free."

Unease swept down Rylana's spine. Maybe all the elves in the city *were* looking for Sylin.

"I don't know where she's staying. I can only pay for up to an hour of work."

"Yes, the assassin *is* a she." He smiled triumphantly. "I suspected you were the one I'd heard about who travels with her."

Rylana clenched her jaw, irritated to realize he'd been fishing, that he hadn't known she was Sylin's friend, and she'd confirmed that for him.

"I only have two gold," she said, "so don't spend more time with it than that buys."

"Perhaps if I need more time, you'll remember where your dubious comrade is staying."

"Perhaps I'll just go find that goblin alchemist." Rylana reached across the counter, wanting to take back the sample, but he drew it out of reach. With peacekeepers and golems all over the square, she decided not to vault into his stand to try to forcibly take it back. "Keep it," she said, and took the pouch and headed down the line.

When she glanced back, the elf was gazing thoughtfully at her.

"I'm starting to have fewer regrets about shooting at their kind during the war," Rylana muttered.

At the end of the stalls rested a small wagon harnessed to a donkey eating from a bucket. A bald, chubby goblin dozed on his back on the driver's bench. There wasn't a written sign anywhere on the side of the wagon, but a painting showed a goblin stirring a cauldron over a fire in a cave. Was he making soup or alchemical concoctions? Rylana couldn't tell but petted the donkey and cleared her throat. The goblin started snoring.

Rylana poked him on the side. "Hello? Are you an alchemist?"

The snoring grew louder.

"If you are, I have a business proposition for you."

The goblin sat up, his yellow eyes opening. "Money, did you say?"

"Not exactly." Rylana held up the pouch.

The goblin held up his hands. "Strictly no returns. Sorry."

"I'm not— Wait, do you recognize this? Is it something you sold?"

"That's one of my sacks. I trade fire salts to my weaver friend for them."

"Well, I didn't buy this from you."

"Aren't you working for the snooty human who came by yesterday?" The goblin took the pouch and peered inside. "Yes, this is my anti-magic powder."

"*Anti*-magic? It's magical, as far as everyone can tell."

"Well, of course *anti*-magical powder would have to be magical itself to succeed in nullifying magic."

"I… see. Did you say it was a goblin who purchased it?"

"No. I— Are we engaged in the business proposition you mentioned?"

"I think we might be." Rylana wondered if Yerin would qualify as a *snooty human* to a goblin. She wished she knew for certain that he *had* been behind the arson and other affronts to the diner.

Jildarin might have more than one rival out to get him. He wasn't exactly warm and friendly with people.

"Then you should be paying me for the information I offer, yes?" The goblin smiled and rubbed his hands together.

"I have two silver." If she could get answers from him, it would save her from having to pay the elf's exorbitant fees.

"Let's see it." The goblin stood on his bench and leaned forward.

Rylana fished coins from her purse to show him, holding them in the air as a promise. "Describe the snooty human who purchased from you. Are you sure it was this pouch and this substance?"

The goblin leaned forward to peer inside and inhaled deeply. "Yes, that is my anti-magic powder. You can try it for yourself if you wish."

"What does it do? If I tossed it into magical spices, could it diminish or nullify their effects?"

"I... suppose that's possible. Usually, my people throw it at powerful shape-shifted enemies like kitsune or selkies to force them to change into their less dangerous native forms."

"Interesting. Could it force a dragon that was shape-shifted into a human to change back into his native form?"

"Yes, but that would be foolish. In the case of a dragon, its native form is much more dangerous." The goblin chuckled. "Who would want to change such a being from a human or an elf into a *dragon*?"

"Someone who wants to see that dragon kicked out of Tranquility," Rylana said with certainty. She placed the two coins in the goblin's hand, then pulled out two more. "Describe the snooty human, please."

"He called my assistant a fleshy shrub, said my prices were ludicrous, and wore spectacles on his beaky nose."

A lot of people wore spectacles, and Yerin was only one of

them, but this gave Rylana enough to believe he was likely the culprit. Nodding to herself, she paid the goblin another two coins.

"Thank you for your time." She turned and almost ran into the elf alchemist. Though alarmed that he'd sneaked up on her, she made herself return his gaze calmly. "I won't need your services, after all."

"Our kind keep an eye on the dragons here," he warned her, his expression cool. "Especially Jildarin-grozanarav."

He must have been listening in on her conversation but misconstrued her mutterings.

"Good. I'm looking out for him too."

His eyes narrowed with suspicion, and he plucked the pouch out of her hand. She hadn't expected that and reacted too slowly to stop him. He secreted it inside a pocket in his apron.

"You will not use this on Lord Jildarin," he stated. "He makes fine food and has broken no laws."

"I hadn't intended to use it on him. I work for him. Someone *else* intended to use it, I think."

Maybe, when the goblin had come to set his fires, he hadn't known that Jildarin would be away with his brother, and he'd planned to force a shape-shifting at the diner.

"Then you will not mind if I take it." The elf turned and walked away, though he again perused the crowd. He also gave her a long look over his shoulder before stepping out of sight into his stand.

Rylana passed a couple more elves on the way out of the market and was glad Sylin hadn't come with her. The next time she saw her comrade, she would have to tell her to leave the city, for her own safety. In the meantime, she would make sure Jildarin knew to avoid anyone running toward him with sacks of anti-magic powder.

21

When Rylana returned to the diner, a surprising number of people were inside. They weren't eating but wielding paint-brushes, brooms, and mops. Gniknik and two gnomes she hadn't seen before squatted in the middle of the floor around a rumbling bronze box with hoses protruding in all directions like octopus tentacles. Some wavered in the air and others drifted across the floor, twisting under tables and between chair legs.

"Gnomish combination air purifier and vacuum," Gniknik explained when Rylana paused to stare at the contraption. "It sucks in smoke, ashes, dander, dirt, and pollen, then incinerates the particles while outputting fresh, pure air, perfect for a dining experience."

The air *did* smell better than when Rylana had left. One of the waving hoses floated over and attached itself to her leg, trying to suck her trouser material into the box.

"I don't want my pants incinerated." She stepped back to break the connection.

"How about purified?" Gniknik winked.

"I thought I'd pay the laundromat to handle that. Who are all these people? I'll run some calculations, but I don't think we can afford to hire handymen." As Rylana waved around the room, looking at faces, she realized she recognized many of them. Wasn't that handsome broad-faced man with a paintbrush the fellow Zalani had been with in the kitchen the night before? And there was the couple who'd come in for soup to help with the husband's impotency problem. He appeared quite cheerful as he fixed a table leg that had been wobbly even before the fire.

"They're volunteering their time," Zalani said, walking out of the hallway with two mop buckets of fresh water. "They're customers who heard about the fire and want to see the Dragon Diner reopened as soon as possible. They like the food."

"Because the food is *delicious.*" Gniknik beamed a smile toward the kitchen. "Chef Jildarin is making smoked-fish and fiddlehead-fern frittatas and black-pepper bacon this morning. He said he would also fry up some of the mesquite bacon he just cured. And the stuff rubbed with his signature onion-garlic-three-peppers blend. That's *so* tasty."

"I won't disagree with that," Rylana said.

When it came to ingredients, she was as suspicious of fiddle-head ferns as spruce tips, but her mouth watered, regardless. With thoughts of bacon in mind, she headed toward the kitchen, hoping to snag a few pieces for herself. She found it encouraging that Jildarin was cooking. The night before, he'd been so dejected that she'd wondered if he might leave the city forever and return to a normal life for a dragon. The thought saddened her.

"You were not here this morning to receive my list of require-ments for replacing storeroom ingredients and equipment." Jildarin gave her a sour look from the stove when she walked in, the scents of frying bacon luring her closer.

"You can give them to me after breakfast. I left early to research something for you."

"Did it involve swilling flavored water across the street?"

"It did not. I asked an alchemist about the contents of that pouch. Someone wants you to change into a dragon."

"We've known *that* for days."

"Yeah, but the other methods haven't worked, have they? The gritty stuff in the pouch was an anti-magic concoction, supposedly, and makes those who have used their power to shift into another form return to their native bodies. I think maybe, after the fire was started, you were supposed to run outside to look for the perpetrator, get pelted with the substance, and turn into a dragon in the street—outside the permissible sanctuary of your lair—as the peacekeepers happened to be in the area." Rylana remembered the pair of uniformed gnomes that had trotted inside during the chaos of the fire. They'd returned later to get a description of the arsonist, and had promised to look for him—as proper peacekeepers should—but she doubted chance had put them in the area when the fire started.

Jildarin didn't answer right away, instead focusing on his cooking. The tantalizing aromas made Rylana's stomach rumble, and she wanted to grab a plate and scoop piles of hot food onto it.

He grabbed a plate and used tongs to arrange several varieties of perfectly cooked bacon on it next to a slice of the frittata. He also plucked a honey-glazed biscuit from a basket that had been covered with a cloth. A ramekin of freshly whipped butter was nestled in it, and her stomach rumbled even more.

"Your reason for being missing is acceptable." Jildarin handed her the plate.

"I'm glad you think so. And I'm extra glad that you're giving me this." Rylana grinned, stuck a piece of bacon into her mouth, and picked up a fork for the eggs. She didn't mind his pomposity when he was handing her delicious food.

"Yes. Did your research reveal who the *someone* is that wants me to change so that the peacekeepers will expel me from Tranquility?" His eyes burned with intensity this morning, suggesting he had decided to stay and fight instead of giving up and leaving.

"I don't have proof, but I have a hunch. You remember the food critic, Yerin?"

"Yes. As I told you, he was also selected to compete in the Golden Whisk."

Rylana nodded. "He sees you as a threat to win, and I think he wants to get rid of you before the contest."

"It wouldn't be honorable to seek the expulsion of a strong competitor."

"No, it wouldn't, but I'm sure he's doing it anyway." Rylana bit into the warm biscuit, savoring the rich buttery layers and a hint of salt with that honey glaze. Oh, that was fabulous. She wanted to grab another biscuit from the basket before she'd finished the first. Considering dragons apparently didn't crave sweets the way humans did, Jildarin had a deft touch with a honey wand.

"He should desire to fairly beat the best competitors," Jildarin said, "else his victory would be meaningless."

"I know, but he wants to win at any cost."

"Because of the monetary prize?"

"I doubt it." Rylana cut a piece of the frittata, eyeing the green spirals dubiously, but when she popped it into her mouth, everything blended well together and tasted wonderful. And was that goat cheese in there? Perfect. "Yerin's family has money, and he's spending who knows how much to hire goblins to assault your diner."

"My diner *is* being assaulted," Jildarin growled. "If one of my rivals is responsible, I will... Cursed golems, I can't *do* anything, not in this city."

"You can win the competition. In Tranquility, the best revenge is personal triumph."

"Without my spices—"

"You can *still* win." Rylana speared a piece of frittata with her fork and held it up. "Trust me."

Jildarin squinted at her, and she expected him to remind her that he did *not* trust her. "By your calculations, you believe this could be possible?"

She almost laughed at the expression, recognizing it as her own. "By my *tastebuds*, I do."

"Taste is subjective. Your calculations interest me more." Jildarin walked to the pantry. He or the volunteers had already cleaned it out, replaced the shelving, and tucked the newly purchased ingredients inside. He gripped his chin and perused them thoughtfully. "If I will not have use of dragon spices, I must take other spices with me to the competition."

"You've decided to stay in it, then?"

"I will not be chased out of the Golden Whisk by a dishonorable competitor who sends *goblins* to do his dirty work."

"Good." A loud *vroom* came from the dining room. The combination air-purifier-vacuum? "Everyone knows gnomes are more reliable for dirty work anyway."

"Yes. I have traditional dwarven, elven, orcish, and human spices, staples of the various species. Many people enjoy the favored spices of other species, but, whether they consciously realize it or not, they have grown up with their own and usually find them more palatable."

"That makes sense." Rylana wondered what *calculations* he wanted from her.

"Traditionally, there are nine judges at the Golden Whisk. Two dwarves, two elves, two orcs, two humans, and often a half-ogre or -troll—someone with mixed blood who's meant to have a less predictable palate."

"No goblin judges?"

"Goblins will eat *anything.* Their palates cannot be trusted."

"But ogres and trolls are more refined."

"They at least have a culinary tradition. Goblins scavenge from other species." Jildarin walked along the shelves, touching jars of spices. "The generally given advice for chefs is to make your best dishes in the contest without worrying about which species will be sampling them, but it's common for contestants to select spices that appeal to certain species, hoping to sway those judges, in particular. One might use elven spices in the first round, dwarven in the second, and orcish in the third, for example. Each judge rates each round separately. The totals are added and averaged to determine the winner. I do not fully understand the math, but I'm told it is possible for someone who didn't win any of the rounds to win the overall competition because of their average." He looked at her with his eyebrows raised.

"Yes, that makes sense. Someone might get second in every round and receive a better total score than someone who got first once and fourth twice, for example."

"Correct. Do you have any thoughts about how the math might suggest I choose spices in an attempt to appeal to the various species?"

Rylana straightened, realizing how he wanted her to help. She was honored that he believed she could be of assistance, but she didn't think *math* could reliably be applied to tastebuds, at least not in this instance. If there had been far more elves than humans among the judges, he could have leaned toward them, but whoever had set up the contest had been going for a panel that didn't favor anyone.

"Do any of the species share favored spices?" she asked.

"The dwarves have eccentric spices that often have different varieties of rocks pulverized in, so they share their preferences with no other species."

"Dwarves eat rocks? Is that true?" Rylana had heard that before but always assumed it was a joke.

"Only in very fine amounts, but it is apparently for the mineral content. Their bodies crave higher amounts than those of the other species." Jildarin selected a jar with a grinder attachment, the label reading *calcium salts*. "Most species find these to be bitter, metallic, and astringent. Dwarves love them, but it takes a talented chef to use them in meals that all will find palatable."

"Maybe leave out the rock spices and hope for the best with the dwarves. What about elves and humans? We like a lot of the same stuff, don't we?"

"Yes. And orcs and ogres also enjoy many of the same seasonings as your kind."

"Who would have thought we have similar tastebuds? Especially since orc tongues are blue."

"Indeed."

"I think you should cook your favorite dishes," Rylana said, "and season everything to your taste, because it's excellent. If you want to take a few spices that the greatest number of judges might especially like, it sounds like those favored by humans and also enjoyed by orcs and ogres would be safest."

Jildarin returned the calcium salts to the shelf. "Yes. I will ensure my dishes have an inherent appeal to as many judges as possible."

"Good. I'm glad you're going to do this. I hope you kick Yerin's ass."

"Since the competition takes place within the borders of Tranquility, physical altercations will not be permitted."

"I know. I meant his metaphorical ass."

"Yes." Jildarin waved for her to take her plate out of the kitchen. "Finish eating elsewhere. I must practice and prepare."

Since Rylana had wanted him to stay in the contest, she didn't complain about being dismissed. She *did* take several more slices of bacon on the way out. For having to deal with such a pompous employer, she deserved a second helping.

22

Rylana spent the day before the Golden Whisk balancing the books and figuring out how much the fire had set the business back. Fortunately, thanks to the enthusiastic volunteers, they hadn't had to spend much on repairs, but having to replace so many ingredients had been costly. The diner was lucky she'd thought to snag a portion of Rolf's earnings.

"If nothing else unexpected happens, we'll still come out ahead for the month," Rylana decided. "Considering the business was in the red for all the months prior to my arrival, that's pretty good."

Yawning, she left the office, peeking into the kitchen on her way past. Jildarin was once again hard at work, stirring, cutting, and muttering to himself as he prepared dishes that would serve both as practice and to sate diners arriving for the evening meal. With only one night left until the contest, Rylana wondered if Yerin would send more goblins to make another attempt to derail Jildarin. It would be his last chance.

Appointing herself a patroller, Rylana walked through the premises. She didn't see anything amiss in the repaired and cleaned dining room, and none of the patrons ambling in looked like trouble. When she passed through the storeroom, she likewise didn't find anything amiss. Outside, there wasn't any fresh graffiti on the doors, nor were any cloaked goblins skulking, but she couldn't shake the feeling that Jildarin's *dishonorable competitor*, as he'd put it, would try something else.

On a whim, she climbed onto the flat roof of the building, where she had a view of the streets in front of and behind the diner, as well as over the dwarven bakery and a tavern to the lake. A corner of her family's castle was visible across the waterway, and she made a face in that direction, the unsatisfactory conversation with her father coming to mind.

When she looked up and down Acorn Street, she was surprised to spot someone else up on a rooftop. Above the coffee shop, a hooded and cloaked figure stood beside a table, leaning a shoulder against a brick chimney.

Rylana's first instinct was to feel alarm, especially since the person was facing in her direction—was someone spying upon the diner?—but the figure sipped from a coffee cup, as if merely enjoying a private rooftop balcony. The person noticed her watching and raised the cup in a salute. There was something familiar about the movement.

"Sylin?" Rylana wondered, then asked, "What are you doing up there?"

She didn't speak loudly, but Sylin's keen elven ears must have caught the words because she pushed back her hood to reveal her forest-green hair.

Since Rylana hadn't spotted any trouble at the diner, she climbed down and headed over to the coffee shop. In an alley to the side of it, she found a metal ladder that led to the rooftop, so she joined her comrade.

"Was it too crowded inside for your tastes?" Rylana asked, sitting in the solitary chair, one Sylin wasn't using. She scooted it around so that she could see across the street toward the diner.

"It *is* quite busy, more so than I prefer, but the quality of the beverages ensures crowds will always be typical."

"Yeah, I think their stuff is good too."

"I'm up here because it would be unwise for me to be observed too frequently in one place. Word might get around, and the elves who seek me out could waylay me."

"But sitting on the rooftop of the place where you've been frequently observed is all right?"

"From here, I can see anyone coming."

"You could vary your routine and visit some other coffee shops in town."

"This one is the best." Sylin sipped from her mug.

"Your addiction might be your undoing."

"We all have to die of something."

"Well, I'm glad to have you around for company. As you saw, my family isn't interested in me, Father at least. And the home I've looked forward to returning to for so many years isn't quite... what I remember." Rylana waved toward the city on their side of the lake rather than looking toward the family estate. Her father had been what she'd expected. But the rest of Tranquility hadn't felt as much like *home* as she'd thought it would, and she wondered if she would be able to recapture the nostalgia of her youth. "I'm not sure if it's changed or I have. No, I guess that's not true. I'm certain I've changed more than the city has."

"Likely."

"How much longer will you stay? I can't imagine that having elves hunting for you on every street corner is that appealing." Earlier, Rylana had mentioned the alchemist elf in the market to Sylin.

"Oh, I don't know. It forces me to stay sharp. Yesterday, I ran from two elven hunters with a hound who thought they would hunt me down. They did not succeed." Sylin smiled at some secret amusement, then sipped again.

"I'd feel bad if they found you and I stumbled across your body outside the diner, all because you'd stayed in the area for my sake."

"For your sake?" Sylin asked, her tone still amused, then sipped again.

"Are you only lingering here because of the coffee shop?"

"Not *only*. Have you tried the offerings from the dwarven bakery?"

"No. I'm not in the mood for a cake with a giant *zerg* stick protruding from the top. Besides, now that I know dwarves like to season their food with rocks, I'm skeptical of their fare."

"The scones are excellent. I recommend them."

"They're not shaped into or decorated with genitalia or other sexually suggestive material, are they? I've had enough of that kind of thing of late." Rylana waved toward the diner, though, with the dragon spices ruined, there hadn't been any of the special soup for a couple of days—much to the lament of a few customers who'd slipped in, hoping to make a deal with Rolf for a to-go container.

"The scones are chaste."

"Good to know."

"The muffins are also nonsexual. The croissants... You may want to avoid the croissants."

Rylana decided not to ask how those might be altered for adult tastes.

"Will you seek to establish a relationship with your father?" Sylin asked.

"Nothing in our meeting suggested he's interested in that," Rylana said, surprised Sylin had asked.

"No? He seemed distressed that you hadn't gone into your family business."

"My father has never been distressed in his life. Disappointed, maybe." Rylana waved her hand, years past caring that she might evoke that feeling in him.

Sylin twitched a finger, not commenting on the distinction. "You're now working in a business. Perhaps that will change his opinion of you and your life choices."

"I'm working for a dragon chef for no pay in a diner located across from a naughty bakery."

Sylin sipped from her coffee. After a pause, she said, "Oh, that *was* your point."

"I'm also sleeping on the floor in a storeroom. I don't think my father would be impressed by the new direction of my life."

"He may *like* naughty baked goods."

"If he does, I don't want to know about it."

"If his primary angst is that you became a mercenary, but you are no longer employed in that field and you are also using the academic skills that you learned from your tutors..." Sylin spread a hand toward the sky.

"Are you suggesting I go talk to him again and tell him all about my new job?"

"Should I be forced to leave, perhaps pursued by crabby elves with hounds, I will no longer be able to provide you with companionship. You might find that less distressing if you reacquainted yourself with your family. There are few in the world that one is tied to by blood, and such bonds shouldn't be torn asunder lightly."

"I'd rather acquaint with Jildarin."

"Perhaps you could take him a croissant."

"I meant *talk* to him, not... two hells, I don't even know what those croissants look like or suggest."

"I'm certain Mya, the baker, could educate you. She's very worldly."

"Jildarin isn't." Rylana waved. "Not in that area."

Sylin gazed at her without comment.

"Not that we've discussed it in depth, but he's said he doesn't have sex *recreationally*. Dragons don't, I mean. Or so he says. That might not be true for all of his kind. His brother has implied that, at least when he's in human form, he gives in to the urges that come with being one of us." Rylana pushed a hand through her hair, feeling flustered. How had they gotten onto this topic? "If Jildarin can be believed, he doesn't have similar urges."

"Is that disappointing? Or a relief?" Did Sylin look amused again? Yes, her eyebrow had moved, and the corner of her mouth was quirking slightly.

"It doesn't matter to me."

"I see. Do you still plan to attend his cooking competition?"

"He ordered me to."

"That wouldn't make *me* inclined to go."

"Yeah, but I may have to watch his back. As I learned during our foray across the lake, Yerin is out to get Jildarin."

Sylin stirred with interest. "With a blade? Explosives?"

"An alchemical goblin powder that could force him to turn into a dragon."

"I suppose that could be exciting. I wouldn't have expected that from a cooking contest."

"The chefs care deeply about their creations," Rylana said. "Do you want me to see if I can get you in to watch?"

"Get me in? Is it an exclusive event with tickets required? Like the final performance in a season of the dwarven opera?"

"I'm certain."

"Fascinating."

"It could be."

Sylin sipped from her cup. "Hm."

23

The night before the competition, Rylana woke in her corner of the storeroom when a knock sounded at the back door. As she sat up, habitually reaching for her sword, the clack of talons on the concrete floor sounded, Jildarin stirring. She felt a whisper of magic from him, and the door opened, a hint of light creeping in from a streetlamp.

From her position, Rylana couldn't see who stood there, but she rolled to her feet in case it was trouble. Remembering that her sword scabbard was tied with a tranquility ribbon, she found her knife instead. Fortunately, her weapons and other belongings hadn't been damaged during the fire.

"Message delivery," called a reedy voice, followed by a gasp of alarm. "Is that a *dragon*?"

Jildarin growled, the deep rumble reverberating from the walls and beamed ceiling. Even though it wasn't directed at Rylana, and enough crates were stacked between them that she couldn't see his eyes, the hair on the back of her neck rose, her instincts promising that he was a dangerous threat.

"I'll just toss it in." The speaker sounded like he was backing away. "No tip required. Have a good night!"

A scroll case arced through the doorway and clattered as it hit the floor.

"I'll get it," Rylana said, more a warning so that she wouldn't startle Jildarin than because she expected him to snatch it up with his talons.

She reached the doorway in time to see a goblin jumping onto a bicycle and pedaling away. As she picked up the scroll case, the great silver dragon she shared the storeroom with bent his long neck, lowering his head to regard it—and her.

She held up the case, not presuming to investigate the delivery without permission. "Do you want me to open it? Or are you expecting something private and personal?"

It may contain an explosive, Jildarin said into her mind, startling her.

Even though they'd spent several nights in the storeroom together, and she'd been aware from her mercenary days that dragons could speak telepathically to others, he hadn't done so with her before.

"I'd consider that private and personal." Rylana held the case toward him in offering.

Jildarin huffed out a warm breath that stirred her hair. Was that the dragon equivalent of a snort? Then his head came closer, and he sniffed the case. Even though she didn't think he wanted to harm her at this point, it was unsettling to have all those fangs so close to her. Regardless, she held the case still.

I do not smell black powder, nor do I sense magic.

Rylana shook the case, hearing the soft sound of rolled parchment inside knocking against the end cap. "It sounds like a scroll. Maybe one of your rivals has some recipe suggestions."

My rivals do not write to me. You may open it.

"One left graffiti on your door." Rylana waved in that direction, though they'd already painted over the mess. She removed the cap, dumped out a scroll, and turned up the lantern by the door so she could read.

A minion was sent to do that.

"Minions are handy. Maybe you should get some."

He gazed blandly at her. Right, his brother had openly called her a *servant*.

"I set myself up for that, didn't I?"

His talons clacked on the floor as he took a few steps back. Magic rippled around him, and he changed into his human form.

"Lord Jildarin-grozanarav of Clan Killcrusher," Rylana read aloud, "we have heard that a foul dragon-hating rival destroyed the spices with which you season your dishes. Though we find it strange that you've decided on a hobby of feeding lowly life-forms —and even stranger that their opinions should matter to you—we consider you an ally after our many years fighting together in the war. We've brought some dried *vagrothmolan* and *xfrayzitor* from the mountains of our homeland." Rylana waved an apology for her pronunciation of the unfamiliar words. "As you are aware, these magical herbs and fungi are rare and have value even among our people, so we would ask a small favor in exchange for containers of them. If you are interested and desire more details on our proposed trade, come this midnight to the Calling Rock in the forests in the foothills of the Icefang Mountains. We will be there with the spices." Rylana lowered the scroll. "It's signed *The Sisters*. Do you know who that is?"

Jildarin sighed. "I am certain I do. They must have found a scribe to pen the scroll since dragons do not typically learn to read and write in the tongues of the two-legs."

That, Rylana decided, was a more flattering term than *lowly life-forms*. "Dragons sent this? How would they have found out that you lost your spices?"

"I told my brother of the incident. He is the only one who

would have had the means to reach others of our kind, but..." Jildarin tilted his head in puzzlement. "As I informed you previously, it is more than a full day's flight back to our homeland where the spices might be acquired. And then, of course, another day to return. *Longer* than that, as you are usually flying against the prevailing winds on the way back. I don't think enough time has passed for the trip, else *I* could have made it."

"Are the sisters the same ones who, uhm, you mentioned your brother setting you up when he invited you out to hunt. Is one of them the female who was waiting for you?"

"That was another female, a friend of my mother's." Jildarin looked pensively at the scroll.

Rylana handed it to him. "It's probably close to midnight now. I don't know where that specific rock is, but it's twenty miles to the foothills of the mountains. They should have sent their message earlier if they wanted you to meet them."

"It doesn't take a dragon long to fly that far."

"Yeah, but there are golems lurking around Tranquility all the time."

"If I leave the city swiftly, and change into my native form as soon as I am beyond its borders, I could reach the sisters tonight. I do not trust them, but if they *do* have the spices..."

"You can win the contest without them," Rylana said.

"Perhaps, but they would help a great deal. Dragon spices were always a part of my plan." Jildarin nodded to himself and headed for the door. "I will go see them and find out what they want to *trade*."

"Do you want me to come along to help in case they're up to something shifty?" Rylana didn't know how much *help* she could be against powerful female dragons, but if she left the city, she could remove the tranquility ribbons from her weapons and use them.

Jildarin paused in the doorway to look her up and down in consideration.

Rylana stood straight and tried to look competent and useful, not like someone in rumpled sleep clothes with her hair sticking out in all directions.

"Will you shoot them if they attack me?" he asked curiously.

Rylana hesitated. "If I say, yes, I'd love to perforate dragons with arrows, I'm afraid it will remind you of our past." She glanced at his temple. "If I say no, then you'll think there's no point in taking me."

"I already *know* that you enjoy perforating dragons. Get your sword and your bow. You will come with me."

24

When Rylana had volunteered to grab her weapons and go along with Jildarin, she hadn't expected to end up riding through the dark night on his *back*. But as soon as they'd passed the last of the pillars at the city's edge, he'd changed into his dragon form and instructed her to get on. Once she'd figured out *how*, which had involved him deigning to lower his belly to the ground and a feat of athleticism on her part, she'd been grinning ever since.

Taking off had been exhilarating, if a touch alarming since there was nothing to *hold on to* on a dragon. She'd nearly slipped off and landed on his wing before flattening to her belly and draping her arms over the curve of his back.

Her bow and quiver were on her own back, the tranquility ribbon threaded through her arrows to hold them in place the only thing keeping them from flying out. Her sword was similarly secured in the scabbard on her belt, and she was glad she hadn't removed the ribbons as soon as they'd left the city.

"I see why elves became your allies during the war," Rylana said as the stars spread out above, a half-moon shining down upon what soon turned from farmlands around the city to forests stretching out from the foothills of the mountains. Some areas near roads had been cut to supply lumber for Tranquility, but they soon flew over virgin forests, the great evergreens creating a canopy that appeared like a carpet from above. When she looked back, the view was even more striking, for the warm glowing lights of the city were visible along the shore of Lumi Lake, which, thanks to its magical life within, also glowed, soft blues and greens making the water visible even from high above and miles away. "This is *amazing.*"

Elves have been allies of dragons for many, many centuries, Jildarin said telepathically, his powerful wings flapping as he gained in altitude. The snow-covered peaks of the Icefangs dominated the night sky ahead, but he turned to parallel the mountains instead of continuing toward them. *They are more akin to dragons than to other two-legs. They do not seek to deplete the world of its natural resources.*

"And they don't try to shoot dragons in the eye?"

They are not so unwise as to attempt that.

"I figured." The implication that humans were inferior in the opinions of dragons couldn't squelch Rylana's enthusiasm for riding on Jildarin's back and experiencing the world from high above. As beautiful as the moonlit night was, she hoped she might one day get the opportunity to ride on his back when the sun was up. How beautiful the landscape would be in even more detail.

As Jildarin continued south, the lake and city disappeared from view behind them. Here and there, campfires burned, or a light or two from a woodland homestead broke up the forest, but overall, Rylana felt like they had vast privacy as they flew. She reveled in the cool spring breeze riffling through her hair and the fresh scents of the pines, spruces, and cedars filling her nostrils.

"Is this where you harvested your spruce tips?" she asked, amused, though he'd probably purchased them at a market.

I was told that a goblin forager selected those, plucking them from the healthiest of trees with the most choice of branches.

"Or maybe just the branches he could reach."

Before she was ready, Jildarin stretched his silver wings wide and glided downward. In the center of a meadow, a great gray pillar of a rock with a mushroom-cap top rose as high as the trees around it. Rylana recognized the spot, having visited it with a neighbor's family that she'd gone camping with in her youth.

"We call that Toadstool Rock," she said.

Somewhat ignoble, considering there is magic within it. Jildarin descended, not landing on the top of the rock formation, as she thought he might, but in the meadow beside it. Fresh grass and clover spread across the ground, damp with dew.

Though it was past midnight, Rylana didn't see any dragons and thought they'd departed. Then she spotted someone and sat up with a start. A voluptuous woman with lush blonde hair that gleamed in the moonlight stood at one end of the clearing. A flowing dress emphasized her full curves, and she looked toward Jildarin with striking eyes like liquid silver, no hint of fear stiffening her body. She held something up in her hands like an offering. Two small sacks tied with twine.

"That looks like a trap to me," Rylana said.

Indeed. I also sense another dragon in the area.

"*Another*? Does that mean *she's* one?"

She is one of the sisters.

"Why did she turn into a human when we're miles and miles from Tranquility's border?"

Despite Rylana's warning that it might be a trap, and the reservations he had to have, Jildarin didn't depart. He'd landed in the shadow of the rock pillar and turned to face the beautiful woman. No, the dragon currently taking the *appearance* of a beautiful woman. So striking was she that if she and Sylin had been walking down the street, *she* might have gotten all the men's looks.

The woman's gaze shifted from Jildarin to Rylana, and a frown compressed her full lips.

"Who are you?" she asked, her tone hard, not matching her youthful beauty.

"I'm the bookkeeper. Who are you?"

"Who are you that presumes to ride upon the back of a mighty dragon? You are not even elven."

"A tragedy, I'm sure." Rylana slid off Jildarin's back to land in the dewy grass.

She serves me, Jildarin stated telepathically. *I am not displeased to see you, Loxvonla, and I am interested in that which you carried all these miles.*

He remained in his dragon form, slitted eyes shifting from the woman to the sacks that she held. Since he was in his native form, her human beauty presumably wouldn't do anything to entice him or affect how he bargained with her, and Rylana wondered again why she'd turned into a human. Surely, more than because dragons lacked pockets, and it was easier to hold bags of spices with fingers than talons. After all, she had to have traveled here as a dragon.

I am pleased that you are pleased, Jildarin-grozanarav. She'd switched to telepathy, and her voice was more musical mentally than aloud—though maybe that was because she was speaking to Jildarin now instead of Rylana.

Since the woman was focused on him, Rylana took a couple of steps back and slid her bow off so she could string it and work out the knot of the tranquility ribbon. In the city, its magic would have made it difficult to remove, but out here, it was a mere knot.

I understand you have use for the dried and powdered forms of the fungi and herbs that grow in our caves, the female—Loxvonla—continued. *I propose a trade.*

While she spoke, a winged shadow crossed over the meadow. Rylana looked up as a huge black dragon alighted on the top of

Toadstool Rock. It—she?—also had silver eyes that glowed in the moonlight, visible when her head lowered and she peered down at them.

Jildarin had been aware of the other dragon's approach, and he didn't react in any way to what Rylana presumed was another sister above them. Perched on, Rylana's mercenary mind couldn't help but note, the high ground.

Be wary, Jildarin whispered into her mind, and she believed the words were only for her. *Female dragons are very powerful.*

Oh, I know, she thought back, trusting he would hear her words. *But you're powerful too, right?*

There are two of them.

Does that mean I should run if they attack? Or take cover behind a tree and shoot them to help you?

Jildarin's head swung around, and he looked at Rylana, but Loxvonla cleared her throat, drawing his attention back to her.

What do you desire in trade? Jildarin asked, but he sounded like he already knew.

We offer what you want, the new arrival said telepathically, her voice booming with her innate power, *in exchange for you.*

Rylana didn't catch her meaning at first, but the way Jildarin stiffened suggested he had.

You seek to mate, he said.

With you, yes, Loxvonla said.

With he who slew many enemies and displayed great prowess during the war, the dragon above added. *He whose strong blood must be, for the good of our people, passed on to the offspring of the next generation.*

The woman looked up at the black dragon—at her sister. *Did you not say it was his striking silver scales, powerful musculature, and sleek symmetry that made you desire him as a mate?*

It is not only *those attributes, else his brother might have sufficed. But he survived the attacks of many soldiers, the traps of those who sought to destroy our kind, and even a betrayal that should have resulted in his death.*

He is blessed by the gods.

Such a blessing might be passed along to his offspring.

Rylana had readied her bow and shifted to untying a few of the arrows knotted to each other and the strap of her quiver. The tenseness of Jildarin's body, his rigid tail straight out behind him, and the irritated power emanating from him all warned her that he didn't care for their proposition. She didn't know if he felt he needed the spices badly enough that he would agree to it anyway, but the cold looks that the sisters kept pointing toward Rylana promised her that she was in danger. Maybe it would have been wiser to stay in the city and let a dragon deal with other dragons on his own.

You will cease speaking about me as if I am not here. Jildarin growled, his muscles bunching under his scales.

You will mate first with Foxvonla, Loxvonla said. *It is her fertile time, but I will also be ready for you afterward. Who knows when the gods may surprise a female with eggs? I will give the spices to your servant to hold. After you've satisfied us, you may depart with them and with her.*

Rylana paused, wondering if she could take the spices and slip away, running back to the city with them, while Jildarin flew off in another direction, leading the dragons away and ditching them. Or mating with them. Whatever he ended up deciding to do.

You will not manipulate me into mating with you, Jildarin said.

The woman had already taken a step toward Rylana, as if she assumed her plan would be acceptable.

We've been told you need these spices, the woman said. *Badly.*

I do desire them, but I will not allow myself to be manipulated into mating. I did not succumb to Sophoneliza's advances, and I will not succumb to yours.

We are desirable and powerful, the dragon atop the rock said.

There is no reason that you shouldn't want to mate with us and create offspring. Our kind need to hatch many eggs, especially now. As powerful as we are, we were not without losses in the war. Her reptilian gaze again shifted toward Rylana. *The humans, in particular, enjoyed targeting our kind.*

Rylana slid an arrow out of her quiver. Could the dragons recognize her? As Jildarin had? And know she'd been an enemy?

You do not think he mates with her, *do you?* Loxvonla's lips twisted with distaste as she also regarded Rylana. *Zilek-grozanarav has admitted that* he *has desires for the two-legs and mates with them when he is in that form. It is appalling.*

Is that not why you *have taken that form, sister?* the female dragon asked. *In case that is what his sensibilities desire?*

We will have him one way or another, Loxvonla said.

You will not, Jildarin said. *And you will leave my servant out of this.*

"It's Rylana," she said.

If she is his servant, she must serve him in many *ways. Can his dragon side be satisfied with mating with a puny human female?*

If she were to die, he might have sexual need for another.

Rylana, not liking the direction of the conversation, nocked an arrow. If only she had mithril weapons with her. Unless she could take one of the sisters in the eye, her projectiles wouldn't harm them much.

A pebble shifted and fell from Toadstool Rock, clattering down the side. Talons scraped at the ledge, and the black dragon looked like she was prepared to spring.

Jildarin growled and shifted closer to Rylana, extending a protective wing. *You two will leave, and you will take the spices with you. I will mate with neither of you, and you will not harm the two-legs.*

Once she is gone, you will have none left to mate with but us. The black dragon dove from the rock, flying straight toward Rylana.

Jildarin shifted and sprang into the air, the beats of his wings rustling Rylana's clothes. She pointed her arrow toward the descending dragon, but Jildarin crashed into her, knocking her into the rock formation.

Instincts shouting a warning, Rylana whirled back toward Loxvonla. Still in her human form, she sprinted across the meadow, fingers curled like talons. Flames sprang from her hands, and gouts of fire streaked toward Rylana.

Cursing, Rylana loosed her arrow at the woman an instant before she threw herself to the side, rolling through the grass as the fire streaked through the space where she'd stood. A furious cry came from her foe, but Rylana couldn't tell if there was any pain in it, if her arrow had struck.

She leaped to her feet and ran for cover in the trees, glancing back to spot Loxvonla with her fists clenched, her eyes glowing, and a slight gash dripping blood on the side of her neck. Had she been a normal human, the arrow would have carved a much deeper wound, maybe cutting an artery, but on a dragon… Rylana was lucky her simple weapon had even drawn blood.

Or maybe, judging by the furious gaze that lanced in her direction, she *wasn't* lucky to have hurt her foe. Magic rippled in the air around Loxvonla, and she shifted into a black dragon, the same as her sister.

Rylana drew another arrow as she leaped between two trees.

Roars and screeches came from above the rock pillar as Jildarin, slightly larger than the black-scaled female, bit and tore into his foe. Wings battered the air as the dragons gyrated and flapped about, somehow staying aloft as they struck for each other's throats. Jildarin knocked his foe into the rock pillar hard enough to make it tremble, pebbles falling into the meadow below. But before the female struck the ground, she roared and got her feet under her. She landed and sprang into the air again, arrowing toward him.

Meanwhile, Loxvonla finished changing forms. Now towering

above the meadow, she roared, the thunderous noise drowning out the battle above. Rylana spotted the bags of spices where they'd fallen to the grass at the dragon's feet, but she dared not run close to snatch them. Loxvonla opened her maw, showing great sword-like fangs, and roared again. Flames roiled in the back of her throat, the only warning Rylana had that more fire was on its way. She sprang backward and ran deeper into the forest.

Yellow light flared behind her, and flames blasted into the trees, engulfing the two she'd first taken cover behind. Heat rolled into the forest, and Rylana leaped over ferns and ducked behind a thick pine as it intensified. Behind her, entire trees burst into flames.

"Why did I volunteer to come out here?" she demanded.

A screech of pain came from the sky above the meadow. Had that been Jildarin? Or his opponent? Rylana couldn't tell the cries of one dragon from another.

As Loxvonla breathed more flames into the forest, new trees catching fire and wood snapping as the others burned, Rylana wanted to run farther away. But she thought of the spices and why they'd come. Ducking low and hoping to stay out of sight, she picked a path parallel to the meadow.

Loxvonla roared and stomped about in irritation, the trees growing too densely for her to follow Rylana into the forest. But, as Rylana tried to circle back toward the meadow without being seen, the black dragon turned her head, wrapped her maw around one of the burning trees, and pulled it up by its roots.

"Two hells," Rylana breathed.

Even though she'd seen plenty of dragons during the war, their sheer power and magic never failed to impress and terrify her.

Again, her instincts urged her to flee, but she mulishly sneaked closer. When Loxvonla was busy hurling the uprooted tree across the meadow, Rylana darted closer again. She spotted the bags of spices near the taloned feet of the dragon and winced. How could she get Loxvonla to move away so that she could slip in and grab them?

A fresh ear-piercing screech came from the night sky. Through the tree canopy, Rylana couldn't see Jildarin battling the other dragon, but she could hear the flaps of wings, the thuds of great bodies coming together, and the roars and screeches of fury and pain. Whatever happened caused Loxvonla to look up.

Bow in hand, Rylana dared run forward, thinking she might snatch up the bags, then sprint away before the dragon could attack again. But Loxvonla's head whipped back down, and those cold eyes locked onto her. Rylana halted at the edge of the meadow, her bow drawn. The dragon opened her maw, flames again roiling in the back of her throat. But her target wasn't Rylana. Her fanged maw aimed at the ground—at the bags of spices.

Even as the first flames rolled out, Rylana fired her arrow. It flew between the dragon's fangs and disappeared into the back of her throat. Loxvonla screeched in pain, but her gout of fire didn't halt. For several seconds more, it blasted into the ground, charring earth and incinerating grass.

A thud came from the other side of the meadow, but Rylana dared not turn to look. Loxvonla's maw lifted and, flames still pouring forth, she stomped in her direction.

Rylana lifted her bow and fired her next arrow at her adversary's eye. Just before it would have struck, a great silver dragon slammed into Loxvonla from the side. Jildarin.

His momentum carried the black dragon to the ground, and they rolled like cats in an alley. *Giant* cats. Slashing and biting, they thrashed about. A tail slammed into a young tree and snapped its trunk in half.

Rylana backed away from the fight but also angled to look for the other sister. She lay crumpled on her side in the grass on the far side of Toadstool Rock.

That must have been the thud that Rylana had heard. The dragon's tail twitched, and she tried weakly to rise, her limbs struggling to support her. Great gashes had been torn in her side, blood leaking from gaps in her scales. A huge chunk of flesh had been torn—*bitten*—out of her long neck.

Bow still in hand, Rylana turned back toward Jildarin and Loxvonla, debating if she could or should help. He had the size advantage and appeared to have more strength, as well. Just as he'd done with the other sister, he hurled Loxvonla into the rock pillar. She struck it, bounced off, and landed hard on her side. Though she immediately started to roll to her feet, Jildarin was too fast. He sprang like a panther and landed on her, pinning her with his weight. His taloned feet curled around her limbs to flatten her to the charred earth.

Rylana risked creeping closer and climbed onto a log for a better view. Jildarin, his foe helpless beneath him, looked at her.

For a moment, fear froze Rylana. What if he'd been overcome by battle fury and didn't recognize her as an ally? Or what if he thought, because she gripped her bow in her hand, she meant to fire at him?

Rylana spread her arms, holding the weapon out at her side. Loxvonla squirmed underneath Jildarin, trying to find a way to free herself. He looked down at her and growled.

You will return to the homeland, and you will not disturb me again, his telepathic voice boomed.

At the far end of the meadow, the other sister had managed to rise. She found the strength to take off, though her flight was lopsided, a hitch to her wingbeats. Jildarin stepped off Loxvonla, watching her warily but without fear. He'd bested both of the sisters, and they would be foolish to try to attack him again.

Perhaps coming to the same conclusion, Loxvonla shifted to face him, lowering her head in defeat. *You have not lost your power or prowess in battle. You remain a desirable sire. When the urge to mate comes upon you, I will be waiting.*

Rylana blinked. Loxvonla still *wanted* Jildarin? After he'd kicked her ass?

Leave now, Jildarin said. *And do not threaten my bookkeeper again.*

"Better than being called a servant," Rylana muttered and lowered her bow, relieved that whatever battle fury Jildarin had felt must have faded. He sounded calm now.

The black dragon summoned her strength, sprang into the air, and flew off toward the south. Soon, Loxvonla and her sister disappeared from view.

Rylana walked into the charred meadow, smoke wafting up from what had been fresh dewy grass, and looked at the spot where the bags had rested. All trace of them was gone. And their contents... Here and there, powder was visible where smoke wafted up from the bare earth. It even glowed slightly. Of course. The spices were—had been—magical. Unfortunately, they were scattered too thinly to scrape up and use. And who knew what they would taste like after a dragon had breathed fire all over them?

"I'm sorry," Rylana said as Jildarin approached, still in his dragon form. A few gashes had torn open his flanks, and one of the sisters had bitten his maw, leaving his snout bleeding, but there was no hitch to his step, no lopsided tilt to his wings. "I was hoping I could get them for you."

I was not willing to trade my pride for the spices. Jildarin didn't sound that disappointed. Maybe he'd figured from the beginning that it would be a long shot if he could get them from the sisters. *I will win the competition without them,* he added.

"I told you that you would." Rylana smiled, as impressed by his battle prowess as the sisters had been, but she didn't intend to bring up mating. She decided she liked his character too. All of him, really. By the gods, maybe Sylin was right. Maybe she was developing feelings for him. How silly.

Jildarin walked closer, muscles rippling under his moonlit scales. *You fought with me.*

"Not very effectively, I'm afraid. I would need magical arrows to do real damage against your kind—their kind."

Yet you distracted one of the sisters so that I did not have to face both at once. That was advantageous for me.

"You might have been able to handle both at once. You're... pretty special." Rylana snorted at herself. Pretty special? Who said goofy things like that?

Jildarin gazed at her for a long moment, and heat flushed her cheeks.

Come, he finally said, not commenting on his *specialness. I will take you back to the city, and then... Then I must prepare.*

25

ON THE MORNING OF THE GOLDEN WHISK, RYLANA WALKED BESIDE Jildarin as he led the way through the city to a venue she'd visited in her youth but didn't remember well, the New God Arena. On a rocky rise overlooking the lake, tiers of worn stone benches offered a view of a field in front of a covered outdoor stage. In ancient times, when it had simply been called the Amphitheater, sporting events had taken place in that field. These days, in the summer months when the weather could usually be counted on to be nice, the arena hosted many outdoor plays, operas, and symphonies.

Rylana remembered how the music could be heard from across the lake, and she felt a twinge of nostalgia, reminded of being a child and playing outside along the shoreline with her brother and their friends. That was when Mother had still been alive and before they'd been burdened by the expectations from Father and their tutors.

"Your elven comrade is skulking along behind us," Jildarin announced without looking back. His fingers strayed to the black knife case he carried, though the blades were for mincing vegetables and cutting meat, not deflecting attacks from assassins.

Not that Sylin would attack him. If she was indeed back there —Rylana hadn't spotted her but wasn't surprised by Jildarin's announcement—she was coming for the entertainment value, not to ply her trade. Rylana didn't doubt that Sylin would find a way into the venue without an invitation or ticket.

"She's a natural skulker." Rylana patted Jildarin's arm, the white sleeve of his chef's coat covering his muscles. In addition to the knife case, he carried a leather bag that looked like a doctor's medical kit but that housed his chosen spices, and he started to move it away from her, as if he worried she would prove she was still an enemy by swiping it, but then he relaxed his arm and left it between them. Maybe someday, he would stop being wary around her. "I believe the elves are still looking for her, so she's not walking openly anywhere," Rylana added so he wouldn't worry that a rival had hired Sylin to go after him—or whatever was going through his mind.

"Ah. She will have weapons?"

"Tied with a tranquility ribbon, probably."

"You did not bring your bow or your sword." Jildarin looked at her as they turned onto a street that climbed toward the arena.

"I almost did, since I suspect Yerin will try something else, but you saw the peacekeepers tie new ribbons on when we got back to the city last night. There's not much point in carrying weapons that can't be used."

"Even a bow with a ribbon may be swung as a staff."

"You think I should have brought it to club your opponents?"

"Only if they attempt sabotage and I am too busy cooking to defend my pots."

"You didn't bring weapons to defend them with, did you? Other than the kitchen knives."

As Rylana waved to Jildarin's case, she admitted the collection of blades inside could take down a small army. It was surprising the peacekeepers let him carry them around without a ribbon, but he wore his chef's jacket and was a known competitor in the Golden Whisk—maybe the authorities had instructions to leave the contestants be.

That morning, the *Lumi Lake Chronicles* had featured a front-page article proclaiming that the competition would determine the city's greatest chef. It had listed the names of the contestants and the diners and restaurants where they worked, though Jildarin's diner had been last and his write-up the shortest, saying only that he was a dragon with an indeterminate culinary pedigree. Yerin's name hadn't been on the byline, but Rylana had a feeling he'd been a part of putting it together.

"A dragon *is* a weapon," Jildarin said.

"Even when he's preoccupied by stirring his soup?"

"Less so then. That is why you are coming. You will yell if you witness skulking, sabotage, or other nefarious acts being perpetrated by my rivals or their lackeys."

"The natural duties expected of a bookkeeper." Rylana smiled, more pleased than offended that he wanted her to watch his back. If all he really desired was for someone to yell a warning, he could have chosen one of the employees that he'd had longer and had more reason to trust. Admittedly, Gniknik and Rolf weren't the kinds of people *she* would choose to watch her back, Rolf because he would accept coin to look the other way, and Gniknik because he might be distracted by an intriguing contraption whirring past.

"A bookkeeper who once *shot* a dragon can handle more duties than calculations," Jildarin said.

"I am versatile."

Though they were arriving early, since the chefs were supposed to receive instructions and set up their stations before the audience came, the arena was already quite full. A peacekeeper and a golem stood at each of the entrances, and a gray-haired man in a chef's jacket was in charge of letting people in through the main gate.

Jildarin looked behind them as they stepped into a short queue. It turned into a long look, and Rylana followed his gaze. Ah, Yerin was approaching the line with a pale-green-haired elven woman, both also wearing chef's jackets. Apparently, it was the chosen uniform for doing battle here.

The pair didn't look toward Rylana and Jildarin, and she debated if they—Yerin, in particular—appeared nervous. The elf did not, but their kind could stride onto a battlefield against far superior odds without looking daunted. Yerin smiled and lifted a hand toward the door monitor. He must have seen Jildarin but didn't acknowledge him. Yerin's smile looked more confident than nervous.

"He's got a plan," Rylana decided as she and Jildarin faced forward again.

"To win the competition? I also have a plan."

"I think his is a little more menacing than opting for elven, human, and orcish spices over pulverized dwarven rocks."

Jildarin eyed her. "I did bring along some of the dwarven spices. Sometimes, their textures as well as their slightly bitter taste can play well into a recipe."

"If you say so."

"I *am* the experienced chef."

"With an indeterminate culinary pedigree." Rylana smirked since that line had affronted him when they'd read the article. He'd growled, saying *indeterminate* described tomatoes, not cooks.

"Good morning, Chef Jildarin-grozanarav," the gray-haired man said and glanced at a clipboard. "You and your assistant may enter and set up at Station Seven. Once the competition begins, she must join the audience. None may have an assistant chef."

"I am aware." Jildarin nodded to the man and waved for Rylana to follow him.

As they headed for the stage, she looked around for threats. She doubted anyone would rise up from the benches and hurl a dagger at Jildarin, not with golems and peacekeepers monitoring the competition, but she didn't believe Yerin was done attempting to get him out of the running. She'd lain awake most of the night, expecting another attack on the diner, and had been surprised when dawn had arrived without one.

The great stone and wood stage was elevated with plenty of room for all the cooking stations, a few feet apart from each other. They offered counter space laden with utensils, tools, and cutting boards, amid burners, grills, and ovens that were in the process of being lit by a couple of goblins also delivering wood. Three men and a woman in white chef's coats had already arrived and were setting their knives out at their stations. In addition to the cooking areas, there were iceboxes and mobile pantries behind them, presumably full of ingredients.

Mirrors above the stations had been arranged so that those seated on the benches would be able to view the chefs working. A row of tables with chairs to the side of the stage, with *Judges* written on a flag, would not, however, be able to see the mirrors. Rylana remembered Jildarin saying that the judges would assess the meals without knowing which chefs had made them. Two people were already seated at one of the tables, one human and one elven, both older individuals.

Behind the stage lay a flat field with folding chairs set up, and a few men and women with press badges sat back there. Enough people had meandered into the arena that vendors were already walking around, selling snacks off trays hanging from straps around their necks.

A couple of geese flew over the lake beyond the tiers of benches, honking and making Rylana wonder why an outdoor venue had been chosen. The weather was decent, but what if it had been a rainy day?

"I will find my station." Jildarin lifted his knife case and pointed to the stage while nodding for her to head to the benches.

Rylana did so, climbing to the top row. A goose had visited that one personally at some point during the setup, and she started to avoid the droppings it had left, but changed her mind and sat next to the spot. Maybe it would keep other spectators from getting close and distracting her. From the elevated perch, she looked all around, taking her self-appointed duty to watch out for Jildarin seriously.

As more people filtered into the arena—chefs, judges, and audience members—she eyed them, debating if any appeared suspicious. In particular, she watched the goblins heading for the benches. They were in the minority and stood out among the humans, elves, orcs, mixed bloods, and more dwarves than she would have expected, though their kind always enjoyed a good feast.

A couple of peacekeepers roamed the area, and two more golems had arrived near the main entrance. Rylana wondered if they would react to anything that wasn't on the law books as a crime. Of course, if someone tried to set Jildarin's station on fire, *that* would qualify, but, with so many people present, she expected any sabotage would be subtler.

Vormalt arrived with a group of people, and Rylana groaned, wondering why he kept showing up in Yerin's wake. Had they become best friends over the years?

Rylana watched intently as the group entered the arena. Maybe *too* intently, because Vormalt seemed to sense her gaze. He looked toward the benches and spotted her. After lifting a hand toward Yerin, who was three stations down from Jildarin and setting up, Vormalt headed toward Rylana.

She groaned again, wishing she could have found a seat with

goose droppings on *both* sides. More people had arrived, some standing while others settled onto the benches, and she couldn't see through them to find a place she could move to where Vormalt couldn't sit near her. A group of dwarves was maneuvering to try to find seats high enough so they could see over the heads of the taller audience members.

Rylana called softly, "There's room up here."

She smiled at them and pointed toward the seats to her left. When they looked up at her, she realized she recognized one of the faces, Mya, the baker. The grandmotherly dwarf waved for her comrades to follow her to the top row, and they sat on the empty bench beside Rylana.

"Hello," Mya said. "Are you here to support Chef Jildarin?"

"I'm here because he ordered me to come," Rylana said but smiled to make it a joke.

He *had* told her to come, but she would have come to watch out for him, regardless. Even if he was a powerful dragon, he was so focused on his craft when he cooked that he might not notice an enemy sneaking close.

Vormalt had stopped to talk to a couple of well-dressed humans, including one wearing wizard's robes. Maybe he wouldn't come up to speak with Rylana, after all.

"It's wise to obey the orders of a dragon," Mya said. "We are here to support the dwarven chef, Mesacor, but I will also wish well to Jildarin. After all, you two gave me a deal on a gnomish oven." She winked.

"That's how friendships are formed, I believe."

"Yes. You should visit the bakery one day. We have many delicious items."

"I've had the scones recommended to me."

The *chaste* scones.

"They are wonderful. As the seasons progress, I add freshly harvested fruit to them." Mya spoke more about her food, but

Rylana returned to perusing the venue and only murmured a few responses, so the baker shifted to chatting with her comrades.

All of the judges' chairs were now taken, and a chef manned each station on the stage. The benches were almost full, and fewer people were trickling in, so Rylana guessed the competition would start soon.

The number of vendors had proliferated, dwarves and gnomes hawking everything from popcorn to skewers of roasted meat to bags of rock candy. The dwarf hefting those around promised his treats were sweet, sour, and hard enough to break teeth if one tried to bite them instead of sucking on them. A girl with her parents waved, apparently delighted by the description.

A pair of goblins in overalls showed tickets at the entrance and were allowed in. Rylana's gaze sharpened. Was that the goblin who'd started the fire in the pantry? With an accomplice? They wore overalls, as if they'd just come from work, and were carrying lunchboxes, but who knew what tools for sabotage might be contained within?

Rylana rose, thinking to confront the familiar goblin, even though they were heading for the benches instead of anywhere near the chefs, but Vormalt had left the people he'd been speaking with and was maneuvering up an aisle toward her. *Straight* toward her.

It crossed her mind to leap off the back of the benches, escape him, and run up to the goblins, but they sat down in the front row, as if they were merely there to enjoy the competition. Further, a golem lumbered past behind the benches and stopped not far from Rylana. She might end up in its arms if she departed that way.

Vormalt smiled easily at her as he climbed, lifting a hand. He sat beside her, not noticing the besmirched spot, and her only satisfaction was that he was sitting in goose poo.

"You're here to support the dragon chef, I assume?" he asked.

"Yes. What are *you* here to do?"

"Enjoy the entertainment, and I suppose I'll root for Yerin, though he's a bit of a self-absorbed twit."

"Which naturally explains why you spend time with him."

"Self-absorbed twit describes a *lot* of people in the upper echelons of society. Though I wouldn't say you fall into that category." Vormalt smiled at her.

Rylana did not return the smile. "I'm not upper anything. I'm a retired mercenary."

"Of course." His smile didn't falter. "There's something I wanted to talk to you about."

What was he up to now? Rylana didn't want to be distracted. She wanted to make sure those goblins didn't wander off to cause trouble.

"I'm busy right now," she said.

"You're sitting on a bench at a competition that hasn't started yet."

"I'm making sure nobody is scheming against my employer while he's chopping vegetables and mincing meat."

Actually, Jildarin had acquired two rags and a spray bottle of water or some other substance and was assiduously cleaning his station. Rylana smiled at the juxtaposition between tidy chef and the fearsome dragon who'd bitten and clawed two other dragons into defeat. Fortunately, the small wounds Jildarin had received during the battle didn't seem to bother him. What had been a puncture wound in his maw when he'd been in dragon form now looked like the kind of cut one might receive while shaving in a hurry.

"Who would scheme at a cooking contest?" Vormalt asked.

She couldn't tell if he was serious or feigning innocence.

"The rivalry can be fierce, I understand."

"Well, a *dragon* surely doesn't need anyone watching his back."

"I think a dragon may need back-watching more than anyone

else here." Rylana had caught a few veiled glares toward Jildarin, not only from his rivals but from the judges. She had a feeling the culinary community as a whole did not want to see a dragon win the Golden Whisk.

"Nobody is going to attack him here with golems on all sides of the arena," Vormalt said. "Anyway, what I wanted to talk to you about is... an apology. That's what I've been trying to get up the courage to do since I first saw you'd arrived back in town."

"Is that so?" Rylana watched one of the goblins opening his lunchbox and leaned forward, but he only drew a couple of coins and waved the rock-candy-selling dwarf over. A half-elven vendor followed with skewers of meat, and the goblins purchased from both merchants.

"Yes. I've long felt distressed about the past—about our past. Did I put too much pressure on you to marry? Is that why you ran away from home?"

Yes, she thought but didn't say it, not wanting him to think he'd had that much power to affect her life. "I was an adult by then. I didn't run away. I departed of my own mature volition."

"You left a letter decrying the evils of expectations and how smothered you were. Your father didn't understand it."

"Dear gods, he didn't let you *read* it, did he?"

"No, but that was the impression I got when he admitted you were gone and told me not to come around anymore, that there was no point. He was distant toward me at work after that, which is why I eventually left his business. I think he blamed me for you leaving. *Was* I the reason? Or did you feel pressured by him? You never seemed that delighted by all those tutors hounding you."

"I wasn't delighted by much of anything that last year at home." Rylana lifted a hand to try to halt the conversation. A silver-haired woman in a chef's uniform had climbed onto the stage with a megaphone.

"All of the contestants are here," she called. "Please take your seats. I will introduce the chefs, and then the first of three rounds of cooking will commence."

As she started the introductions, telling the judges and audience about a human chef at the first station, Vormalt tapped Rylana's shoulder and pointed behind them. She looked, thinking the golem might be doing something, but he was gesturing across the lake. Toward her family's estate?

"I heard that you ran into your father the other day," Vormalt said.

"Yes, so?" Rylana eyed him warily, wondering if he'd also heard that she'd been in the Molingvar family manor when he and Yerin had been chatting in the kitchen. She didn't think he'd ever seen her, but others had and might have identified her later.

"Did you go inside? See your old room?"

See whatever rooms *he* was interested in having access to? The library, perhaps?

She only said, "No."

The announcer finished the introductions, asked the chefs if they were ready, then said, "The first round shall commence. Timer, set the hourglass. The ingredients that will be required for the first dish are mutton, mushrooms, and grapes. Chefs, you may begin… *now*."

None of the cooks looked stumped by the ingredients. They went straight to work, pulling items out of the iceboxes and mobile pantries. Jildarin wore a determined expression and nodded to himself as he extracted everything he planned to use in his dish.

"Are you going to make amends with your father?" Vormalt asked. "Return to living on the estate?"

"Not likely."

"Where are you living now?"

"Nowhere you'd want to visit. I assume you're not looking for a hook-up after all this time."

Vormalt snorted, his gaze drifting to the hair he'd called too short. "I am not."

"Good." Trying to think of a way to get Vormalt to go away, Rylana almost missed noticing that one of the goblins had disappeared. The arsonist goblin. "Damn it."

26

THE COOKS HAD STARTED SAUTÉING, GRILLING, AND FRICASSEEING, and delicious scents wafted into the air, but Rylana barely noticed. She'd slipped away from Vormalt to prowl around the arena, looking for the goblin that had disappeared. She should have leaped upon him as soon as she'd recognized him, peacekeepers be damned.

But the uniformed gnomes eyed her as she moved away from the benches, probably wondering why someone from the audience was leaving their seat so early in the competition. She lifted a hand toward one of the vendors to pretend she'd come down for a snack, but she surveyed the area intently and looked behind the stage as well. A few of the men and women with press credentials were writing while others yawned and chatted, probably wondering why they'd been assigned to cover a cooking contest.

"Rock candy, ma'am?" the dwarf she'd flagged down asked. "One copper."

Rylana produced a coin and almost grunted at the heft of the bag that he plopped into her palm. "You sure this is rock candy and not just rocks? This must weigh ten pounds."

"No more than five, certainly. But good candy has the *heft* of rocks, yes, ma'am." He shifted the box in his hands. Its weight was probably the sole reason for the thick muscles on his arms and in his neck. "It's a traditional dwarven dessert."

"You could knock out an elephant with this."

"Maybe a small rhinoceros, ma'am."

As the dwarf turned away, it occurred to Rylana that the bags might make decent projectiles, at least at short range. She had excellent aim but could only throw such a weight so far. "Wait."

He turned back.

"I'll take three more bags." Rylana held up a finger while she dug for more coins.

"You haven't tried the first yet."

"I'm a woman who can appreciate a dessert with heft."

While Rylana extracted three more coppers, a boy with a coin trotted up to him.

"One, please."

The vendor accepted his coin and gave him a bag, but he fumbled it and dropped it on his toe.

"Ouch," he yelped, grabbing his foot and hopping around on one leg.

"A *large* rhinoceros," Rylana murmured as the kid hobbled away.

The dwarf smirked, filled her arms with the rest of her order, and headed toward the seats. Aware of a golem passing nearby, Rylana opened one of the bags and pretended to inspect the contents while she searched for the missing goblin.

"One minute's worth of sand left in the hourglass," the announcer called through her megaphone, then turned toward the stage. "Plate your dishes, chefs."

The goblin wasn't with the press. He *could* be lurking behind the stage, and Rylana wouldn't be able to see him from her location. He also could have gone to the lavatory and not be up to anything nefarious, but she doubted it.

The announcer banged a mallet on a gong. "Time is up! Back away from your dishes, chefs."

"You'll need to return to the seats, ma'am," a uniformed gnome told Rylana, a towering golem behind him.

"Yes, of course." She went as far as to stand at the end of the front bench while the dishes were delivered to the judges. Each plate had a number but nothing else to indicate who had cooked what. Since their tables were to the side of and below the stage, they shouldn't have been able to see much of the actual cooking.

The judges picked up their silverware to sample the offerings, then scribbled ratings in pads. Reminded of the night Jildarin had asked her to assess his meals, Rylana decided he must have done his research in regard to how the contest would unfold.

Rylana looked at him. He gave her a confident nod as each judge received a small portion to taste.

"As we wait for the results from the first round," the announcer said, "chefs may begin thinking about the second. The ingredients that will be used are orcish fieldthrash, freshwater octopus, and maple syrup."

Murmurs went through the crowd, the audience agreeing that the required ingredients were growing more challenging. Rylana was fairly certain that the fieldthrash was a weed, maybe even one that was poisonous without proper preparation. Jildarin tapped his chin thoughtfully.

Two men tallying up the ratings took a piece of paper to the announcer.

"We have the results from the first round," the woman called through her megaphone. "Right now, the three chefs in the lead are Lady Saslin, the elf chef from Twigs and Bears, Yerin, food critic for the *Lumi Lake Chronicles* and chef at Celestial Ceremony, and, finally, Jildarin, the chef of the Dragon Diner."

Cheers, murmurs of surprise, and an indignant, "What about Chef Doxlor?" came from the crowd.

Rylana gave Jildarin an approving gesture, but the announcer had said they could begin the second dish, and he was with the other chefs, gathering ingredients from the pantries and iceboxes.

"Isn't that Jildarin a dragon himself?" someone murmured.

"I didn't think dragons could cook," someone else said.

"They can roast humans without trouble."

"That wouldn't be allowed here."

"Are you sure? They haven't announced the ingredients for the last meal yet."

Rylana spotted the goblin coming out from behind the stage and ambling toward his fellow goblin who'd remained on their bench. She was tempted to pounce on him and ask questions, but a golem stood ten feet away from her. Even though she told herself that neither the goblins nor anyone else would be likely to start a fight or do anything illegal with so many peacekeepers around, she couldn't help but glower suspiciously at the arsonist. He was still on Yerin's payroll and up to something; she was certain.

The goblin spotted her and stumbled, but he recovered quickly and looked away, hurrying to join his comrade in the front row.

Hadn't he had a lunchbox with him before? He wasn't holding anything now, and his buddy wasn't holding an extra one.

Rylana looked toward Yerin and caught him lifting his head to meet the gaze of the goblin. He gave a curt nod, then returned to mixing and cutting.

Oh, yes, they were up to something. Rylana longed for her mercenary days when she could have subdued an enemy, dragged him back to her camp, and questioned him at knifepoint.

"You have ten minutes left to complete your meal in this round," the announcer called to the chefs.

The judges rubbed their hands together, ready for the next

offering. A few servers walked to their tables to collect the plates. Because they had so many submissions yet to taste, they hadn't finished the offerings from the first round, and the servers distributed the leftovers to people in the front row, waving for them to share the food around. That elicited cheers from the crowd.

One of the people who received a plate was the arsonist goblin. He lifted it with a whoop, took a bite, then turned and walked up into the rows of benches, offering morsels to people seated higher. Something told Rylana he wanted to avoid her coming over and grabbing him, not that he cared about sharing.

She shifted the bags of rock candy in her arms, half-tempted to hurl one at the back of his head and see if she could knock him out. He wouldn't be able to enact whatever Yerin wanted if he was unconscious. But she couldn't think of a way to make braining a goblin look like an accident, and a couple of peacekeepers were still watching her, probably because she was standing on the side instead of sitting, cheering, and eating bits of food.

"One minute remains," the announcer called. "If you haven't started plating your dish, you'd best do so now."

Rylana caught Vormalt looking at her. He patted the bench next to him and raised his eyebrows in invitation. Wanting her to sit down where he could keep an eye on her? Or question her further about her father's estate and if she might take him for a visit? That was what she thought he'd been angling toward and deemed it more likely.

The servers jogged to the stage with trays to collect and number the second round of entries. After his dish was taken, Jildarin cleaned his knives, then shifted and stretched, like an athlete keeping limber for the next round in a boxing match. When their gazes met, he gave her a confident nod.

Rylana nodded back; though, as the judges sampled each of the entries, she eyed the goblins again, worried she would miss her opportunity to stop them. The one who'd distributed food had ended up sitting on the top row near Vormalt. They weren't speaking with each other, but Rylana wondered if, through Yerin, they knew each other and were both part of his plan.

"The judges are tallying!" the announcer called with excitement.

Murmurs of speculation came from the crowd.

"Ah, here we have the results of round two. Once again, Chefs Yerin and Jildarin have been selected for the top dishes, with Jildarin's scoring one more point than Yerin's. Chef Higlyar had the number one dish but, due to a lower score in the first round, is now in sixth place. The contest may come down to Yerin and Jildarin, with the dragon chef surprisingly two points in the lead at this time."

Surprisingly? How offensive. It wasn't a surprise that Jildarin's food was wonderful.

People in the benches called out for samples.

"For round three," the announcer said as the servers took dishes to distribute, "and the final meal, the chefs will use the ingredients of turtle eggs, sea lettuce, and tarragon. Time starts now!"

Without hesitation, Jildarin strode to the pantry. Yerin shot him a dark glower and tossed a significant look toward his goblin ally before retrieving his own ingredients.

Rylana picked a route up through the benches, intending to squeeze in to sit right beside the arsonist and make sure he didn't do anything. But when she drew close to him, the goblin turned and rose, pointing out at the lake.

"Dragon!" he cried. "A dragon is flying toward Tranquility."

As one, the people in the benches also stood and turned to look. The judges did, too, and some of the chefs paused. Others, determined to win, did not.

Rylana didn't see a dragon in the sky, despite the goblin

jumping up and down, and shouting, "There, there! It just flew behind the castle on the far side of the lake."

Rylana turned in the opposite direction—toward the stage—and jumped onto a bench. She was positive the goblin was trying to distract everyone because... Because why?

There. An unassuming man with a press pass rose from his seat behind the stage. He pulled a crossbow out from behind him, no sign of a tranquility ribbon knotting it, and pointed it at the contestants. No, at *Jildarin.*

From her elevated position on the bench, Rylana could and *did* hurl one of the bags of rock candy over the stage and at the man. But it was a long way to throw such a heavy projectile, and she doubted it would reach.

"Get down, Jildarin!" Rylana shouted as she leaped to the ground and ran toward the side of the stage.

The crossbow fired, but it wasn't loaded with a deadly quarrel. Instead, a cylindrical glass vial flew toward Jildarin's station.

He'd heard her warning and ducked low. The projectile sailed over his head and landed on the ground beside the judges' tables. It shattered, gritty gray-green powder flying up.

"Keep cooking," the announcer cried, though she dropped her megaphone and waved for the peacekeepers to investigate the trouble. "Once the sands of the hourglass start, they cannot be stopped!"

Closer to the press seating now, Rylana threw another bag of rock candy. The crossbowman had reloaded and was aiming a second vial, and he didn't see her projectile coming. It smacked him in the forehead. He pitched backward, dropping his weapon. It fired wildly as it fell, and a vial landed on the stage and shattered several yards from Jildarin. He only glanced at the spot and continued cooking.

Several uniformed gnomes ran toward the crossbowman with two golems stomping after. Rylana lifted another bag of rock candy, but she'd hit the attacker hard enough that he remained down, curled on his side and grabbing his forehead.

When Rylana checked on the goblins, the arsonist was jumping off the top bench. He sprinted away from the arena, darting down the rocky slope toward the lake and out of view.

On the stage, Yerin lunged toward the vial that had shattered. He grabbed some of the powder that had fallen out and looked toward Jildarin.

"Watch out!" Rylana warned again and ran toward the stage.

But a golem and two peacekeepers intercepted *her*. One of the gnomes wore the rank of captain, and she cursed. He was probably in charge of the entire security detail here. And he was after the wrong person.

"I'm helping," Rylana said, attempting to dart around them. "Yerin is trying to sabotage Jildarin. He knows he's going to lose!"

Though she was fast, the magical golems had even greater speed, and a stone-like hand clamped onto her arm, halting her. On the stage, Yerin ran at Jildarin with the powder clenched in his raised fist. As Rylana tried unsuccessfully to escape, her gaze raked over the vial that had hit the ground near the judges' table. That gray-green powder. She recognized it. Two hells.

While in the middle of whisking eggs, Jildarin took several steps back from his station, his implements still in hand as Yerin approached. Yerin hurled the powder at him, but Jildarin sprang lightly away, easily avoiding it. Instead, the flying particles struck the chef at the station next to Jildarin's. The person yelped and dropped what she'd been working on, then backed away as magic rippled around her. Before everyone's eyes, she turned into a huge jaguar.

Shocked and confused cries came from the judges, crowd, and nearby chefs. Tan with black spots, the jaguar bunched its muscles and sprang at Yerin. He cried out, throwing his arms up, and the great feline crashed into his chest, knocking him off the stage.

"That powder forces shape-shifters back into their native form!" Rylana yelled as the peacekeepers gaped, seemingly not knowing how to react.

The jaguar didn't stick around. She loped out of the competition area and into the city.

All the while, Jildarin kept whisking his eggs. As the peacekeepers recovered and advanced on Yerin with their golem assistants, Jildarin returned to his station. He gave Rylana another nod before he redoubled his focus on his dish. She was relieved when the peacekeepers hauled Yerin away, but she remained in a golem's grip.

"Will you let me go?" she tried to ask calmly and reasonably. "I didn't do anything."

"You took the law into your own hands by turning an innocent bag of candy into a weapon." The captain of the peacekeepers, who remained nearby, pointed toward the press area. The crossbowman still lay on his side, gripping his head and groaning. Somewhat melodramatically. Was he *trying* to get her arrested?

"He's fine," Rylana said. "And *candy* can't be considered a weapon." Though maybe those heavy bags *should* have come with tranquility ribbons knotted around them. "Besides, I was protecting Jildarin."

"We do not allow vigilante justice. You will be taken to—"

"She's my friend, Captain Laridon," came a familiar voice from behind Rylana.

Sylin had appeared, and she carried more of the glass vials in her hand. Had she recovered them from the crossbowman? Rylana hadn't even seen her at any point during the day. Sylin held the vials out toward the gnome captain, as if offering the evidence for consideration.

"Rylana is a retired mercenary, not a vigilante," Sylin added.

"Like *you* are retired?" the captain added dryly.

It took Rylana a moment to realize they knew each other. Even so, it was another long moment before the gnome captain signaled to the golem and said, "All right. Let her go."

As soon as her arm was freed, Rylana stepped back to stand beside Sylin, though she was confused about why her elf-assassin comrade had any sway with the peacekeepers.

"You called me your friend," she said.

"To simplify matters, yes. The gnomes would be confused about the complicated nature of our relationship."

"I knew you liked me."

Sylin snorted.

"But how do you know him?" Rylana pointed to the captain, though he'd turned and was directing his troops to round up the crossbowman and look for the goblin that had run down to the lake.

"Since we've arrived, I've assisted a couple of times with locating heinous criminals that have been vexing the city and that the peacekeepers were having trouble finding."

Was *that* how she'd earned those gold coins? Rylana had assumed she'd taken on a new mission on her own.

"*Just* locating them?" she asked.

Sylin smiled enigmatically. "As the captain would be quick to point out, vigilante justice isn't permitted in Tranquility."

The announcer rang the gong, startling almost everyone since they'd been distracted by the chaos. Nonetheless, Jildarin and six of the other chefs had completed their dishes. They stepped back, nodding their readiness when the servers trotted up to the stage.

Several of the judges had scattered when the jaguar had appeared, but they returned, noses twitching at the aromas wafting through the air. Those passionate about cuisine couldn't be distracted for long from tasting delectable new dishes.

"I've seen a handful of elves in here," Rylana murmured to Sylin as the judges dug into the dishes. Jildarin stood with his chin up and his arms crossed, as if already certain of the outcome. "Is it safe for you to stand there with your hood down and your ears aggressively poking through your noteworthy green hair?"

"My ears are elegant, not aggressive."

"That one is sticking out almost three inches."

"It's not *that* long," Sylin said dryly. "It's not like elves are jackrabbits."

"No, the wolves would have eaten you if you were."

"If it had been winter when they found me, and they'd been hungry, they would have eaten me regardless." As if to make Rylana's earlier point, Sylin gazed at one of the elven chefs who was gazing back at her with a suspicious frown. "As to the rest, you know I'm planning to leave Tranquility soon. I won't stick around and let elves or anyone else capture me."

"You keep saying that, but I keep finding you at the coffee shop."

"True."

"Maybe you *like* the challenge of having people hunting you down. Weren't you mentioning that you've felt listless and bored since the war ended and we left the mercenaries?"

"I do enjoy challenges, but I would be foolish to remain when elves are seeking me out. We are preeminent hunters."

"Foolish, yes, but also challenged."

"The results are in," the announcer called, having recovered her megaphone. "The winner of the last round *and* the grand winner of this year's Golden Whisk is the dragon chef, Jildarin!"

The applause wasn't raucous, but it was polite, and several people nodded.

Someone yelled, "We want to try his dish!"

But the judges were devouring it and didn't look like they would share with the audience.

Wondering what had happened to Vormalt, Rylana looked at the tiers of seating where he'd been. But he'd disappeared. Whether he'd departed the same way the goblin had or simply walked out one of the entrances when she'd been distracted, she didn't know, but she doubted she'd seen the last of him.

Once the judges had finished the final course, one of them stepped aside to retrieve a glowing golden whisk from a wooden box. He took it up on the stage to bow to Jildarin and award it to him.

Jildarin, who'd remained calm and composed throughout the competition, even when vials of magical powders were being shot at him, held it aloft and roared. Given that he was in his human form, it was an impressively deep and resonating roar. This time, some people *did* cheer.

"You can enjoy his cooking at the Dragon Diner on Acorn Street," the announcer informed the audience.

Ah, free publicity. That would be worth more than the prize money for winning.

"He should come up with a more memorable name for his diner." Rylana wondered if Jildarin would accept advice on such matters from his bookkeeper.

She turned to her side to ask Sylin's opinion, but she had disappeared. Perhaps because two elves in green cloaks had wandered through the front entrance, as if telepathically summoned by the elven chef.

"Well, I'm sure I'll see her later," Rylana murmured to herself. "On the roof of the coffee shop, perhaps."

EPILOGUE

Jildarin hung the glowing golden whisk in the front window of the diner, its light bathing the street outside and inviting people to come in. He emanated pride as he backed up and studied its placement.

"We will have to hire more staff," he said. "Once the word of my victory and culinary excellence spreads, we are certain to have an increase in clientele."

"And they won't even be here for the soup." Rylana decided not to point out that he sounded pompous. She didn't think he was wrong.

"Not *only* for the soup, at least. You will perform calculations to determine the proper prices for menu items based on our new notoriety."

"One usually prices based on achieving a certain margin above the expenses of running the establishment and making the dishes," she said.

"In the culinary world, the reputation of the chef *also* must be factored into the prices."

"Are you looking to become wealthy?" Rylana didn't know how

long the diner could expect a boost in business from Jildarin's victory. Would it be lasting? Or would people eventually forget about the competition? His food *was* good, and she expected that repeat customers would be frequent. Maybe hiring more staff *was* a good idea.

"I seek to have enough reserves that I needn't worry about paying the rent and buying necessary equipment and supplies. *Without* needing coin from my manipulative family."

"You don't want to be coerced into mating for money, huh?"

"Certainly not."

"That's understandable."

"Yes." Jildarin considered her for a moment, then waved for her to follow him into the hallway. "I have something for you."

"Like... a gift? Or work?" Rylana envisioned him leading her to the office and her accounting books to record his winnings.

"It is not *work*," Jildarin said with amusement. "It is to show my appreciation for your assistance this past week."

"I didn't know dragons knew how to show appreciation," she said before she could tamp down her natural snark. She didn't want to offend him, not if he was beginning to see her worth—and that she wasn't plotting his demise.

"Our kind are capable of being appreciative, but you are correct that we are not a demonstrative people."

Having mostly seen dragons raking enemies with their claws while breathing fire and biting with their fang-filled maws, Rylana couldn't imagine *how* one of them demonstrated affection. She tried to imagine two dragons snuggled together with their tails entwined but snorted at the unlikelihood. It hadn't sounded like their mating had anything to do with what humans would consider romance and love.

In the kitchen, Jildarin stepped into the cold room and returned with a covered pan. He removed the lid to reveal a side of bacon rubbed with a brown powder mixture that smelled sweet and also of...

"Is that coffee?" Rylana lowered her nose for a closer sniff.

"That is the main ingredient in this new rub that I am experimenting with. This slab is still curing, but I've another that just came out of the smoker." Jildarin returned to the cool room, switched pans, and returned with a side of bacon ready for frying. "I thought to reward you for your work here."

He walked to the stove, placed a pan on the cooktop, then rested the bacon on a butcher block to slice it.

Even though it still had to cook, Rylana's mouth watered. "I would pretend to be offended at the idea of being rewarded with a treat like a loyal hound, but... coffee-rubbed bacon sounds way too amazing to be offended by."

"Yes. And loyalty should be rewarded in *all* species." Jildarin looked over his shoulder at her, his eyelids drooping.

If she hadn't known better, she might have thought he had bedroom thoughts in mind. But he'd made his feelings on sex clear. Besides, he didn't *have* a bedroom. They would be storeroom thoughts. Or perhaps lair thoughts. Either way, Jildarin returned to slicing, and she decided she'd been hallucinating by reading anything into his look.

"What will you do now that you've won the contest after practicing so long for it?" Since Rylana had only been in town for a week, she didn't know *how* long Jildarin had been practicing but trusted he'd diligently trained for months.

"Continue to use my cooking to inform the various peoples of Tranquility that dragons are capable of culinary greatness and that our kind are more than mindless predators as so many believe." Jildarin laid four strips of sliced bacon in the pan and activated the gnomish ventilation fan. He hadn't fired up the stove, but the surface had heated regardless, and Rylana leaned forward in anticipation as the sizzling of bacon began.

"I look forward to watching the diner's success and seeing you get the recognition you deserve for your hard work," she said.

Jildarin considered her for a moment, then lay two more slices in the pan.

"Do I get more bacon when I compliment you?" Rylana wouldn't complain.

"As we discussed, all species should be rewarded for good behavior."

The bacon was starting to smell wonderful, of coffee and salty pork and was that maple he'd used to add sweetness? Had she been the hound she'd mentioned earlier, she would have been wagging her tail if not thumping her leg on the floor.

"Does your appreciation mean you've decided to keep me on permanently as your bookkeeper? And that you trust that I'm not out to get you?" Rylana knew he'd started believing the latter for a while, and she *thought* he valued her ability to balance his books and improve profits, but it would be nice to have that confirmed. Once she knew her job was permanent—maybe she could talk him into paying people in more than tips, as well—she could look for a more long-term place to stay than in the corner of the storeroom. She could settle in to start the next phase of her life.

"Had you been *out to get me*, you would not have stepped in often to keep me from changing into a dragon where the peacekeepers could see."

"I'm glad you realize that."

"As to the rest, I am still not entirely certain why you have desired to help me and work for me, but..." Jildarin trailed off as he flipped slices of bacon, then pulled down a plate in preparation for taking them off the heat.

"I like a challenge," Rylana offered, hoping he would finish his thought.

"That is undoubtedly true. Most people would not have

chosen rock candy as a method of defeating an enemy from a distance."

"There wasn't anything else on hand."

"Yelling for me to duck was sufficient." Jildarin moved the cooked bacon to the plate to cool.

Rylana was tempted to pounce on it immediately, hardly caring that it was hot. "If I hadn't done something, the guy might have gotten away."

She lamented that the goblin had. At least Yerin had been taken away by the peacekeepers, but she doubted he would be punished for his scheme. Forcing a magical being to change shapes was not, as far as she knew, against the law, even in Tranquility.

"Perhaps," Jildarin said. "To answer your question, I desire you to become—"

"Greetings, dear brother," Zilek said, entering the kitchen.

Rylana stepped aside to make room for him, though she wished he hadn't appeared until Jildarin had finished speaking with her—and handed her the plate of bacon.

Zilek's nostrils twitched. "What is that wonderful meat you are cooking? And do I also smell the human stimulant coffee?"

"The coffee is *in* the meat." Jildarin took tongs from a ceramic utensil holder, plucked a piece directly out of the sizzling pan, and extended it toward his brother.

Not hesitating, Zilek took it with his bare fingers. The heat didn't bother him, and he inserted it directly into his mouth.

"Oh, that's exquisite." Zilek chewed happily. "What wondrous flavors to put together."

Rylana eyed his chewing with envy, but she trusted Jildarin intended to give her several pieces. And she, not being a dragon who was impervious to fire and heat, would prefer to wait until they wouldn't burn her tongue.

"Now I feel even greater remorse," Zilek added.

"For what?" The expression Jildarin shared with Rylana while his brother finished chewing suggested he also would have preferred if Zilek hadn't shown up at that moment.

"I came to apologize for the mishap you had with the sisters in the mountains. When I asked them to bring some spices, I may have suggested that you would be grateful and might grant their wishes for your vaunted sperm—"

Rylana groaned and would have stepped out of the kitchen if not for the magnetic allure of the bacon rooting her near the stove.

"—but I didn't think they would *bribe* you with it. Or *attack* you. I suppose I should have foreseen that, as they're quite determined in their quest."

"How did you know I would need more spices?" Jildarin's tone wasn't exactly suspicious, but he did regard his brother intently. "You would have had to tell them three days ago for them to travel all that way and return, and it's only been two days since the goblin arsonist destroyed my pantry."

"One of your rivals attends the wine conclave. We were discussing the increasing popularity of your diner, and he mentioned that you would likely run out of your secret ingredient soon and that your business endeavor was sure to fail after that. In hindsight, it should have occurred to me that he might be plotting its demise, but you know dragons aren't great schemers and don't tend to anticipate that others will be. We aren't *usually* ones to employ bribes either, of course."

"I hope the sisters' failure to entice me to mate will cause them to return to our homeland and find another suitable male."

"I'm not sure about that. You left deep claw marks on the flank of one and bit the other in the shoulder, tearing a hole that will take time to mend. In short, you impressed them anew with your ferocity, and I believe they want you more than ever." With a grin, Zilek stepped forward and reached for the plate of bacon.

Jildarin caught him by the wrist. "The remaining pieces are for Rylana."

Zilek looked at her as if he'd just noticed she was there. "Your servant?"

"My..."

Rylana waited for him to finish with the traditional *enemy*.

"Ally," was what he said.

She smiled, her heart warmed.

"*She* hasn't bribed me, nor set me up to be bribed," Jildarin added.

"She did shoot you." Zilek waved to Jildarin's temple.

"Not recently. Further, she assisted me with my rival at the Golden Whisk."

"Well then, I'm pleased my insistence that you take her on to help with your books has worked out." Zilek gave the plate a longing look, but he stepped back, and Jildarin released his wrist. "You are most welcome," Zilek added, heading for the doorway. "Perhaps you'll join me at the wine conclave next month."

"Do you believe him?" Rylana asked when they were alone again. "That he was trying to help, not set you up for anything?" She wasn't sure she did.

"We have been rivals since we were hatchlings but have also always watched out for each other," Jildarin said. "I do not think he had anything to do with Yerin's scheme or intended for me to fail in the competition, but he has not supported me as fully as some." He nodded to her, and the warmth returned. "As I was saying, I desire for you to become—"

"Rylana?" Zalani stepped into the doorway. "There's a man here to see you."

Rylana huffed in exasperation. "It can wait."

She wanted to know what Jildarin *desired* her to become.

"He says he's an important lord. And, er, your father." Zalani raised her eyebrows. "When you mentioned being a mercenary and fighting in the war, I assumed— I didn't think you had any family left. Are you *sure* you're not related to the Avandars that live across the lake?"

Rylana grimaced. She didn't want to see her father but knew making him wait wouldn't improve his mood.

"I'll be back in a minute," she told Jildarin and grabbed a piece of bacon. Before she'd more than turned toward the door, she rotated back to grab a second slice, popping one into her mouth on the way. Oh, yes. That was every bit as good as she had expected.

"Do you want some to share with your sire?" Jildarin asked as she walked into the hallway.

"No."

Rylana wasn't sharing her reward with *anyone*. It was delicious. And *hers*.

She chomped down both slices on the short walk from the kitchen to the freshly painted dining room. Even though it had been cleaned and tidied, showing no signs of the fire, her father stood near the door with his coat folded over his arms, looking around like he couldn't wait to depart.

"What is he doing here?" Rylana murmured.

Zalani had walked out with her and smiled, extending her hand toward the glowing whisk in the window, as if the answer were obvious.

"I doubt he knows anything about the contest," Rylana said, though her father always read the newspaper, so that probably wasn't true. He would at least be *aware* of it.

As Rylana approached, Jildarin exited the kitchen, but he remained in the hallway and didn't look like he would interfere with her conversation. He'd probably come out to watch. Rolf and Gniknik, who appeared to be arguing about a tip left on a table, also turned to look.

Rylana had no idea what her father wanted but wished he'd sent a note and invited her to meet somewhere else.

"I have heard," he said without preamble, "that you are now a bookkeeper."

She couldn't tell from his tone if he approved or thought that was as lowly a job as being a mercenary.

"I'm helping Chef Jildarin with the numbers, yes." Though Rylana doubted her father cared about anyone present, she pointed around to make introductions, finishing by stepping aside so that he could see into the hallway. "That is Jildarin-grozanarav of Clan Killcrusher. Jildarin, this is my father, Lord Gavlin Avandar."

"The contest winner." Ah, Father *had* read about it in the newspaper.

"And the owner of this establishment, yes."

"A legitimate business that earns its money through the distribution of meals?" Father arched his eyebrows, something in the expression making Rylana think he might have heard the rumors about the diner from its dragon-spice days. Days in the very recent past.

"That is correct." Jildarin looked at Rylana, as if asking what *illegitimate* way a diner might earn money.

She didn't look at Rolf.

"The family business has expanded from being primarily a shipping carrier," Father said, "to also offering logistics management, providing warehousing, and even building rails and roads in landlocked nations desiring access to the global markets." He paused and waited expectantly.

What did he want Rylana to say?

"Congratulations," was what she offered.

"Should you seek employment that is more challenging and offers the potential for upward mobility, and should you be willing to return to your studies to learn what is required, the family would have an opportunity for you."

Oh.

Rylana tried to smile, but it must have come out as more of a grimace. This was exactly what she hadn't wanted. Not seventeen years ago and not now. The job sounded stressful even without the added tension of working with her uptight father.

"Rylana is employed as my bookkeeper," Jildarin said. "She is required here."

Father gave him a condescending look. "Employment at a diner is *not* upwardly mobile."

"Based on her recent contributions and the fact that she's not attempted to slay me," Jildarin said, "I have decided to make her a partner in my business."

Rylana blinked. Had he *just* decided that? Or had that been what he'd been about to tell her in the kitchen?

Jildarin, looking a little smug, met her gaze with a slight smile and nodded at her. She had the urge to run over and clasp his hand, or even hug him, but she didn't, not with her father looking on. Besides, she had no doubt that he wanted a *business* partner, not anything romantic. Still, he was quite handsome when he smiled and looked warmly at her.

Father was also blinking and taking a moment to recover, though it may have had more to do with the words *not attempted to slay me* than the partnership news. He looked toward the golden whisk in the window, considering it thoughtfully for a moment, then turned back to them.

"You'll accept that position?" he asked Rylana.

She recovered from her own surprise, glanced at Jildarin, then said, "Yes. This place is... more challenging than you might expect."

A *thunk* came from one of the tables. The tip money had disappeared, but Rolf and Gniknik were now engaged in an argument over clearing dishes.

"I see," Father said.

He looked toward the door, and she thought that would be the end of the visit, but he turned back again to ask, "Do you wish to get coffee?"

Rylana's first instinct was to object, but she thought of Sylin's words about blood ties and bonds. "All right," she said.

"I see there is a new shop located across the street," Father said. "Or perhaps you would prefer a pastry from that bakery."

"The coffee," Rylana hurried to say, "is excellent."

And it wasn't *shaped* into anything suggestive.

Her father nodded, and they walked across the street together. Rylana looked up toward the rooftop and caught a glimpse of a hooded figure sitting up there, keeping an eye on things.

THE END

www.ingramcontent.com/pod-product-compliance
Lightning Source LLC
LaVergne TN
LVHW091030080826
845145LV00002B/434